New Beginnings at Rose Cottage

Erin Green

REVIEW

First published in Great Britain in 2019
by HEADLINE REVIEW
An imprint of HEADLINE PUBLISHING GROUP

1

Cataloguing in Publication Data is available from the British Library

ISBN 978 1 4722 6355 1

Typeset in Sabon by CC Book Production

Printed and bound in Great Britain by
Clays Ltd, Elcograf S.p.A.

MIX
Paper from
responsible sources
FSC® C104740

HEADLINE PUBLISHING GROUP
An Hachette UK Company
Carmelite House
50 Victoria Embankment
London EC4Y 0DZ

www.headline.co.uk
www.hachette.co.uk

*To those of us who have sought and
experienced new beginnings*

Come not to sojourn, but abide with me.

Reverend Henry F. Lyte, 1847

Chapter One

Saturday 18 August

Benjamina

As I step from the bus, I'm nervous yet relieved. Relieved that the kindly driver helped me offload my oversized suitcase, avoiding the embarrassing situation I'd been anticipating throughout my journey from Paignton station. And relieved to see the street sign: Lower Manor Road. I'm in the right location.

This isn't my usual Saturday afternoon. This is an adventure I've talked myself into over the last few weeks. A holiday I'd have loved someone to try to talk me out of booking but, sadly, my life doesn't contain such loyal friends. Just family.

Turning to my right, I view the steep incline of Lower Manor Road – the route to my holiday cottage. I can't see the end of the road, simply a double row of pastel-painted cottages lining the cobbled street, which stretches skywards before disappearing. It looks picturesque, the perfect setting for a two-week holiday, but it'll be a bugger to walk up. No one mentioned that Brixham is so hilly, though I doubt my family are aware of such details.

I should have booked a taxi. Not because of my oversized wheelie case, but because when your exercise routine consists of nothing more strenuous than pushing a shopping trolley around a supermarket, you doubt your physical prowess. I have what I prefer to call a curvy, somewhat ample figure – voluptuous, some might say – certainly not one that's accustomed to steep hill climbing.

What I do know is that one step in front of another always gets me where I need to be. So off I plod. I'll pace myself. Stop for a breather whenever I need to, but I'll get there in my own sweet time.

My suitcase wheels provide a comforting rattle to my trek. I switch hands numerous times as its plastic handle cuts deep into my sweating palms. I count my steps as I walk, a habit from childhood; it helps to pass the time.

I stop several times to take deep breaths and appreciate the stunning views of the harbour, the cliff face opposite with its stacked cottages, and the deep blue horizon. I smile at passing folk striding down the hill, knowing that my freckled cheeks are bright red, my blonde ponytail is sticking to the nape of my neck and a trickle of sweat runs the length of my back to soak my elasticated waistband. But still, despite my ballet pumps digging into my swelling feet, one step at a time gets me to the top of Lower Manor Road, which leads into Higher

Manor Road, then Church Street, before a sharp left presents a glorious view of Rose Cottage.

Despite my nerves, it's a welcome relief to view the lilac paintwork, the wrought-iron gate and the plethora of pale roses growing above the bay window. The narrow street doesn't have a pavement, so I stand in the road and admire the cottage, playing for time in order to slow my heartbeat and renew my ability to speak before meeting my holiday housemates. I'm aiming for a good impression. I'm hoping to portray the adult I should be, rather than the naïve child I continue to feel like.

I recall the holiday let's small online advert in my mind's eye.

Cosy, picturesque cottage available for solo holidaymakers, offering a comfy home from home with new friends guaranteed.

Which is exactly what I need. It's not the holiday option I'd have chosen for my mid twenties. Growing up, I always imagined lying with a group of close girlfriends on an exotic beach filled with toned, tanned bodies whilst overstimulated holiday reps cajoled drunken males fortified with beer to participate in ludicrous sports. Sadly, nearly a decade after leaving school, all my friends are either married, pregnant or AWOL – away with other ladies. And I, desperate for my first holiday as an adult, am going solo.

I fish my mobile from my pocket and quickly text my brother to let him know I've arrived safely, after which I find the email containing my arrival instructions and note the combination for the key safe, which the attached diagram pinpoints beside the front door.

I retrieve the key and enter Rose Cottage.

This is it . . . Let my holiday begin.

Emma

This bar isn't my usual scene. I stare at the darts board, the numerous framed photographs of winning pub teams jostling for wall space alongside a small wooden shelf lined with trophies and tankards. I admire the humour of the young bartender's quirky comments in response to the free-flowing banter from the cheeky guys leaning against her bar. She dashes back and forth behind the counter, her plum-coloured mane flowing attractively about her delicate features. I couldn't do her job for all the tea in China. I watch as she pulls pints, delivers change and stands her ground, all with a pleasant smile and a polite manner. At her age I'd have blushed and run for cover – which probably explains why I'm not front-of-house material. I'm happy backstage, hidden from public view. It's tough enough earning your corn each day without having to interact with the general public.

'Another?' asks Ruth, the stranger sitting opposite me. Her kindly green eyes look eager to please, her greying brown hair is pinned behind her ears and her growing smile is enhanced by the large glass of rosé I carried to our tiny table thirty minutes earlier.

'Yes, why not. She can't be much longer, can she?' I say, nudging my empty wine glass towards her outstretched hand.

'I shouldn't have thought so. My email did say we would all be arriving on Saturday. It must be gone half five by now,' says Ruth, before heading to the bar. I watch her careful step, her knee-length brown skirt swinging gently from her hips. I imagine she's a good twelve years older than me, fifty-one . . . fifty-three at the most, though looks can be deceiving. Her soft, placid voice is lost to the sound of the men jeering at the TV's football results.

It's not that I'm disappointed by first impressions – Ruth seems very pleasant, easy to chat to – but I was hoping for people my own age, late thirties or thereabouts. I hope the third woman, when she arrives, is more on my wavelength. If not, I suppose I'm in for a busy two weeks of avoiding my holiday housemates and doing my own thing. That isn't out of the ordinary for me, but I'd set my heart on a bit of excitement; a fun holiday spent with other people. Alone time is the last thing I need. I only booked this fortnight because I knew there'd be other solo holidaymakers, though it didn't enter my head to ask questions regarding their ages. I don't know what I'll do if the third woman is in her fifties, or even sixties. I won't be impolite. I'll simply accept the situation and make my own plans.

Ruth

I stare at the array of drinks lined up neatly behind the bar. I could stick with rosé, but with such a variety to choose from, maybe I should try something new. I am on holiday, after all.

'What can I get you?' asks the young woman behind the bar.

'One large rosé and . . .' I scour the bottles, unsure of what I fancy. 'Oh, I don't know.'

'We have a good selection of gins. Can I tempt you there?'

'Gin . . . It's not really my thing, but why not!'

'We've got Bombay Sapphire, Hendrick's, Gordon's or a very nice rhubarb and—'

I don't let her finish; rhubarb sounds divine.

'Rhubarb, please.'

'With ginger ale or tonic water?'

I shrug. I haven't a clue regards taste.

'The ginger ale is a nice mixer with rhubarb,' she adds.

'OK.' I simply hold out a ten-pound note and wait as she prepares our drinks before handing me the change.

I'm as proud as Punch delivering the glasses to our small table, Emma eyes her rosé and then points to my rather bulbous glass of pale pink liquid.

'Rhubarb gin,' I say, popping my small bottle of ginger ale alongside. 'Apparently they go well together.'

'I usually lace my rhubarb crumble with ginger – it smells beautiful while it's cooking,' says Emma, sipping her wine.

'So you said you're a chef?'

'Yes, but not the kind I trained to be,' she says as I pick up my gin.

'Where do you work?'

She waves her hand dismissively. 'In a poky roadside joint

where everything on the menu is fried at least twice and served with a side order of chips ... Seriously, it doesn't bring out the best in my talents, but hey ho, it'll be a different story in a few weeks.'

'Why's that?' I ask eagerly, buzzing from the unexpected zing from my first sip of chilled gin.

'Redundancies. After forty years of ownership, my boss has sold out to a guy who wants to convert the place into an Indian restaurant ... which makes sense given that the car park is huge. It's been a long time since we've managed to fill it anywhere near to capacity. And you're in banking?'

'Yes, a clerk for NatWest ... I'm mainly on the till, serving customers and handing out leaflets, you know the sort of thing.'

Emma nods but seems lost in a world of her own. Her rich auburn hair bounces with life; what I wouldn't give to have such a fine head of hair. Instead mine's got as much grey as brown and is looking listless and lank of late.

'And do you enjoy it?' she finally asks, seeing me watching her.

'Not really. I did in my younger days – banking was a different industry back then – but now I feel it's more like glorified shop work.'

'No chance of a change of career?'

'I doubt it, not at my age.' If only that were a possibility. But how do you venture to pastures new when all you know is banking? I've spent a lifetime asking customers, 'Is that in tens or twenties?' and now I have to do battle with the younger generation, who only ever want to use the automated machines. I'm virtually redundant, sitting behind my counter, smiling and making small talk about the weather. It's not how it used to be when I could name ninety per cent of the customers who came through our doors, many of whom I could identify by their signature alone.

I notice Emma doesn't ask how old 'my age' is, so I assume I look all of my fifty-two years. My dress sense is a little dowdy and sensible compared to her vibrant off-the-shoulder top, but I mustn't complain. I'm still agile and have kept my figure – though given all the running about I do, it's hardly surprising.

Benjamina

I stand outside the Queen's Arms, my hand poised above the handle of the double doors, unsure if I should enter. I never go into bars on my own. Never. I rarely socialise at all, come to that.

Can I do this?

I need to go inside, but here lies the biggest problem: who will I be looking for? It'll be two females for sure. But what happens if the pub is full of female pairings sipping wine and laughing? Do I then walk up to every table to ask each pair if they are the other two occupants of Rose Cottage? Or do I simply dash through, heading for the ladies' toilet, only to linger for a minute in a locked cubicle before slinking back out towards the exit?

I reread the scribbled note I found on the kitchen sideboard of Rose Cottage.

Hi, hope you had a good journey. We've popped over the road for a drink. Join us when you can. TTFN.

There is no name signed, no mobile phone number ... nothing.

Who still writes *TTFN*?

Maybe, if I hold the note before me as I enter, the author will recognise her scribblings and beckon to me across the pub.

I take a deep breath and wrench open the door.

The pub is much smaller than I imagined. One step in and I'm in the middle of the floor with a short bar to my right and several small wooden tables to my left. Instantly I spy the sign for the toilets – useful in case I need a bolthole. A group of men lean against the bar; another crowd stand beneath the plasma screen blaring football results. The only other occupants are two women seated on the far side, both staring in my direction.

Is it a toilet dash or a cheery hello to the pair of staring strangers?

'Hello, I'm Benjamina,' I say, walking straight towards their table. My smile is firmly fixed in place and won't falter even if I've made a giant faux pas and they sheepishly exchange a glance signalling 'Who the hell is this?'

'Wow, finally! We thought you'd got lost,' jokes the younger woman.

'Lovely to meet you,' says the older one, her hand wrapped about her gin glass.

'Benni for short,' I add, uncertain which side of the table to sit. I opt for the chair beside the older lady.

'Emma Grund,' says the younger woman, her brown eyes holding my gaze.

'I'm Ruth. Ruth Elton,' offers the other lady, before sipping her gin.

'Well, Benni, why don't you grab yourself a drink and we'll introduce ourselves properly,' says Emma, her dark eyes blinking quickly. She appears pleased to see me; I'm hoping she's not one of those people who can be overfamiliar in a heartbeat.

I leave my seat, nudging the table as I sidle past it awkwardly. Maybe I should have gone to the bar first before joining them, but then what if they weren't the right females? I'd have looked a plonker standing alone, drink in hand, or worse still, dashing into the toilets with it.

As I approach the group of men near the bar, I avert my eyes and focus intently on the wine taps. I know if I lift my gaze for a fraction of a second, I'll see them noticing me. I might see their sideways glances, their heads nodding in my direction, and even worse, their mouthed comments, which they think are funny but which I know from past experience can be hurtful and unnecessary. So I continue to stare at the wine taps while the pretty bartender delivers change to her previous customer and receives a grateful 'Cheers, Marla' in response.

'What can I get you?' she asks, her row of perfect teeth framed by a wide smile.

'A large glass of medium house white, please,' I reply,

dividing my attention between the bartender and my purse. I don't need to witness any unpleasant gestures or comments from those further along the bar.

A colourful display of crisps and nuts stands beneath the optics calling my name and luring me to buy. I could murder a large bag of scampi fries or dry-roasted peanuts, but ... I can't. I shouldn't. I mustn't be tempted.

I talk myself into just having the wine. I don't want to be crunching while the two women are talking to me. I'm trying to give a good first impression.

'That's all, thanks,' I quickly say, before my brain can request the much-wanted snacks.

Back at the table, the two women look up and smile as I approach. I'm not disappointed by my fellow holidaymakers; I get along better with older people. I automatically feel inferior to women of my own age, not because of anything they do, but more due to my own insecurities.

'Sorry I'm late. My train journey involved three changes, and then I had to catch a bus – not to mention the hike up that huge hill,' I joke, gratefully sipping my wine.

'I caught the train but got a taxi from Paignton station,' says Emma, looking at Ruth.

'Same here, though just one change for me.'

I can hear a unifying tone in their accents.

'Are you both from the Midlands?' I ask.

'Rugeley,' says Emma.

'Tamworth,' says Ruth.

'Wow, no way – I'm from Burntwood.' I laugh. Emma and

I can only live ten miles from one another. 'How the hell does that happen?'

'You travel to the other side of the country only to meet people from your own doorstep; how funny is that?' says Emma, unceremoniously spluttering her wine across the table.

We laugh and shake our heads at the bizarre nature of coincidence.

Or is it fate?

Emma

'Seriously, you contemplate booking a holiday, which you are in desperate need of, but then you start thinking: but with who? All my girlfriends are married or busy raising their children, some refuse to do British holidays any more, so I kept putting it off. It was only when I saw the advert—'

'The one about cosy comforts?' interrupts Ruth eagerly.

I nod before continuing.

'Yep, the very one. Emma, I said to myself, just bloody do it – stop faffing about and pay the deposit . . . and that was that!'

'I did the same. It took me two weeks to get myself sorted, though, as I had to make arrangements for my mother. We live together . . . she has dementia,' says Ruth, giving a tiny shrug after her explanation. 'My father was killed in a car accident when I was twelve, so I look after my mum.'

'Oh dear, is it difficult for you to be here?' asks Benni, her tone softly comforting.

'Yes, yes, it is. I haven't had a holiday in years, so it felt like a huge decision for me to come away and organise for Mum to go into respite care for the two weeks . . .' Ruth's sentence fades; she seems to be struggling to justify her own needs.

'Will she be OK?' asks Benni, a look of concern eclipsing her features. I've taken an instant liking to this young woman. She's not the age group I was hoping for, but still, she seems a genuine sort.

I watch as Ruth seems to shrink into herself. 'I'm not sure.' She shrugs. 'Her doctors assure me she'll be fine, and the care home seems lovely, but you never know what she's thinking or feeling. She might do very well for a few days and have a good sense of clarity, but then suddenly relapse. She's steadily getting worse.'

'I'm sure she'll enjoy herself. The time will fly by,' says Benni, sounding uncertain of her words.

'Good for you,' I add quickly, hoping my delayed reaction doesn't imply that I think badly of Ruth.

'You deserve a break from the daily routine just as much as we do,' chimes in Benni, obviously catching my drift.

'And you, Benni – have you got a job?' I ask.

'Of sorts. I do agency work at the local vinegar factory near to where I live.'

'Agency?' I ask, taking in her appearance: a natural freckly complexion, a defined dimpled chin and a blonde ponytail, the fullness of which I'd kill for. Her cotton T-shirt is simple but unflattering given her fuller figure, but as long as she's comfortable, what does it matter?

'Yeah, there's very little chance of a permanent job at the moment, so I have a contract with an agency, who send me wherever I'm needed. It's all a bit up in the air most of the time, but I get called back to the vinegar factory most weeks.'

'Won't they employ you directly?' asks Ruth, playing with her empty glass.

'It's difficult. The agency tie you into their contracts, and if you get offered a full-time job with the company, there's a release fee to be paid. So to employ me, the factory would need to pay more upfront, but then they'd save money because the agency charge so bloody much to send me there. It's ridiculous, if you ask me.'

'Sounds like a rip-off,' I say, shaking my head.

'It means I'm stuck for the time being,' agrees Benni, adjusting her T-shirt to cover her elasticated waistband.

Our three glasses sit empty before us.

'Shall we have another drink here, or should we mosey on over to the cottage and I'll rustle up something to eat for us all?'

Ruth and Benni exchange a quick glance and a decision is made.

'To the cottage!' announces Benni, pushing her chair back.

Ruth

I feel awful as we walk the short distance back to Rose Cottage from the Queen's Arms. It's literally twenty steps, and yet my silence seems so obvious. I need to start coping with this. I believe the term is 'self-care'. I need to start looking after myself a little better, but as soon as I mention my mother, that wave of guilt washes over me and I could burst out crying.

Emma unlocks the key safe and lets us into the cottage. It's such a sweet cottage, and suitably named. I wish our climbing rose at home blossomed and bloomed as this one does above the lounge window. Though I suppose it would be awkward to dead-head each year, a ladder job for sure. I wouldn't cope well with that task; it would definitely be overlooked whilst I cared for Mum. Sadly, every job is overlooked in favour of Mum's care.

I follow the other two into the hallway, past the staircase, and head for the galley kitchen at the rear of the cottage, which leads off the dining room.

'I dumped my belongings in the lounge when I found your note,' explains Benni. 'Have you both chosen a bedroom?'

As Emma explains the bedroom set-up, I listen, hoping to chase away my negative thoughts.

'Ruth has taken the first bedroom on the first floor, me the second – but I didn't unpack in case you didn't like the large bedroom with the en suite on the top floor. The choice is yours. I'll happily move rooms.'

I watch Benni's eyes widen at the mention of an en suite. I secretly wanted that room, but felt it looked a little pushy to ask when Emma and I were deciding. I should be grateful that I'm on holiday at all, I remind myself sternly.

'I'll go take a look, shall I?' says Benni, hastily leaving the dining room as Emma wanders through to the kitchen and opens the fridge.

'The owners have left us a welcome hamper: eggs, cheese, butter, milk . . . some button mushrooms and cherry tomatoes – sounds like an omelette to me!' calls Emma, her back end poking out from the fridge door.

'Sounds fine to me, though you might want to run it past Benni too,' I say, settling myself at the dining table, unusual by design given its rustic, artisan style.

'Phuh! I'm sure she eats anything,' calls the muted voice from the kitchen.

I wince. I'm sure Emma didn't mean to be rude, but that sounded a little offensive, given the young woman's size.

Emma's head pokes around the kitchen door.

'*Sorry*, did that sound a bit . . . ? What I meant was, who doesn't like omelettes? Eggs, cheese and milk – surely everyone eats those.'

'Of course, but she might have allergies or such like,' I say, pushing the original comment aside. No offence caused or meant, plus Benni didn't hear the remark.

'Yes, right you are . . . allergies – I'll ask.' Emma disappears and I hear the sound of frying pans and cooking utensils being gathered. I hope she doesn't start cracking eggs before she checks with Benni.

Benjamina

I climb the staircase to the first landing, then take the second set of stairs up to the final floor, which opens into a massive bedroom complete with a stunning view of the surrounding rooftops and the harbour beyond.

I linger by the window, getting my breath back.

Two flights of stairs might be an issue, but I want this room. I hope I don't have to be polite and give it up for Emma. I feel like a child excited purely by the prospect of waking up in the morning and seeing this is all just for me. My bedroom at home, being my mother's bungalow, is the tiny box room that first-time buyers use as their nursery. I'm still in my nursery aged twenty-five – how bad is that! Though given my crap wages and employment prospects, it's hardly surprising.

I lean against the window ledge and admire the sky-high view. To my right I can see a tier effect of pretty cottages built into the hillside looming high above Lower Manor Road up which I'd struggled to walk earlier. To my left is the local pub from which we've just walked. It looks tiny from here, yet seemed so big as I stood plucking up the courage to enter. I was lucky that Ruth and Emma were literally inside the doorway waiting for me. How awful would it have been if I'd walked in and straight out again, then had to greet them back here at the cottage after they'd witnessed my faux pas! Cringe-worthy or what?

Emma

'I'll take the top floor, if that's still OK with you, Emma?'

I turn at hearing my name to see Benni entering the kitchen, her face all smiles and freckles.

'Sure thing, I don't mind either way. Are you OK with omelettes?' I ask, eager to begin cooking.

'Sounds good to me. I'll volunteer to be the official washer-upper, given that I can't cook.'

'Can't or won't?' I ask, looking at her under my fringe.

'Can't. I burn everything.'

'Didn't you have home economics lessons at your school?' I ask, unsure how anyone can get to their mid twenties without learning how to cook.

'We did, though it's called food technology now. I didn't join in every lesson . . . my mum didn't always have the right ingredients in the cupboard. I dropped it in Year Nine when I chose my options, so I still burn everything.'

'It's just a matter of getting your timings right . . . For a second there I thought you were one of the new generation who refuse to cook,' I add, seeing Ruth standing behind Benni's frame. 'It's not the done thing, apparently. It sounds to me as if you've simply never had the right guidance or instruction. I'll happily teach you; you never know, you might enjoy it.'

'I despise cooking, it just feels like another daily chore to me,' says Ruth, over Benni's shoulder. 'I always end up cooking the same things; it's easier and quicker than faffing about with anything new.'

'I have a go sometimes,' Benni says, 'but I'm not organised enough and I never understand the recipes properly, so normally I do the shopping and my mum cooks. The only time I enjoyed cooking was for a school charity event – the school provided the ingredients and I made tiny chocolate truffles to sell to the parents.' There's a sudden flicker of pleasure in her voice.

'Ladies, I promise you that for the next two weeks I'll be in my element as long as you don't ask me for twice-fried chips, breaded mushrooms or chicken Kiev,' I say, cracking eggs into a mixing bowl.

'I'll wash and tidy after you produce the goods then,' says Benni.

'And I'll ... well, I'll keep the cottage clean and do the shopping, so fair's fair,' offers Ruth.

'That sounds perfect,' I assure them.

As I whisk the eggs and add a little seasoning, my earlier reservations are forgotten. Despite the age differences, I think we'll be fine together for the next fortnight.

Chapter Two

Sunday 19 August

Ruth

I wake with a start just after 5.30 a.m. A quick glance around the unfamiliar bedroom and instantly I feel lost. Alone. Panicked. My heart is racing. Desperately recalling yesterday's events in order to explain the here and now.

My recall is swift: Brixham. I lie back and stare at the dusky shapes of unfamiliar furniture arranged around the room. My heart rate is easing, my sense of belonging returning.

Is this how Mum feels each time she forgets herself – like an almighty jolt from dreamland to a reality she doesn't recognise or understand? Does she experience this exact confusion a million times a day? Or is panic a memory from her childhood that has faded too?

A lump clogs my throat. I feel like crying.

I need to stop doing this to myself. Berating myself every

minute of the day. I have spent the past five years caring for her needs. I give her every free hour I have, and yet here I am feeling as guilty as hell for making time for myself. Two weeks to do as I please, when I please, and yet ...

A creak outside my bedroom door distracts my thoughts. Who is it, Emma or Benjamina?

I can't tell whether the direction of movement is from along the corridor or down from above, but either way somebody is up and wide awake.

Seconds later, I hear the front door click.

Boy, someone's an early riser.

I throw back the duvet and hobble to the window. My back isn't as good as it used to be, as much as I try to stay active. I can't combat the strain of lifting Mum in and out of the bath. We need to think about changing the bathroom to facilitate her needs.

I pull aside the bedroom curtain and peer into the darkened road below.

Benni.

The sun isn't even up yet, but she's out and about. That's unusual for the younger generation in my experience: my son, Jack, gets up as late as possible, every day of the week.

I watch her saunter down the hill, not a care in the world, so lucky to have her entire life ahead of her.

I sigh.

If only.

Shopping or sightseeing? Surely, it's too early for either. Or simply wishing to escape her daily life to enjoy the sea, sand and sunshine. Or like me, with no plans, no hopes and no dreams.

I return to bed, chastising myself for not being gracious at fifty-two, mature in my outlook. Instead, I harbour resentment deep within. It's difficult, even with Jack. He doesn't understand that he should make the most of life, stop wasting his days. While he's free from a mortgage, free from worries, ill health and . . . responsibilities.

'Stop it.' The words leave my mouth, my conscience sick of hearing the same broken record of woe and self-destruction that is my internal monologue.

Youth is wasted on the young, just accept it.

Benjamina

I pull the front door closed behind me, having checked that there is a key in the safe. I'm sure neither Ruth nor Emma will be happy if I have to bang on the front door on my return.

Usually on holiday I'm a lounge-about person, I take my time doing things, but this morning I had a sudden urge to be up, dressed and out. I can't say I have ever done this before, but why not? I'm on holiday, I can do as I please for the next two weeks. I have no one to answer to, no one shouting their orders and no restrictions about spending time doing whatever I please. Bloody hell, this is a first, and I'm determined to make the most of it.

Before I know it, I'm halfway down Church Street, bracing

myself for the steep incline, which is just as difficult to walk down as it is to walk up. Go figure that one! I'm wearing flat ballet pumps, but still it's no picnic. Shoes are a major concern for me given how swollen my feet can become. I live in ballet pumps. No heel, no ridged seams, but sadly no cushioning insole either. I can feel every bump and edge of these cobbled streets, which will play havoc with my feet as the day goes by. I might need to invest in a decent pair of sturdy shoes if I'm to walk these hills each day.

I weave my way down amongst the quaint cottages, stopping at benches that appear like magic at various points, before reaching the main road. I have no idea where I'm heading, but taking a gentle stroll in the soft morning light seems like the thing to do when staying in a harbour town. I've never been to Brixham before and if it wasn't for the advert I'd spotted offering a sense of security amongst other solo holidaymakers – I probably wouldn't be here now.

I pass shop after shop, all closed given the early hour, but I assume they will be busy with tourists and locals alike once nine o'clock arrives. Gift shops, charity shops and fish and chips shops line my route as I gently plod through the empty streets. It's comforting to see the familiar names – the Co-op, Costa Coffee and Superdrug – hiding amongst the local shop frontages.

My usual routine on a Sunday is a long lie-in, followed by several hours dedicated to a box set and maybe a leisurely afternoon spent flicking through magazines. Early evening is spent dreading Monday's shift on the production line at

Vine Yard's vinegar factory. A factory floor filled with rowdy women bantering back and forth about their kids and noisy machines pounding in your ears followed by a bus ride and a lonely walk home contemplating my prospects.

I stop walking.

What prospects? I don't have any. I haven't any hobbies as such. When was the last time I heard from my school friends? I used to speak to Lesley Crawford every Sunday, but not recently, in fact not since the weekend when we discussed the Olympics opening ceremony. When did she stop calling? Does everyone lose their school friends once they reach their mid twenties?

Laid bare as pure facts, my daily existence is even sadder than I imagined.

I resume my walk. In the far distance I can see various landmarks – a lighthouse, the harbour wall, an ancient-looking sailing ship complete with complicated rigging and crow's nest – any one of which will be a welcome destination when I finally arrive. I'll sit and quietly watch Brixham wake on a Sunday morning.

Crossing the main road, I arrive at the harbour wall, where hoardings announce that the *Golden Hind* will open at 10.30. I'm not usually interested in museums and such like, but it might be worth a look around if the weather turns nasty one day. Looking towards the dawn inching across the horizon, I doubt I'll need a rainy-day pursuit today.

I continue to plod along the length of the harbour wall, watching the high tide lap at the edges. The sound is so relaxing, reminding me that I can forget about everything for the next fortnight – as if I haven't already.

I glance at my watch: 5.55. No doubt my mum will be fast asleep after a good night at the Liberal Club with her friends, and Dan, my older brother, might still be out with his cronies, having pulled an all-nighter at a dingy poker game. A wave of guilt snags at my conscience before I hastily chase it away. For the next two weeks I'm not responsible for anyone else in my family; just myself. I won't need to struggle on the bus with the weekly shop, or keep a cautious eye on the recycling box to make sure there aren't too many empty bottles visible to the neighbours. As for the daily mess around the bungalow, they'll need to sort themselves out; a quick run-around with the vacuum and a spot of washing-up won't harm them. I can't imagine that Dan even knows where I keep the clean tea towels.

I focus my attention on the fleet of boats in the distance heading towards a point further ahead. I quicken my pace, interested to see what lies around the corner from the harbour. I pass shops and pubs all with their metal shutters tightly fastened, but as I follow the harbour wall around the corner, I see that the boats are docking at the far end. Several are already anchored there, and a number of men are energetically throwing white plastic boxes to one another before the final guy in the line piles them on to the harbour's edge.

Is this the morning's fishing catch?

I stand a short distance from the nearest boat and watch, mesmerised by the busy nature of the scene. Men old and young, dressed in heavy coats and woollen hats, with brightly coloured dungaree waders, bantering light-heartedly as they play catch with the plastic boxes.

Each boat is top heavy with equipment and metal work as the busy bodies beneath unload quickly. On the harbour side, other men stride back and forth wheeling trolleys piled with crates. It looks like an ants' nest, where everyone has a job and everyone knows his role.

I linger a while before seating myself on the large concrete step beside the harbour. I can rest my legs, watch the dawn lightening the morning sky and enjoy seeing the catch brought in.

How perfect. A million miles away from a Sunday morning at Redwood Drive, Burntwood.

'Are you all right there?'

The voice startles me. I didn't see the man approach.

I point to the boats, as if that answers his question.

'It's not a good haul today; we did much better yesterday,' he explains, removing his woollen hat and stuffing it into his pocket. 'You visiting, are ya?'

Once revealed, his brown curls tumble in large loops, and his gentle hazel eyes stare inquisitively. I don't reply, but simply stare back.

'Are you OK?'

'Sorry, I'm just watching . . .'

'That's fine. I thought . . . Oh, never mind.' He turns away to look at the nearest boat before turning back to face me.

'Is that your boat then?' I ask, unsure of myself, wondering if I've caused offence.

'Trawler ... it's a fishing trawler.' He laughs, a smile spreading across his wide mouth. 'Don't let my dad hear you calling it a boat; he'll put you out to work for a night so you never make the same mistake again.'

'Trawler,' I correct myself. 'Yours?'

He shakes his head, his curls dancing.

'Nah, my dad's ... and his dad's before that. She's bloody ancient, to be fair, but she's got plenty of years in her yet. She might be mine one day.'

'And you've been out all night?' I ask, thinking of another male who could well be dragging himself home after a skin full – though I doubt Dan has netted any return for his evening.

'Since one o'clock this morning. We didn't go too far today, but some nights we leave at ten o'clock and return for the fish market.'

'The fish market?'

'Yeah, just in there. They'll be auctioning our catch to the local restaurants, and maybe some top-notch London kitchens. Our catch might end up being sent anywhere and used for all sorts of posh nosh, or for simple fish and chips sold literally over there.' He points to the nearest row of shops and pubs.

'So you're a fisherman?' I ask.

'Yeah, that's me and many more around these parts. We go out every day and net what we can, when we can. It's a real job.'

It's my turn to laugh.

'Sorry, that was such a stupid question,' I say, 'but where I live, people like me don't ever think about ... fishing.' I nod towards the trawler.

'And what do you do?'

'Nothing much ... I work at a vinegar factory back home. I'm on the bottling production line.'

He gives a small laugh. 'And here, people like me, don't think about the likes of you doing such a job.'

'I suppose not.'

He smiles and extends his hand towards me.

'I'm Ziggy. Nice to meet you.'

'Benni,' I say, taking his hand for a brief shake. I can feel the calluses at the base of each finger, his rugged nails and weathered brown skin. Quite different from my podgy white fingers complete with French manicure.

'You arrived yesterday, I take it?'

I nod.

'Most folks come on a Saturday. One week or two?'

'Two.'

'With family?' he asks, removing his woollen hat from his pocket.

'No ...' I hesitate, unsure how to explain the three solo holidaymakers in Rose Cottage. 'With friends, actually.' It isn't entirely a lie; after last night I'm sure we'll get along just fine.

'That's nice ... Right, I'd best make haste so we can finish for the day. It's been good chatting to you; see you another time.'

I repeat the sentiment and watch as Ziggy does a slow jog back towards the outbuildings of the fish market parallel with the row of bobbing trawlers.

I scan the horizon; the morning's blue sky is nearly in place. Behind me, row after row of cottages painted in pastel shades stare out across the harbour. Somewhere amongst them is the steep road I need to navigate in order to claim a decent breakfast and a morning cuppa.

I get up from my concrete seat, adjust my baggy T-shirt to cover the tops of my leggings and set off slowly back along the harbour wall.

Emma

I don't want to seem pushy, but I might as well use my strengths during the holiday rather than ignore them. I mash the tea while flipping the waffles, delighted that my early morning stroll to the local Co-op has resulted in maple syrup and a bounty of local produce for our holiday cottage.

As the sweet smell of the waffles fills the air, I feel on cloud nine. It seems so long since I've taken delight in preparing food – five years, ten years at a guess – but this feels right. *This* is where my heart lies, cooking good food to be enjoyed in a ... I look about the tiny galley kitchen ... in a location where the vibe is positive and my talents will be appreciated.

'Morning!' Ruth makes me jump with her sudden interruption. 'That smells wonderful.'

'Good morning, did you sleep well?'

'Not too well, but that's to be expected given that it's a new bed, a new house and new ... friends.'

29

I smile. That's nice to hear. I bet she's been worrying about her mother's first night in the care home.

'Benni went out very early this morning; is she back yet?' asks Ruth.

'Nope, but I hope she's ready for a fine breakfast when she does roll in. I've made waffles, or there's fresh bread and local honey if you prefer.'

Ruth perks up at the sound of honey. She seems a simple soul, and yet I noticed last night how forlorn she became whilst talking about her life at home.

'Have a seat and I'll bring it all through,' I say, not wanting the kitchen to be cramped with bodies.

Ruth disappears into the adjoining dining room, her pink quilted dressing gown pinned about her slim frame. She seems frail today, altered from my first impression. Maybe she's homesick already, or suffering the effects of last night's gin.

I remove the warm bread from the oven, pile the waffles on to a serving plate and carry it all through to my waiting diner.

'Here we go! Tuck in, don't stand on ceremony,' I say, returning for the cutlery and honey pot.

'Emma, this is quite a spread. I hope you're not on a busman's holiday without a rest from the day job.'

'Phuh! No such thing for me. I adore proper food. Making this is a lovely change from the fried crap I serve every day. I've thought about starting my own business with my redundancy money, though I fear it might all get swallowed up by the astronomical cost of setting up. I could always seek additional investment with a business partner, I suppose, but it wouldn't be purely mine then, would it?'

'Anything in particular?' asks Ruth, choosing a waffle and eyeing the maple syrup.

'I'm torn between a small bakery and a coffee shop. I know there are plenty of each along any high street, but I'd make mine different by using my talent for taste.'

Ruth looks up, intrigued.

'It's a knack I have for putting flavours together. However odd the combination first sounds, once the delicacies and textures are blended, then bingo, it's a winning combination! Don't ask how I do it, I just can. I believe my paternal grandmother could do the same.'

Ruth's green eyes slowly close with pleasure as the waffle melts in her mouth.

'This is gorgeous,' she murmurs, taking a second bite.

'Ah, bless ya for saying.'

'Waffles were always a favourite with Jack when he was young.'

I raise a curious eyebrow.

'My son, he's twenty-five.' Ruth shakes her head. 'Boy, how the time has flown. He's recently left home and is renting a place with his girlfriend, Megan, which allows me a little more freedom when Mum's not needing my attention . . .'

She falters. I see her struggle to complete her sentence, as if her train of thought has been distracted away from Jack and his new living arrangements.

'How lovely,' I say, unsure if I want to reveal my own circumstances. 'Married?'

'Jack? Oh, sorry, you mean me. No. I never married. I was
twenty-seven when I had Jack . . . on my own. His father said
he wasn't ready for such a commitment – some men are and
some aren't, don't you think?'

I give a knowing nod. I can imagine it's been difficult.

'Mum looked after me when I needed her support. There
was never a question of me not keeping the baby; it was more
about how we could remain respectable in the eyes of the
neighbours. She grew up at a time when social stigma was
prevalent; I think those attitudes were ingrained within her
upbringing. I suppose without my father to help guide her,
she probably felt we were already different from the rest of
the street. Being a single parent due to my father's death was
socially more acceptable than my unplanned pregnancy, so I
followed her plan. I never questioned it.'

'I know what you mean,' I say. 'Some people have a knack
of getting exactly what they want in a subtle manner by over-
ruling others. They appear to have all the answers, so you
simply go with the flow, and before you know where you are,
you find they're running your life. I've had a man dominate
me in much the same way. Friends and family thought he
was great for me, so charming and handsome, when really he
controlled everything I did. Thankfully there was never any
violence or aggression, yet his jealousy and insecurities dictated
every choice I made.'

'Exactly. And now the tables seem to have turned and I'm

making all Mum's decisions for her. I know I've got nothing to worry about – the care home is a reputable one and came highly recommended, so they'll be looking after her well – but still . . .'

'It doesn't stop you worrying, does it?' I say, sensing her guilt.

Ruth nods her head and continues to eat.

I note her despondency. She should be proud of herself given the effort and responsibility needed to bear such a situation alone. I'll do what I can to ensure she has a great two weeks, if nothing else.

Simultaneously we hear a key in the front door.

'Hello!' calls Benni, bounding into the dining room. 'Boy, have I had a walk and a half.' Her cheeks are rosy red, a healthy glow glistens upon her brow and there is a vigour to her step.

'It seems to have done you the world of good,' says Ruth.

'It certainly has. I never knew a harbour town could have so many pretty landmarks yet be so compact,' says Benni. 'Have either of you been here before?'

'Me, when my son was very small. I was desperate to provide him with a proper family. I thought I might be lucky enough to meet a decent man in the same situation and in a new place . . . Well, you know . . .' Ruth's sentence fades.

Both Benni and I turn to view her blushing cheeks.

'Ay ay, someone had an agenda,' I tease her.

Ruth's blush deepens. 'Not at all. Back then I needed to make the most of my free time. I've always worked. Even when

33

Jack was tiny, I went straight back to work and left him with my mother all day.'

'You were young. You wanted to enjoy yourself,' says Benni, her beaming smile fading somewhat.

'Exactly. Some dreams are pie in the sky, though, aren't they? I never met anyone I was taken with.'

'It's not too late . . . you never know who you might meet,' says Benni, her smile returning. 'I intend to let my hair down while I'm here, try new things and enjoy getting to know the two of you.'

'And so we shall!' I say. 'Here's to being ourselves, doing as we please and enjoying the time we have together.'

Ruth

It's 10.30. From my reclined position on the sofa, I watch the wall clock. I've struggled through ten pages of the Jane Austen I found on the bookcase, which I hoped would reignite my reading habit. It hasn't. Instead, my gaze keeps diverting to the hands of the clock.

The landmark hours of my usual day with my mother are etched upon my mind. Events around which our existence revolves. Breakfast, which is a good barometer for determining the day ahead. Her bath routine, likewise a mood indicator. Her medication. Her mid-morning snack. Her repeated refusal of fruit squash to help with her hydration levels. And of course, her constant questioning: 'What time is it?' asked approximately every seventeen minutes. It used to be every twenty-three minutes, but it's even more frequent now. I've learnt to cope. To answer without a hint of frustration or impatience. Sometimes I'm honest. At other times I'll say any old thing – Mum never queries my answer regardless of how dark it is outside. I don't think she knows the difference any more.

I stare about the lounge, unsure where Emma and Benni are. I heard neither go out.

I close the book; there's no point pretending. I'm on holiday and I am bored senseless.

What do people do on holiday? Eat, drink and what? What do *I* do on holiday?

My last one is so long ago now, I've forgotten where we went. Was it Ilfracombe or Barry Island? Either way, it definitely involved a twelve-year-old boy, his mum and his gran. It seems a lifetime ago. Mum, Jack and I happily filled our week with penny slot machines, beach balls and live entertainment on stage at the caravan campsite bar.

I can hardly fill this holiday in the same way.

In the silence of the lounge, I hear the ticking of the clock, the rumble of passing traffic and my own steady heartbeat.

I suppose I could go for a stroll along the harbour wall, venture to the local shops or take a paddle at the water's edge. Sadly, none of those things interests me.

So what am I going to do to fill the next thirteen days?

I didn't think about it before I arrived. I didn't plan like Emma and Benni clearly have. I didn't count down the days or even buy new holiday clothes. I literally thought my holiday would be cancelled at the eleventh hour due to unforeseen circumstances relating to Mum and I wouldn't find myself in this predicament. Bored.

I could stare out of the window at the passing tourists and watch the world go by. I could take a little siesta. I could browse the clothes shops for a few holiday items. I could phone Jack and ask how he is. I could, but I won't.

Actually, I might do that if I can't think of anything else to do.

Who in heaven's name is ever bored on holiday?

This is the story of my life. Empty.

I want to cry.

For the first time in years, I have free time, the chance to do as I please, and yet I can't think of a single thing I want to do. Typical. Back home, I'm busy juggling a full-time job with my caring role and my head is filled with a million tasks I wish I could do other than bathing, feeding and constantly telling the time. And now I'm free, I'm at a loss.

I might as well be back home.

I glance at the clock: 11 a.m. Time for Mum's mid-morning snack, which I usually leave prepped on our kitchen sideboard. Today, a kindly woman in a uniform will deliver it in the care-home lounge. It's comforting to know Mum has proper company and not just our kindly neighbour who drops in a couple of times a day.

I sigh.

I despise myself for allowing this to happen. I'm an invisible person who is kept busy doing things for others, and that alone justifies my daily existence. I'm needed. I'm useful. Yet outside of that, who am I? Remove Mum, remove Jack, and what's left? A woman who hasn't a clue how to fill her hours by herself. Who can't even name what she'd like to do. A lost soul amongst strangers. I shared my life story with Emma at breakfast, so what else is there for me to chat about? I've said it all.

If I stay here, I'll end up ruining Emma and Benni's fortnight. If *I* don't like me, why should others take an interest?

Emma

It's one thing to stroll by and wistfully watch the excited children and their accompanying parents crab-fishing over the harbour wall. It's another level entirely to impulsively purchase a new plastic bucket, a crab line and a bag of bait to indulge one's inner child.

I drop my line into the water and wait, enjoying the view. I bet Rugeley isn't looking so beautiful, despite the overshadowing beauty of the old power station's cooling towers, which have hogged the skyline for decades.

There are moments in my life when borrowing a well-behaved child from a neighbouring family seems reasonable: seeing the latest Disney remake at the cinema, visiting Legoland or queuing to speak to Santa. Today, I simply ignore the strange looks aimed at the woman crabbing alone. Hopefully my bucket of sizeable crabs will suggest a talent absent in the families either side. I'm praying that one of their brood doesn't accidentally knock it over during a tantrum after having been refused permission by their father to hold the nylon line for fear of friction burns to tiny fingers. Though I suspect it's more about the father's reluctance to relinquish his enjoyment to his offspring.

I have no such worries; I'm going solo.

It's amazing how therapeutic it is, despite the noisy neighbours. With the sun on my face, an azure sky overhead and the delicate lapping of the waves, I let my worries pass me by. Redundancy isn't what I asked for, nor what I hoped for, but I have to be honest. I haven't been happy since my very first shift at the roadside chain of 'Fry it, grill it, eat it!', with a menu filled with trice-fried chips, side orders of trice-fried onion rings served upon wipeable plastic cloths. In fact, I'm surprised I stayed so long. It was supposed to be a pit stop between catering college and my dreams as a sous chef within a classy hotel. It'll take time to find what I truly want, be it a coffee shop or a small bakery, but that's the least of my worries. My redundancy money is safely in the bank awaiting my decision, and ... well, the other stuff can wait.

I feel a gentle tug on my crab line, similar to the painful tug on my heart strings; both appear empty when inspected but I know from experience both are a waiting game.

The little lad in the neighbouring family squeals with delight as his father raises a crab pot with a healthy horde of snapping occupants. The boundless energy, the excitement at such small achievements – it never ceases to fascinate me. The boy is thrilled beyond belief as his hero nets the catch of the day. Does the guy realise this might be his most treasured memory? If he doesn't, then someone should nudge him, in case he's so absorbed in the retrieval of a crab pot that he misses the admiration on his young son's face, that one-in-a-million moment.

The dad reels in the crab pot, abruptly asks for the plastic bucket and then scolds the boy for spilling half the contents down his new shorts, wetting them through. The boy's face drops. The memory moment is gone. Missed. Lost for ever.

I smile at him before returning my interest to my own line – empty and forlorn in the water.

Within twenty minutes, I've had enough. I need some light refreshment, given the soaring heat.

I say goodbye to my collection of claw-clacking crabs before tipping them back into the harbour water. I shake the bucket for dramatic effect, splashing the father beside me, who glares before resuming his new-found sport. Pity his young son's delight didn't win his interest.

'Sorry,' I mouth, before wrapping my nylon line inside the bucket and setting off on the trek back to the cottage.

I'm unsure what I want to do. A siesta? Sun myself whilst reading on the back patio? Or treat myself to a cheeky vino alongside a plate of cheese and crackers? It all sounds good, but nothing piques my interest.

I continue my stroll along the quayside, window-shopping as I go. That's when I spot it: an old-fashioned ice cream parlour, its frontage as colourful as a box of wax crayons.

Instantly, I know what I want. My pace quickens as a long-forgotten childhood song spins about my head: 'I Scream, You Scream, We All Scream for Ice Cream'. I don't read the sundae menu pinned inside the window; I enter without hesitation.

I'm met with a mind-boggling black-and-white tiled floor with a distinct geometric pattern that plays tricks on my eyes like an Escher drawing. Thankfully the welcome from behind the serving counter steadies me.

His olive skin crinkles about his eyes, his bright smile accentuates a direct gaze and he's wearing the cleanest catering whites I've seen in a long time.

'Hello, madam . . . how can I help you today?' he says, in a smooth, rich Italian accent.

A nice touch, signalling authenticity for any ice cream parlour. Instantly I'm transported to Rome and the best gelato I've ever tasted.

I browse the array of plastic tubs filled with a multitude of popular flavours. My mouth begins to water at the thought of their taste and texture.

'Today's special is chocolate and chilli ice cream.'

'That sounds delightful.' I look up into dark, smouldering eyes watching me peruse the selection.

From a table in the corner a shriek of laughter fills the air, and we both glance over to see a group of teenagers, heads locked together, shoulders juddering, six bodies crammed around a table intended for four.

'I'll have a double scoop of the chocolate and chilli, please.'

Retrieving a note from my purse, I wait as he manhandles the tub and firmly scoops and rolls two large dollops into a waffle cone.

'Good choice. We've only just introduced this flavour.'

'Luca, how about we try—' A second man, wearing identical catering whites, enters the serving area from a back room, and stops when he sees me waiting. 'Hello.'

I give a polite smile. His grey eyes twinkle beneath a pale but heavy brow, he's obviously local given his accent, and somewhat alluring given his charismatic smile by which I'm transfixed. How can a mere smile, like the Mona Lisa's, draw you in within a heartbeat? I wonder.

'It's such a beautiful day; are you enjoying your holiday?' he asks, leaning both arms on the glass counter and staring at me intently. His confidence emanates from him, creating a magnetic field around his strong but slender frame.

'Yes, the harbour is absolutely stunning,' I reply, but find I have to look away. One glance and he seems to know everything about me.

Luca is still waiting to hear the end of his direct question, his dark gaze flipping between me and the stranger.

'I'm Martin . . . nice to meet you.'

His hand extends awkwardly over the top of the counter towards me. I raise my own hand, but due to the angle of the display case and my short stature, I can only reach part way, pinching the tips of his fingers in a feeble introductory handshake.

I instantly regret falling for his persuasive action.

Who shakes hands like a teeny tiny mouse?

Martin looks down at my hand and then back to my eyes. Yep, I bet even he is now questioning the kind of woman I am, based on that last action.

'And your order is . . . ?'

'Ready and waiting, boss,' says Luca, holding the chocolate sauce ladle aloft, offering to embellish my cone.

'Oh no, thank you, chocolate and chilli is enough for anyone's taste buds,' I laugh.

'Surely you wouldn't question Luca's choice?' asks Martin, pulling a quizzical face. 'His family are renowned for the finest ice cream in Rome and he's brought all his expertise to us here in Brixham.'

'Oh no, sorry, that was rude of me. I'm a chef by profession. I pride myself on excellent taste buds and—' I don't have a chance to finish my sentence as both men fire questions at me, while I reach for my double scoop delight from Luca.

'Now, you're talking, lady . . .' says Luca, still holding my cornet with a tissue.

'How excellent is excellent?' asks Martin.

'It might sound boastful, which isn't my intention, but pretty damned excellent actually – a born talent, for sure.'

'And you use this talent . . . where?'

'Please don't judge me, but sadly, I waste it serving fried food morning, noon and night in a cheap roadside café in the Midlands.'

Both men stand and stare.

'May I?' I ask, indicating my double cone, which is starting to dribble. I take it from Luca, place my five-pound note on the glass counter and unceremoniously lick the melting ice cream. The creamy texture is divine, the flavour so rich and the . . . I cease analysing the cone. Instantly I'm aware of two sets of male eyes widening slightly as they watch. I blush profusely.

How naïve am I?

The teenagers burst into raucous laughter, I suspect at my expense. I can imagine the social media post winging its way across the ether involving a sassy lady, an ice cream and an avid male audience.

'*Anyway . . .*' says Martin, breaking eye contact.

'Yes, anyway . . .' repeats Luca, coughing to clear his throat.

I want to die of embarrassment. I didn't mean to be suggestive, but sadly I have been.

'Keep the change,' I say. 'Pop it in the charity box or something, and I'll see you another day.'

As I turn to leave, Martin calls out, 'Visit us again soon. We need to discuss your amazing talent because—' The door cuts off the last of his words.

Head down, eyes low, I continue to eat my delicious ice cream as I begin the trek back to Rose Cottage.

Boy, will my housemates laugh at this little anecdote!

Benjamina

I'm not one to don trainers usually, but my latest purchase is definitely more comfortable than my ballet pumps. As I climb towards the cottage, I feel like a child with new school shoes, though my floaty cotton skirt with its elasticated waistband might not be the perfect accessory. I watch the pink laces bob up and down against the grey quilting and feel like I'm moon-walking on a layer of cushioned air, my abandoned pumps swinging in the shop's paper bag.

I've already stopped twice on my homeward climb but am grateful when I spy another wooden bench. I'll sit for a moment, breathe deeply and enjoy the view over the aged stone wall. I can see for miles: the harbour, the marina, the lighthouse and a grand-looking building framed by dense vegetation. Under a clear blue sky everything looks so wonderful. I could sit here all day and never tire of the view. I retrieve my mobile and snap a couple of panoramic photos.

Back home, I'd feel too self-conscious to sit here pondering the view, afraid of people staring, hearing their unkind remarks about my size or fitness level, but here, in one morning, I have acquired a laissez-faire attitude.

Is it the sea air? Or simply being more independent?

I have new trainers; what else matters?

'Hello, Benni!' The voice lifts my mood higher. I watch as Ziggy glides to a stop in front of my bench, tipping his skateboard on to its end before he grabs the top edge. 'How are you?'

He's the definition of cool in faded jeans, a white T-shirt and unlaced trainers, so different from this morning's fishing garb. And a skater boy – wow!

'Ziggy!' I exclaim, pleased by his sudden appearance. 'I'm great, thanks . . . just pacing myself.'

Ziggy's dark curls sweep low over his eyes. 'Wise decision. You'd be amazed how silly some of the tourists can be – they seem to forget how unfit they are. Last week, an old guy had a heart attack when he attempted to jog to the top of this road. He should have phoned for the ambulance before he started!'

'No way.'

'Yes way! He got an entirely different bed and breakfast than the one he'd booked.'

'I'll heed the warning, though I can't ever see me attempting to jog, so there's no worries there.'

Ziggy grimaces and frowns.

'You're tough on yourself, aren't you?'

I shrug. I call it honesty. The guy has eyes in his head; how can anyone ignore the rotundity of my frame? Even the kindest of people describe me as big-boned.

'Maybe,' I mutter.

'Where are you walking to?' he asks, filling the growing silence.

I hesitate before answering, unsure if it is wise to confirm details to a stranger who I've known for less than a day, but he seems so open and trustworthy.

'Rose Cottage.'

'I know it.' A smile lightens his expression. 'I used to have a paper round on this stretch. Carrying a huge bag up this hill felt like army training, especially on a Sunday with all the supplements inside. It's a holiday let nowadays, but back then it used to be a family home,' he adds.

I smile politely, slightly embarrassed that I've clammed up.

Along with buying trainers and hiking up steep hills, casually chatting with males is not my usual forte.

'In fact, any cottage with a decent view around these parts is a holiday let now, but hey, mustn't complain.' He shrugs. 'It attracts more tourists, so it's good for us locals.'

Suddenly being here with Ziggy doesn't feel so awkward. I shouldn't be so self-conscious.

'Anyway, I'd better get going,' he says. 'I'm heading down to catch up with my mates.'

'It's nice seeing you again, Ziggy,' I say, collecting my paper bag from the bench.

'You too. Maybe I'll see you down at the fish market one morning . . . I could give you a guided tour of the auction.'

'That would be lovely,' I say, beaming.

'See ya, Benni.' And with one fluid foot flip, his skateboard lands on the tarmac before he pushes off, zigzagging down the steep hill towards the main street.

I continue my climb at a gentle pace, my mind replaying his kind invite. If I leave the cottage at five tomorrow morning, maybe I'll be at the fish market in time to see his trawler landing their catch.

I wonder if the locals get sick of tourists parading along their harbour, enthralled by their daily lives.

I know I'd be none too pleased showing countless visitors around the vinegar factory whilst I monitor and maintain maximum production on the bottling conveyor belt.

Ruth

Having wasted three hours sitting on the sofa failing to read a book and staring at the clock, I give myself a good talking-to. I struggled yesterday when introducing myself to Emma and Benni because I couldn't think of anything to say about myself. I'm a mother, daughter and carer. I work full time as a bank cashier, my first and only job. And that's it. I rarely go out or do anything remotely interesting outside of my family role. I never spend money on myself or my appearance. I refuse every invite offered to me, be it a quick coffee with the girls after work, a wedding anniversary party or even, for the last ten years, the staff Christmas party.

Now, with time on my hands, what do I want to do? I decide to compile a list. After twenty minutes of thinking, it consists of one thing: painting.

So before I can talk myself out of the idea, I pull on my shoes and go out to find the nearest art supplies shop.

'Can I help you?' asks the young girl with the tri-coloured hair. I stare boggle-eyed at the racks of brightly coloured pencils in every shade of the rainbow, the sketchpads, watercolour palettes, acrylics and tubes of oils.

I'm happy to browse, unsure of my needs, but my polite smile and bashfulness don't dampen her eagerness to help.

'We have a great offer on graphite pencils for this week only – a complete beginner's set for only . . .' I tune out and continue to look around. But she persists, describing the quality, the tonal range and the reputation of the manufacturer.

My heart rate is elevated, my palms itching to create. I can't remember the last time I entered an art shop, but I know it was years ago, before I had Jack. I recall the joy I used to feel every time I stared at a blank sheet of paper, the scope of possibilities bewitching me prior to touching the paper with any material. It seemed so indulgent at the time, to allow my imagination to run riot as the first mark can signify such possibility – anything from a simple mindless doodle to a detailed landscape. The composition didn't matter back then – landscape, portrait or still life; all that mattered was my ability to capture an image, a moment in time, much like a photographer as he presses the shutter-release exposure.

In time, I duly select the recommended weekly bargain of graphite pencils, a decent-sized sketchpad and a putty eraser, promising myself that I will return if this impromptu project sets sail into something more. If not, I've only wasted twenty-five quid, which will hardly wreck my bank account.

My second stop is a clothes shop, for a couple of pairs of linen trousers and a few colourful tops, not unlike those Emma wears, though not her off-the-shoulder style. Then I hastily return to the cottage, sneaking my purchases up the stairs and into my room before the other two can spy my carrier bags.

Tomorrow I will attempt to sketch the marina. It'll be my first creative piece since my A-level days. Before a deep-seated love of all things creative was eclipsed by the offer of a full-time job and the staff entitlement of a mortgage rate one per cent lower than the customers' rate. A fine reason to accept a career in banking, or so my mother said.

Emma

'Quick, otherwise you'll lose this one,' I joke to Benni as Ruth rushes towards the barbecue to claim her second burger.

'Oi, wait your turn!' calls Benni, nudging her aside. 'This one is mine!'

'You said you couldn't eat any more,' retorts Ruth feistily, grasping her plate and returning to settle at the small table positioned on the patio. 'You said—'

'I've changed my mind, I'm allowed,' says Benni, squeezing ketchup on to a burger bun. 'In fact, if the truth be known, I'm changing my mind about a few things.'

I flip Ruth's next burger over to brown on the other side. The evening has unfolded in an impromptu way, after we all drifted from our rooms slightly uncertain of the others' plans but without any of our own. A warm summer evening spent in the courtyard became even more appealing once the first bottle of wine was uncorked. The delightful scent from the rambling rose decorating the trellis and the potted lavender provides a pleasant ambience.

'I bought new trainers today – I haven't owned a pair of trainers since my school days, and those were hardly worn,' continues Benni. 'Every week I used to produce a note from my mum excusing me for the PE session.'

Neither Ruth nor I interrupt, I continue to turn the meat on the barbecue not wishing to offend or make a social faux pas.

Benni glances between us before continuing. '*Anyway,* I was impressed that I only stopped three times while climbing the hill today.'

I can hear the pride in her voice; now is the moment to speak.

'Good for you! And tomorrow ... more of the same?' I ask, unsure if Ruth can hear what I can decipher in the young woman's voice.

'I think so. If I can walk every day and enjoy the experience, then maybe I could develop better habits before I return home. I rarely walk anywhere there – a trek to the bus stop and back at the most.'

'I felt exactly the same today,' Ruth says. 'I bought a set of graphite pencils for sketching, but I'm tempted to go back for some watercolours, a canvas and a couple of brushes. I loved painting when I was younger. I've promised myself I'll do as much as I can in the next two weeks. Who knows how many drawings or paintings I can manage before returning home. I also bought a few pairs of holiday trousers, which I desperately needed.'

I turn from the coals, tongs in hand, to view my housemates.

'Well, *I* actually got excited at the prospect of a chocolate and chilli ice cream. My mouth watered uncontrollably and I had a sudden urge to create a new flavour. It's been ages since I truly felt passionate about food.'

On the tiny patio, we all nod in acknowledgement of the others' achievements, so different and yet so alike.

'I say we make these our holiday goals. I'll paint or sketch every day, you might rediscover your food passion and Benni will . . .' Ruth hesitates before blushing profusely.

'Attempt to wear out her new trainers!' I say diplomatically, removing the browned burger from the barbecue.

'Deal!' Benni and Ruth chorus.

'You can mention the dreaded exercise word, Ruth,' Benni says. 'I won't take offence – or blag a note from my mum.'

'Sorry, I always do that. I faff about choosing my words rather than saying what I actually mean. It annoys me as much as others,' says Ruth meekly.

'You don't have to tread on eggshells; just say what you mean,' Benni tells her. 'I'm a big girl, in more ways than one.'

There's a moment's silence before Ruth begins to laugh, and I join her.

'Thank you for being so open, Benni. It's really refreshing,' she says.

'I don't kid myself,' Benni says. 'I know exactly what I see in the mirror and I don't like it. I need to do something about it, and today's highlighted that for me.'

'Good going for one day,' I say, flipping Ruth's burger on to a bun and adding cheese.

'I figure if I can make a few small changes during this holiday, I can continue once I'm home in Burntwood, and then who knows . . . I might enjoy life at last, join a group activity and start socialising, possibly even . . . dating.'

My heart melts for her; she seems nervous even mentioning the word.

'Focus on yourself first and what makes you happy – the rest will follow in good time,' I say as Ruth collects her second burger. 'Don't you agree, Ruth?'

'Phuh! Don't ask me . . . I haven't been on a date since way before the millennium.'

Benni and I exchange a brief glance.

'And you?' asks Ruth sheepishly. 'When were you last in love, Emma?'

I pretend to calculate in my head, buying time. I'm not ready to explain myself, so play-acting seems the natural way to go. I can admit to myself it's been a while since I was in love, and I'm unsure when I fell out of it. But I've definitely known love since the millennium.

'Mmm . . .' I glance between them. 'Bloody hell, who am I kidding! It's been so long, I've forgotten. There, let's settle for that,' I say, relieved that a feasible answer came to mind.

'Sounds like we're each stuck in our ways,' says Ruth, settling herself at the table.

'Each in search of new beginnings at Rose Cottage,' says Benni, holding aloft her wine glass.

'In whatever form we choose,' I add with a giggle. 'It's never too late for a fresh start!'

'Hear, hear,' says Ruth, raising her burger.

Our toast is interrupted by the sound of chiming bells. We all fall silent and listen, cocking our heads as if it will help us to hear more clearly.

'I'll name that tune in three,' says Ruth, taking a huge bite of her burger.

'I've heard it several times today. It's familiar, but I couldn't name it,' adds Benni.

'You're showing your age now, Ruth,' I joke, knowing her TV reference flew straight over Benni's ponytailed head.

'*Exactly*, and sadly it feels like yesterday . . . which is why I need to focus and not waste a moment of this holiday.'

Chapter Three

Monday 20 August

Benjamina

What am I doing?

Having tiptoed down the creaky stairs from the top landing, I swiftly pass Ruth's room and descend to the ground floor. I'm literally up with the lark again, pulling on my new trainers and checking that the key is safely in the safe before clicking the front door shut.

This is not me.

And yet here I stand, observing the dusky hue that surrounds Rose Cottage and the neighbouring homes; even the sun hasn't shown willing at this unearthly hour. I can almost hear faint chuckles resounding in my mind. If my family could see me now, they'd be laughing their socks off.

I walk quickly down the hill towards the harbour front and its fish market, an internal monologue justifying my actions.

I'm doing this for me. I need to establish a routine. I need to exercise. I need to be comfortable exercising while other people aren't around so they can't discourage me with their negative comments about my appearance and efforts.

I stop.

Am I kidding myself?

Is that really the motivation for my early rising, or has Ziggy's offer of a tour of the fish market altered my sluggish behaviour?

I answer my own question: absolutely me and my desire for change.

I resume my walk. Ziggy may have provided an end reward for this early-morning excursion, but ultimately I want to be more active, out and about before other holidaymakers or even the locals are awake. I'm free to do as I please without judgement.

And that is liberating. I've spent my entire youth waiting on the sidelines of life, wanting to join in with the crowd. A crowd who have ignored me, failed to offer me friendship and then stood back to criticise me without getting to know me. Thankfully Ruth and Emma are different.

Although I'm alone, I blush.

I'm not about to announce it to the world, but Ziggy's invitation to the fish market is a first for me. Most women my age have been invited to prom nights, dinner dates or outings to the cinema, but not me. Nothing. I've never been asked to dance, never been asked to make up a social group or be a plus-one at a party. It probably won't be the most exciting event, but to me it's a big deal: someone wants to spend time in my company.

Within twenty minutes, I'm approaching the concrete area dedicated to the fish market. Along the quayside, trawlers of all sizes are moored, and a row of men snake from each, as plastic boxes are flung along by hand from one to the other and finally arrive stacked upon the concrete dock. The herring gulls call noisily from above in an excited state, darting and dipping, attempting to bag free fish from the distracted fishermen. None are successful.

I'm out of breath; I didn't stop once on my descent from Rose Cottage. A metronome count set the pace in my head and I stuck with it. Now I'm positively glowing but deliriously happy with myself for making the effort.

'Benni!' calls a voice to my left.

I turn to view Ziggy waving energetically from his father's trawler. His beanie hat is pulled low, and he's wearing a bulky jacket and waders – gone is the skater-guy look. I raise a hesitant hand as other fishermen glance in my direction before returning to their unloading.

I settle myself on a bench nearby to wait. I pull my mobile from my pocket and take a couple of snaps of the choppy sea, the amber horizon in the backdrop and the noisy herring gulls dive-bombing for food.

This is pure heaven. See what happens when you are active and say yes to an invite.

*   *   *

'Are you ready?' Ziggy bounds over energetically to where I'm sitting. 'You're OK with the smell of fish, I take it?'

'Er, yep, my brother's feet smell like gorgonzola, so if I can stomach those, I can stomach anything!'

Ziggy leads the way through a large open doorway hung with a curtain of thick plastic strips into a vast space occupied by piles of white boxes stacked upon each other. Around each pile stand fishermen and men in white overalls clutching clipboards. The space is filled with noisy banter, deep-throated laughter and the sound of forklift trucks whizzing back and forth.

'This way,' says Ziggy, pointing to a nearby mobile coffee bar around which a scattering of white plastic chairs are placed.

'Are they haggling?' I ask as we stride through.

'Yeah, the fishermen need to get the best price for this morning's catch – we did pretty well today, so Dad's hoping for a lucrative deal. Fingers crossed he'll be happy with the outcome. Woe betide them if it's low like last week's takings were. Coffee or tea?'

'Coffee please, white with one sugar,' I say to the serving guy.

I can't believe this process happens every morning in order to get fresh fish into shops and restaurants the width and breadth of the country. It's a hive of activity. The nearest I normally get to fresh fish is visiting Morrison's in Burntwood.

Ziggy pays and we wander towards the seating area.

'Is it what you expected?' he asks, sipping his coffee.

I shake my head. 'It's a new world to me. I had no idea this went on.'

He nods knowingly.

'Most people have forgotten that fishing is still an industry in this country. The fish simply arrive in a supermarket and they don't question how.'

'Have you always done this?'

'Since I was a teenager. I used to finish school on a Friday and then sleep during the early evening before my dad and his crew took me out and showed me the ropes on Friday and Saturday nights – and sometimes Sundays as well.'

'What about school on Monday?'

Ziggy raises his eyebrows. 'I was never academic, so Dad didn't worry. I could have achieved more if I'd applied myself, but like he used to say, if you're going out to sea, what's the point of GCSEs. And you?'

I hesitate, wishing we could continue to focus on his life choices.

'I'm contracted, so the agency organise my hours and tell me what shifts I'm on. It's a bit of a no-brainer really, doing the same repetitive thing each day, but needs must.'

'And you enjoy that?'

'No, but it's all that was going at the time. The factory folk are quite nice, and the work is OK too. I dislike the agency part – it means I'm never quite sure when I'll be needed next. It's always wait and see, but if I get lumbered with loads of shifts I have to take them in case I'm not needed next week.'

'Unpredictable then?'

'Yep. I always say to my mum, I'm sure they must know . . . that they play games with us half the time pretending they aren't sure. I've learnt to take each week as it comes.'

'And you're happy staying there?'

I pull a face. 'Not really. I'll need some security at some point in my life.' I realise that I should add job-hunting to my to-do list for when I return home. 'And you . . . will it always be fishing?'

'Pretty much, unless the government lets the industry die a death. It's getting harder and harder to make a living from the sea.' He sounds genuinely saddened at the prospect.

'And your dad?'

Ziggy laughs. 'He'll probably plop off the edge of the trawler one day and be lost to the sea . . . much like his old man was.'

'No!' I'm horrified that he should joke about it.

'Don't worry, he'd love that – it'd be a fitting end to a lifetime working at sea. Feed the fishes, so to speak.'

I start to giggle, which soon develops into a joyous laugh. He's funny in such a natural way.

'Come on, let's show you the kind of produce we haul in. Have you ever eaten oysters?'

'No,' I say, grimacing at the thought.

'Fresh cockles, mussels or whelks?' continues Ziggy.

I shake my head.

'Bloody hell, what have you been living off all these years?' he asks, leading the way through the groups of haggling traders to a guy stacking his produce. 'Here, Smithy, have you got a handful of cockles going begging? This one has never eaten fresh shellfish by the sounds of it.'

Smithy looks up, pushes his woollen hat back from his brow and peers at me.

'Yer pulling my leg, man!'

'Seriously, works with vinegar but has never eaten anything that can be pickled in the stuff,' says Ziggy.

I stare as Smithy opens a plastic box, plunges his callused hand amongst the ice chips and lifts out a handful of glimmering blue shells.

'Here, will fresh mussels do?'

'I owe you,' says Ziggy, putting his coffee on the floor and pulling a small penknife from his pocket.

I watch as he works at the edge of one shell before pulling out the creamy orange flesh; he discards the empty shell and pulls a tufted bit from one end.

'Here, try one.'

This is a first for me.

He holds the mussel to my lips. I open wide and he pops it in.

I chew, and swallow. The taste of the sea floods my senses.

'Good?' he asks, opening one for himself.

'Amazing.'

'You don't know what you've been missing, girl!' He laughs heartily, popping the mussel's flesh into his mouth.

My heart rate quickens as his gaze meets mine and lingers.

He quickly works at the edge of another blue shell, removes the mussel and puts it to my lips. As I take his offering, his thumb gently strokes my lower lip.

I blush profusely.

He winks.

Things like this don't happen to me.

Emma

I loiter outside the Co-op trying to look inconspicuous to passers-by whilst blatantly eager to enter the moment the shop opens at seven o'clock. I have literally run down the hill as my taste buds prepare to greet the culinary masterpiece I've dreamt up overnight. I've read the store's opening notice five times and glance at my watch continuously – if they haven't got ripe figs in stock when I enter, I will be flummoxed for sure.

I'm inches from the glass as the assistant unlocks the door with various keys. Finally, I'm in. I grab a plastic basket, though I don't need one, and stride to the fruit section as if I'm doing a sponsored trolley dash.

Found: twelve ripe figs. A quick turn sends me in search of double cream, vanilla pods and a few other essentials. I'm at the till before the assistant has even got there. In, out and gone in under a minute, that's me when I'm on a mission.

Ruth

I scurry from the cottage straight after breakfast. I don't want to be rude, but I can't waste time with pleasantries. I have less than a fortnight to do as I wish. And today, I want to draw.

As I leave, Emma and Benni are sitting on the patio enjoying another round of breakfast tea amongst the roses and the potted lavender plants, Benni eagerly recounting her morning's jaunt to the fish market. I'm surprised she had the nerve to walk about on her own in such a bustling environment. I thought her too shy for that, but maybe she's coming out of her shell.

I had wanted to leave probably an hour ago, if I'm honest. They both compliment my new clothes, saying they suit me, which is nice to hear – but still I should have been on my way.

I have no idea where I'm heading, but having spied the marina yesterday whilst shopping, I've made it my priority.

On the wooden walkway, I find a plastic crate to sit on, and plonk my sketchpad on my knee. Ahead of me is a sea of bobbing masts and complicated rigging on the main wooden gangway of the marina. I'm not causing an obstruction on the walkway for those accessing their beautiful boats, but I have an attractive view to draw. I'm at eye level with my subjects, which will focus my attention on the boats and their idyllic backdrop.

I'm nervous. Eager to begin, and yet my insecurities hold me back from starting the composition.

How ridiculous am I? There's no one to judge me – the nearest person is some thirty feet away, cleaning his decking – yet my hands shake and my stomach twirls.

Emma's right. I must be myself and enjoy my time, as brief as it is. No expectations, no demands, no responsibilities.

Within twenty minutes, I've made a tentative start. I've captured the outline of several large boats in the foreground, and have blocked in the horizon and a number of interesting cottages high up on the craggy hill.

My pencil glides across the page, the paper's surface providing a comforting feel beneath the edge of my right hand. The graphite lines blur and smooth as I blend them, changing the texture and softening the appearance.

I sit back and ponder.

'Not bad,' says a male voice behind me.

I turn with a start. I didn't realise anyone was in the vicinity.

He stands a foot behind me, casually dressed in deck shoes and faded jeans. He shades his blue eyes from the morning sun as he stares down at my sketch.

'Sorry, I didn't mean to make you jump.' His greying hair is closely shaved, like a silverback's fur.

I instantly apologise for being in his way.

'No, no ... I spotted you from the quay. You were so absorbed in your work I didn't want to disturb you,' he says, extending his free hand. 'Dean Harris, nice to meet you.'

'Ruth Elton, likewise,' I say, wiping my palms against my trousers before shaking his hand.

'Your preferred medium, is it?' he asks, peering at my open hold-all and art pencils.

'No, I love watercolour, though I'm not very good, to be honest. I haven't dabbled for a long time.'

'I'd let others be the judge of that, Ruth.' He laughs, a deep, rich tone suggesting a younger man.

'No, seriously. I want to indulge myself whilst on holiday, that's all.'

'If you're looking to exhibit a finished piece, you'll find me at the Quay Gallery over the way.' Dean points towards the main street.

'Thank you, but that's out of my league.' I'm humbled, flattered by the very idea. This is obviously his practised spiel to gain customers for his business. You can't blame him, with an ever-changing footfall of holidaymakers – I'm sure he has to try every tactic to fight off competition.

'Any time you're passing, please drop by. With regards to your project – just remember, always complete the composition before finding a new scene on which to focus.' With that, he sets off along the walkway, chatting to boat owners as he passes.

I return to my sketch, adjusting a line here and there, studying the rigging to get the details right.

The sky is a dazzling blue, not a cloud to be seen, the water laps gently against the sides of the boats and the herring gulls glide overhead.

What more can I ask for?

As I sweep away the eraser debris from my page, I can see Dean laughing heartily with the man who was earlier scrubbing his decking. Both look happy, content with their lot and enjoying a lazy Monday morning.

It must be strange having all the time in the world to navigate your day without demands from others.

I continue to watch their body language, and decide they're probably friends of old, possibly naughty boys dating back to the school playground.

A pang of jealousy ignites within my chest. I haven't got that. There're no friends who remember my younger years, my schooldays or even my craziest moments, though they were few and far between given my strict upbringing.

I'm suddenly aware of warmth at the base of my neck. The midday sun is blazing down, and I forgot to bring my sun screen. I won't be best pleased if I burn, so I start to pack away my pencils and promise myself that tomorrow I'll get up extra early, like Benni, and continue my composition.

I'm pleased with this morning's efforts. The sketch might not be perfect, or anywhere near finished, but I've accomplished something in a few hours and enjoyed myself into the bargain. On my trek home, I'm tempted to nip into the art suppliers and price up a basic set of watercolours and an easel. They might offer a package price for a starter set.

Emma

'I thought it would be brown,' exclaims Ruth as I peel the lid back to reveal the creamy beige confection. 'Surely fig ice cream should be brown.'

I don't answer, knowing the colour is determined by all the ingredients, not just one.

'Would you like some?' I ask.

'Absolutely! It looks like rum and raisin.'

I scoop a roll of ice cream and deliver it in a tiny glass dish alongside a teaspoon.

'Fig and balsamic vinegar,' I announce. Ruth's face is a picture as she cautiously eyes my offering, which has taken all morning to freeze properly. 'Seriously, it might sound strange, but I promise you, this is a delightful combination.'

Ruth spoons the tiniest amount into her mouth, tasting it gingerly. I've seen this reaction so many times when I offer people food. People often taste food mentally prior to *actually* tasting it; some talk themselves out of even trying. I know exactly what'll happen in the next sixty seconds.

'Oh my God, that is gorgeous!'

There it is. All the confirmation I need. Ruth's subsequent mouthfuls are rapid, and each spoonful is heaped. I watch as she scrapes the tiny glass dish of every smear.

'More?'

'Yes please. Who'd have thought balsamic vinegar could taste so lovely in a dessert?' She hands me the empty dish, then waits impatiently at my elbow like a child wanting to lick a mixing bowl clean. 'Are you sure there'll be enough left for Benni?'

'I'm sure,' I say, proud that once again my culinary ideas have borne fruit. 'I'll dish us each a decent portion then Benni can enjoy the rest later on. Do you want some double cream on top?'

'Think of the calories,' stutters Ruth, but she's almost drooling.

'Bugger the calories – we're on holiday!' I take the remains of the double cream from the fridge and garnish the ice cream with a little extra. Ruth doesn't protest, but grabs her spoon and tucks in.

This is my pleasure in life. Dreaming up combinations, experimenting with ingredients and creating delights that bring happiness to others. I want to burst with pride as Ruth scrapes her dish clean for a second time.

Benjamina

'Dan, it's only Monday! I've only been away for two days ... OK, three if you count travelling down,' I mutter into my mobile. I'm trying desperately to sound bright and cheery with Ruth and Emma sitting opposite me in the Queen's Arms. 'Surely you can cope?'

I pause, listening as my older brother rants on about my selfish behaviour. I'm embarrassed to look in Emma's direction but I can sense her frown deepening. I should have ignored the call. Kept my phone on silent.

'No, I'm not coming back. You'll just have to manage,' I say, as he finally draws breath. 'Now if you don't mind, I need to go. Bye, Dan.' I tap the screen, cutting his call short, and instantly burst out crying, much to the surprise of Emma and Ruth. Hot, angry tears race down my cheeks, and I frantically dab my eyes with my sleeve, mortified at reacting so emotionally in a public place. We were supposed to be enjoying a lunchtime drink before looking for a quiet restaurant for dinner later on.

'Hey now, what's all this?' soothes Emma, reaching for my hand.

'Here . . .' adds Ruth, offering me a tissue, as Emma removes my hand revealing my teary eyes.

I take the tissue, dab my eyes and glance about the pub to see how many customers are staring or remarking on my behaviour. No one seems to have noticed. The crowded bar continues as it was before my phone call.

'Take a deep breath . . . have a sip of your drink,' urges Emma, rubbing my forearm, as I dab at my eyes.

Ruth sits in silence, watching.

I feel such a fool. Who the hell am I kidding? I thought I was grown up and independent; that I could go on holiday amongst strangers and have a good time. I had such a wonderful morning down at the harbour, which left me feeling revived and energised. But all the time, the realities of my life are there in the background, ruining what I've chosen to do. Maybe I should feel blessed that I've managed to enjoy myself for three days.

Within a few minutes, I feel calmer. I know I can be honest with the others; their expressions show concern for my wellbeing.

'I'm so sorry, I should have ignored his call,' I say, not knowing where to start. 'He knows exactly how to wind me up.'

'That's family for you,' says Ruth, playing with her gin glass. 'Anything we can do?'

'No. I should be used to it by now, but . . .' I pause, unsure whether to continue or to offer to fetch a fresh round of drinks.

'Benni, you can tell us if you want to,' says Emma, giving me a warm smile.

'My mum's gone on another bender and ... apparently, she's been ranting since the moment I left for the station on Saturday about my selfish behaviour. My brother's demanding I return home tonight. I don't want to,' I say quickly, before I can change my mind.

'She drinks?' questions Ruth in a whisper.

'Yeah, always has. Dan reckons she's downed a bottle and a half of vodka each day since I left. She'll be completely sozzled, but why should I cut my holiday short?'

'You shouldn't,' states Emma. 'Couldn't your brother call on support from elsewhere ... someone closer to home?'

'Phuh! That'll never happen. It's as if she's my responsibility. Usually I'm the one at home, but on this occasion Dan will just have to cope, won't he?' I ask anxiously, needing reinforcement. 'I've had to do it on previous occasions, he's never dashed home to support me. It feels like my punishment for daring to enjoy myself. They know how I'll react; they know me too well.'

Both women are nodding sympathetically.

'He's twenty-eight,' I continue, 'he's not a child, but oh no, Dan's got better things to do – probably involving gambling until the early hours of the morning in some seedy back room or a pub lock-in. But if Mum needs me, maybe I should go ...' My voice cracks as my inner turmoil surfaces alongside my annoyance.

'Hang on a minute, Benni. Do you deserve this upset?' asks Emma.

'No, I don't. I deserve a decent holiday.' I sob into a paper serviette. 'That's the first call I've had in three days ... Dan didn't even reply when I texted to let them know I'd arrived safely. I wish they could be happy that I'm doing something in life rather than staying at home.'

'So let them get on with their drama,' says Ruth.

'I agree,' adds Emma, squeezing my hand before releasing her grip.

'Better still, switch your phone off for the rest of the holiday. I could be made to feel guilty about leaving my mum in the care of others but I'm not going to let myself. You're no different to me, Benni – you need time out to enjoy yourself. It isn't too much to ask, is it?' says Ruth, in an emphatic tone that seems unlike her. 'I haven't called the care home since I arrived. I desperately want to, but I've stopped myself. They'll let me know if I'm needed.'

'Exactly! You both deserve this. Let others pick up the slack for a while.' Emma finishes her wine in one mouthful. 'I say we go back to the cottage and find something to take your mind off the situation.'

'But what happens if he can't cope?' I ask.

'He'll cope – like you've had to,' says Emma. 'Come on, we're going to cheer you up.'

'Emma has exactly what you need ... it's gorgeous!' giggles Ruth, getting to her feet and collecting her handbag.

'You're both too kind. I don't deserve this.'

Emma lifts an open palm to stop me.

'Nonsense. You're worth it. Now get your stuff. We've got a treat waiting at the cottage, and if it doesn't put a smile on your face, I promise to nip to the shop and make a batch of your favourite flavour.'

I'm intrigued but immensely grateful that fate has delivered two strong women with whom I can share my troubles.

Emma

'Hello!' I call, entering the ice cream parlour to find the counter area bare of staff. It's late, just before closing time, and there are no customers. Half the chairs are turned upside down on the tables. A bucket and submerged mop stand abandoned beside the counter, and a section of tiled floor gleams wetly.

Martin appears in the doorway from the back room.

'Hello again, sorry I didn't hear you come in. What can I get you?' He begins to wash his hands in the tiny stainless-steel sink unit.

'I thought you were closed.' I indicate the mop bucket and empty tables.

'No, not quite. It's been a quiet kind of day, but there's still thirty minutes to go until we officially shut up shop. Still enjoying your holiday?' he adds as he dries his hands.

'I am. My first time visiting Brixham and I'm impressed with the scenery.' I'm stalling. I can sense this conversation isn't going how I intended, and I need to take control before I climb the hill, returning my offerings to the cottage for swift consumption by Benni.

'Good to hear. I'm a local, born and bred in the area, and

I think we forget how beautiful it really is. Did you enjoy the chocolate and chilli ice cream yesterday?'

'I did, very much. So much so that it got me thinking about other flavoursome combinations, and this morning I was up and out buying fresh produce to create my own.'

'Honestly?' Martin's eyes widen and his mouth gapes as I open my bag and retrieve the small tub of home-made ice cream, which I offer over the glass counter.

'Fig and balsamic vinegar – it sounds a bit weird . . .' I wiggle my hand before continuing, 'but my two housemates have devoured an entire tub between them. It's my first attempt, but it shows the kind of flavour blending that interests me.'

Martin takes the tub, conjures a small spoon from nowhere and digs it into the ice cream. As he tastes the first mouthful, his eyebrows lift into his hairline and a look of surprise dawns.

'That . . . is beautiful!' He continues to scoop greedily, testing and tasting each spoonful noisily. I'm one to vocalise food tasting, but his response outweighs mine any day. I'm mesmerised. 'Wow! I agree you have a talent for taste.'

'Thank you, I am rather pleased with the results—'

I didn't finish my sentence regarding my plan to create others.

'Sold!'

'What?'

'I'll take as much as you can make. How do you want to work this financially?'

'Are you serious? Just like that?'

'We could agree a purchase price or arrange a percentage of sales, whichever you prefer.'

'You want me to make a fresh batch for sale in here?'

'That's exactly what I want.'

One minute he's sampling my ice cream, the next we're talking money and I'm staking claim to the cottage's kitchen for an entire day of ice cream production. Talk about a cottage industry appearing from nowhere!

We settle on a price for two large tubs of ice cream to be delivered as soon as humanly possible and I dash from the ice cream parlour and head straight to the Co-op to purchase fresh ingredients. It's amazing how a busy mind can eliminate all distractions, even when you're lugging four heavy shopping bags up a steep hill. The urge to share my success with Ruth and Benni outweighs the painful stitch I have under my left rib.

Ruth

Benni's emotional reaction earlier has unsettled me. I make my excuses soon after Emma returns to the cottage and head for the bathroom. I slide the lock across, lean my back against the closed door and breathe deeply.

I didn't think I would react in this manner. Witnessing Benni's anxiety about her alcoholic mother has made me jittery about my own responsibilities. Is Mum eating? Sleeping? Taking her medication as she should?

I cross the bathroom, tastefully decorated in blue and white and accessorised with a nautical theme, and turn the shower on full blast despite the fact that I won't be getting undressed. Hopefully the noise will cover the sound of my phone call; if I have to raise my voice to be heard over the water hopefully Emma and Benni will assume I'm singing. I fold the hand towel in half and place it over the closed loo seat, making it more comfortable, then settle myself and take my mobile from my pocket.

I promised myself I wouldn't do this for another few days. Earlier I told Benni to switch her phone off, and now look at me. Am I a hypocrite? Or simply a concerned daughter who should have called earlier?

It takes ages for the care home to answer. Is the delay due to a staffing shortage? Or is it unrealistic of me to expect every establishment to answer their phone within the standard three rings stipulated within the banking industry?

'Hello, Acorn Ridge Care Home . . . how may I help you?'

'Ah yes, it's Ruth Elton calling to enquire how my mother, Violet Elton, is getting on,' I say as calmly as I can despite my anxieties.

'Thank you, if you hold the line I'll put you through to the carers.'

A blast of 'Greensleeves' fills the hiatus while I'm connected elsewhere.

'Hello, Ms Elton?' comes a mild-mannered voice.

'Yes, speaking.'

'Hello, I'm Jenny, I'm happy to report that your mum has settled in nicely. She's slept well each night and has spent most of her time in the lounge enjoying the activities with our other guests. She's currently in the conservatory having a cup of tea.'

'That sounds wonderful.'

'She appears quite happy to join in. Not everyone wants to, but your mother seems eager to socialise. Is there any message I can pass on?'

I feel stupid. Over-protective in every manner. I'm utterly ridiculous, I'm pretending to have a shower to cover up my phone call, and all the time Mum hasn't a care in the world. Basically, she's having the time of her life.

'No, no message. Sorry to disturb you,' I say curtly, eager to end the call.

'No worries, call at any time – you're not disturbing us. We know it's a worry when relatives come to stay, and if we can answer any of your concerns, we're happy to help.'

'Yes, thank you ... Goodbye.'

I sound rude cutting her short, but the jitters of guilt are instantly chased away by relief. I shouldn't worry so much. Mum is fine. I'm now fine. I should call whenever I want, instead of sneaking around up here. Keeping up appearances and worrying what others might think, hasn't that always been the problem with our little family? Well, no more! I'll mention my phone call when I go downstairs – no one will judge me for caring, I know they won't. And Benni really shouldn't switch off her phone; instead, she needs to find a way to cope. That's better advice; I should have said that earlier.

I switch the shower off. What a waste of water, too.

From tomorrow, I'll phone first thing each morning. I'll

make a routine of it, then I can be worry-free for the rest of the day.

I replay the short conversation in my head. I find it strange that Mum seems to be enjoying participating in activities. Whenever I suggest attending social groups or clubs, she flatly refuses, coming up with an endless string of excuses to remain at home with me. And yet now, amongst strangers she's acting entirely differently. Typical.

Chapter Four

Tuesday 21 August

Benjamina

I hold tight on to the warm duvet cover. Today, I won't go to the harbour. I won't dash down the hill to chat with Ziggy at first light. Instead, I'll relax, chill out and have a well-deserved lie-in, a rare treat when juggling shifts at the vinegar factory.

It takes great willpower to remain in situ.

About an hour ago, I heard footsteps below so assume that either Emma or Ruth are up and about. But I'm going to stay here and enjoy my lie-in. What's a holiday unless you enjoy at least one lie-in?

The bedside clock tells me it's eight o'clock. Hardly late, and yet unusually I'm itching to be up and out of the front door. At this time on a typical weekday, I'd be heading towards the bus stop to catch the bus into Burntwood, followed by the five-minute walk to the vinegar factory. First stop, the changing room, to don my regulation uniform. Never a flattering option, or at least not for the fuller figure. I hate the blue cap with attached hairnet, and the pale blue tabard is simply hideous.

I close my eyes and watch the daily routine unfold in my head: the white wellingtons, the scrubbed hands and finally the tsunami of employees as we clock on at the main door of the production room. I'm usually on bottling. Not the most glamorous of roles, but the sight of bottles passing by at speed to be injection-filled with malt vinegar is mesmerising. I can watch it all day; I often do.

I've been hired via the agency for so long, I can recall the injection sounds, the pungent smell and the noisy hum of the chattering work force – like a living breathing monster churning out bottle after bottle. They tell me it sells for less than a quid, which seems remarkable given the number they produce each day, month or year.

I glance at the clock again: 8.18. I wonder if any of the production crew will miss me. Or will the agency send a replacement who'll quit the shift by 10.30 due to the factory floor banter? I giggle at the very idea. The older women are the worst culprits, always a tad suggestive – verging on crass – with the young males. Strictly speaking, I've witnessed one or two near misses with regards to comments verging on in-decency but Sandra, the supervisor, possesses the magic touch to bring her wayward ladies back in line. I'm sure the human resources department has been grateful on many occasion for her no-nonsense approach.

A sudden rapping on my bedroom door disturbs my thoughts.

'Yes?'

'Benni, have you got a moment?' asks Emma, her voice muffled by the wooden door.

'Sure . . .'

She enters looking flustered in a lacy blue shower cap, from which tendrils of auburn hair hang loose, and a plastic bin bag fashioned roughly into a tabard.

'Fancy dress?' I ask, conscious that I have bed hair and puffy eyes.

'No, I just haven't brought my chef's whites with me.' She indicates her outfit. 'Do you fancy helping me in the kitchen, just for one day? I'll make it up to you tomorrow.'

'I'm supposed to be on my holidays,' I groan. 'Can't Ruth help?'

'She's not in her room – I've checked.'

'So I'm not even your first choice? Jeez, thanks for that,' I mutter, turning over and pulling the duvet over my head.

'Please, Benni. I've made a promise, which I'd like to keep.'

I can hear the desperation in her voice. I'm intrigued.

Slowly the corner of my duvet lifts to reveal Emma's pleading face.

'Go away!'

'I'll make you waffles for breakfast,' she coos.

Sold.

Erin Green

Ruth

I frantically erase a huge section of pale blue sky from my drawing. It isn't right; I've over-layered and applied the colours too heavily for the subtle effect I'm after.

What's wrong with me today? Nothing's going to plan, despite my first stop being the art shop to purchase a range of coloured pencils to complement my graphite set. Sadly, my new purchase wasn't on offer. I'd got up early and hastily made tea and toast before sneaking out of the door without disturbing my sleeping housemates. I felt a tinge of guilt as I snuck out knowing I hadn't invited them. They're so generous in asking me to join in and tag along with everything they plan. It's as if they need to be sure I'm OK with plans of my own before they disappear out the door. Yet, I scurry from the cottage for fear of being spotted. It's just that I want to submerge myself in my sketching without distractions. I don't want to explain myself. I've spent my entire life explaining myself to others, mainly Mum.

Last night, I was open about my call to the care home. I'm glad I told them, and relieved that I changed my advice to Benni too. And they didn't judge me. I knew they wouldn't. What was it Emma said afterwards? 'I'm a true believer that you create the weather in your world, if only in your head.' Instantly, her line struck a chord with me, so today, I chose full sunshine without a single cloud to blot my horizon.

I also called the care home during my walk towards the marina. Everything is fine; nothing's changed.

I quickly select another pencil and begin applying a subtle blend of colour, my hand barely touching the paper to create a blue that is barely visible and yet essential in depicting the delicate skyline. I sit back from my work, turning my head this way and that to view the landscape from various points.

I like it.

You can't always appreciate the effect when you're in close proximity to a composition, but as soon as you sit back or view it through different eyes, it's obvious where the flaws and the beauty lie.

I look around at the surrounding boats bobbing listlessly upon the waves. I've never seen the attraction of boats and water until this holiday. But sitting here listening to the tide lapping against the supporting joists of the wooden walkway has given me a new insight.

My eyes drift towards a boat moored at the far end. Its owner is busy waxing the decking with a vigour that defies reason, and yet his smile is as broad as they come.

Simple pleasures. That's where the joys of life lie. Drinking decent coffee. Laughing heartily with others. Feeling the sun on your face. Looking at the clock not because you have to administer medication but because you need to know the time.

Instantly, I feel sad.

Nowadays I never look at a clock face without thinking about Mum's routine. When did that start? When will it—

I stop myself.

The very thought makes my blood run cold.

After all she's done for me over the years, I'm sitting here contemplating a time when ...

I retrieve my pencil and attempt to clear my head by defining a small boat in the distance.

I can't be thinking like that, not now, not ever. I should be grateful for everything I have. What is it they say? 'Count your blessings', and so I shall.

I have Jack, and Megan, if she's his choice.

I have my mother.

I have my health.

I have a home, food and enough money to live on.

What more do I need?

I don't answer my own question. I simply refuse to acknowledge the situation.

The spell seems to have been broken and has affected the fine weather inside my head. I no longer wish to draw, so I begin to clear my equipment away.

If only I'd kept my focus on the water, the reflections and the clouds, I might have finished my sketch.

Never mind, I'll come back early tomorrow morning and see if I can complete it in one more sitting. Though if I purchase the watercolour starter set I looked at earlier, I could use this as a preliminary study sketch for painting a much bigger piece. I rarely spend money on myself, which is why I'm holding back. But I'm tempted, very tempted.

Benjamina

'Don't beat them like that!' screams Emma, grabbing the balloon whisk from my clutches and dripping egg yolk on to the tiled floor.

'I beat as I beat, OK? I'm no professional.'

'Be gentle, loving,' she instructs. 'It's a rhythmical action, not an erratic zigzag.' She returns her attention to weighing a mountain of sugar.

'It's egg yolks,' I mutter sulkily, slowing my whisking action to a minimum speed, mocking her instruction.

Emma huffs for the umpteenth time during our fifteen minutes of prepping.

'It may only be egg yolks to you, but it's a key ingredient.' She peers intently at the tiny LED display, tipping minute amounts of sugar from a tablespoon.

'Are you like this at work?' I ask, wedging the mixing bowl into the crook of my arm and quickening my now rhythmical action. The bowl sticks to the bin-liner overall that Emma has made me don, though my bandana looks more fetching than her lacy shower cap.

She doesn't answer, focusing on her task.

'Oh my God, you are! You're a shouty chef.' I snigger.

'Stop it. Most chefs are shouty . . . we can't help it. When it's a busy shift, food flying in and out of the kitchens and waitresses demanding orders quicker than they can be humanly cooked, then yeah, it gets a bit manic and I can get a bit shouty.'

'Great, and I'm your unpaid lackey for the day.'

'Yeah, but I won't be . . .' Emma falters. 'Forget it, just shout back if I do.'

Bloody right I will.

I watch as she clears away milk cartons and egg shells and gathers a medley of dishes and jugs containing chopped figs, caster sugar, double cream and balsamic vinegar into a neat line on the countertop. She meticulously wipes the surfaces, then gathers saucepans from the cupboards and collects utensils from a large drawer.

'For a holiday-let cottage this really is home from home in terms of cooking equipment,' she says, admiring the array of items on the worktop.

I don't answer but simply take in her excited expression. Have I ever looked at a kitchen counter in such a way? Never. Have I ever prepped ingredients before baking like that? No, which probably explains a lot. On the rare occasions when I attempt to bake, I tend to grab each item from the cupboard as and when it's mentioned in the recipe. Which explains why I have to scrap ideas halfway through when I find there's no caster sugar, or gelatine, or vanilla pods in the house. I smile. As if I've *ever* lived in a house containing a tube of vanilla pods. *Those* homes were the same ones that put sticky-back plastic on the weekly shopping list. That said, I'm not entirely sure I know what sticky-back plastic is. And I only know how to use a vanilla pod because I watched a Nigella's 'all day special' four Christmases ago.

'Is this what you're supposed to do?' I ask, taking the chance to learn.

'What do you mean?'

'Lay it all out?'

Emma looks puzzled.

'Yeah.'

'That explains it then,' I say, shrugging. 'You won't find this amount of clear workspace in our kitchen, so no wonder we're all crap cooks.'

She smiles politely. She clearly thinks I'm joking. I'm not. I'm being honest. Back in the sixties, when our bungalow was built, the kitchen wasn't the main feature. A spacious lounge with interconnecting doors to the dining room and a tiny serving hatch into the kitchen was far more important. Nowadays, some family kitchens are bigger than our front and rear gardens put together.

Emma begins to create.

I lean against the fridge door watching her. If I treat today like a school cookery lesson, I may pick up one or two hints – though given my lack of culinary skills I'd probably mess it up if I try to emulate this back at home. Or spend the rest of my life eating only ice cream which goes against my recent health kick.

'Would these flavours work well alongside chocolate?' I ask as she begins blending the ingredients.

'Perhaps, though the bitterness of the chocolate would need to be balanced depending on the quality and percentage of cocoa butter.'

'I wouldn't mind experimenting with chocolate. When I was at school, I enjoyed making chocolate truffles for a charity event – I made loads and sold every bag. It's funny what you remember from your school days.'

I see her eyebrows flicker, but she doesn't comment. I don't ask what she means about percentages; I was never any good with numbers and my teacher provided the block of chocolate for me to melt over a pan of boiling water.

Within minutes, she's apparently made a custard, added flavourings and figs. She asks me to gently stir it while she adds yet more cream to the warm mixture on the stove.

'You've hardly got a flame,' I say, trying to be helpful.

'I know. The aim is to avoid scrambling the eggs,' she says, eyeing me cautiously as she pours. 'So a low heat is essential.'

I nod as if I knew that. I didn't.

'Keep stirring, don't stop,' she says, piling her used jug next to the sink. 'Not until I say.'

As I stir, I watch her peeling the lids from brand-new plastic boxes. They're the deep-sided kind that my older brother used to have as a teenager for his packed lunch. He could fit three rounds of jam butties, a Club biscuit and a pack of Mini Cheddars inside and still be starving when he arrived home at four o'clock. I hated jam butties so opted for the tuck shop instead. Two Bountys, one Mars bar and a bag of Twiglets would do for me.

Emma washes and dries each box, placing them on the counter beside me.

'OK, you can stop,' she says, nudging me out of her way. I

resume my position leaning against the fridge. It's like baking with my mother – except it isn't. I've never baked with my mother.

Emma kills the heat, lifts the saucepan from the stove and gently pours the creamy beige contents into the boxes. Nuggets of chopped fig plop into the mixture as it slowly fills the containers. She gives each one a gentle bang on the worktop before looking up at me.

'Here, taste,' she says, offering me the saucepan.

I wipe my index finger around the edge of the warm pan, collecting a bobble of creamy mixture. Emma does the same, her eyes closing as she tastes the rich fig and balsamic vinegar blend.

'That's delicious,' I say, wanting more, much more.

She nods, her expression one of sheer joy.

'We need to let it cool and then pop it into the fridge freezer for about three hours before we deliver it.'

'We?'

'Yeah, *we* . . . You helped to make it.' She beams.

'Benni, help me! We've got a problem.' Emma's voice is frantic as she knocks on my bedroom door.

I hastily answer, moving faster than I have in years.

'What?' I'm imagining the disaster and how much compensation we'll need to pay to the cottage owners: for fire, flood or an act of God.

'Come with me.' She grabs my hand, pulling me down two flights of stairs, causing me to trip and stumble in her wake.

She drags me into the kitchen, opens the fridge door and says, 'Look!'

I look. I observe the inner door containing milk cartons, fruit juice and a half-finished bottle of wine. I view the shelves, neatly ordered by food category, thanks to our resident chef. I don't understand her issue. I haven't spilt the milk and left it to dry. I haven't put an empty juice carton back in the door – one of my brother's tricks. I have covered the butter pack. I have even cling-filmed the half-emptied tin of beans.

I can sense her rising panic, but I can't see an issue. I'm going to have to ask for a clue.

'What am I looking at?'

'The freezer!'

My gaze lifts to the slimline plastic flap at the top of the fridge, and then shifts to where Emma is pointing to the two deep-sided tubs sitting on the counter.

'Oh.'

'Exactly!' Her shoulders slump. 'What a waste of time – they're going to think I'm an utter fool. Why does this always happen to me? I have such great ideas, yet this kind of thing happens every time I try and accomplish anything in life. *This* . . .' she thrusts her hand between slim-line freezer and deep sided tubs of cooled ice cream, '. . . is the story of my bloody life!' Her voice breaks on the final words, hot, angry tears cascading down her cheeks. 'Every time I try and better myself, improve my prospects in life, or simply enjoy myself – it all goes wrong. Every bloody time!'

Emma covers her face, as her shoulders heave up and down.

'Emma, we'll find a solution, don't worry. There must be smaller tubs in the supermarket. I'll go and buy four and we'll repackage the ice cream. It's not the end of the world.' I gently rub her shoulders. I'm unsure whether a full-on hug is necessary, though given her loud sobs, it could be.

This isn't the Emma I've come to know. This Emma seems vulnerable and frustrated by life; stressed by the simplest error.

'Emma, don't.' I wrap my arms about her shoulders and squeeze. 'It isn't ruined. Another ten minutes cooling on the worktop won't hurt. I'll nip to the Co-op and be back before you know it. It'll taste as good as ever, no harm done.'

She mumbles something into my shoulder, but I ignore her, knowing it's probably negative given her current mood. I lead her into the dining room, pull out a chair at the large wooden table and plop her on to the seat, manoeuvring her like a rag doll.

Who'd have thought it? Emma was so in control whilst blending and creating, but now she's good for nothing.

I return to the kitchen and rustle up a cup of tea before she can resume crying or deepen her negative thoughts.

'There you go. Now have a quiet sit and a sip of that little beauty and I'll be back in no time, OK?' I quickly push my feet into my new trainers and grab my tote bag. 'See you in a bit.'

I open the front door, my plan fully formed to the point where I can see myself returning up the hill carrying a bag of plastic tubs. But before I've even stepped outside, my intended mad dash towards the shops and supermarket sweep for new plastic containers is wiped from my mind.

'The Queen's Arms,' I whisper to myself.

What a bloody good idea! I nip across the road and am dashing through the double doors into their lunchtime session quicker than a rat out of a trap. I make for the bar; it's the same bartender as the other day. I wait patiently while she finishes serving her customer, then make my request.

'Hello . . . it's Marla, isn't it?' I say. 'Would you mind doing me a favour?'

'Emma, we're sorted.' I dash into the dining room, delighted with my five minutes of work. 'Grab the ice cream tubs and follow me – we're going over the road.'

Emma puts down her mug and stares.

'Quickly, put your shoes on.'

'Now's not the time for a quick half! The ingredients will be ruined if—'

'Hurry up, will you!' I snort, my patience beginning to wear thin. 'Follow me.'

I pick up the first container with both hands and, careful not to slop it, walk through from kitchen to dining room towards the hallway, Emma following with the second tub. In the Queen's Arms, Marla kindly beckons us through the bar's hatchway and along a corridor towards the pub's large kitchen – complete with huge catering freezer.

I gently slide my plastic container on to the white wire shelf.

'Are you sure you don't mind?' I ask as Emma follows suit with hers.

'I'm sure. Two tubs hardly take up any space. I'll mention

it to the landlord when he drops in later, but it won't be a problem,' says Marla confidently.

'Thank you. We owe you one,' I say, before we retrace our steps back to the bar. 'And you don't mind if we nip over in an hour to check how it's going?'

'No problem. Just go through. I'll warn the chef when he comes in later.'

'You don't serve food at lunchtime, do you?' asks Emma, nervously anticipating another disaster.

'Nope, only in the evenings. We offer bed and breakfast to our guests, but they tend to disappear out and about until early evening, and there's really no call for food amongst the regulars.'

'The tubs will be gone by then,' I say, and we leave Marla to her bar of waiting customers.

'Thank you,' says Emma as we saunter back across the road to Rose Cottage.

'No worries. You get het up about nothing, don't you?' I tease.

'And you don't?' asks Emma, as we enter the cottage.

'Not really. When you work for a temping agency, not knowing if you have work from one week to the next, you get used to living with the unknown. There's no stability in my life. Yeah, I still live at home, and my mum's unreliable due to her drinking. There have been so many times when we've switched roles and I've had to be the adult while she's ... well, inebriated. My brother's hardly supportive or protective towards me either, so I just get on with life as best I can. You witnessed the phone call last night. I've survived by becoming stronger. I'm used to crisis – it's all I've ever known.' I fall silent to find Emma watching me; she's calmer now but there's a tiny glint in her eye.

'Sounds . . . hard,' she says, blinking quickly.

I pause. 'Yeah, it has been. I can't plan for the future. I certainly can't save on a basic wage, but hey, at least I have a reputation for being a good worker – which is why the agency keep calling me back to the factory.'

'Good for you, Benni . . . that's worth so much nowadays.'

'It is, but it won't ever provide me with a deposit for a property,' I say, brushing away the image of me aged forty still living at my mother's.

Ruth

Each step is a saunter; there's no rush or hurry. I allow myself to wander through the streets towards the cottage. Without realising, I've taken a different route each time I've returned. This walk is no exception.

The Quay Gallery stands directly before me, its vast window dominated by a painting of the lighthouse. I stop and admire it. The brushstrokes are proud and plentiful upon the wide canvas. The image depicts a choppy sea, which lifts and sprays a cacophony of colour against the aged sides of the lighthouse.

It is quite a composition.

If I ever paint anything as amazing as that . . .

'Afternoon. Are you well?'

His voice breaks into my thoughts.

'Dean – you startled me! Yes, very well, thank you. I was admiring the lighthouse.'

'Stunning, isn't it?'

'The way the artist has captured the fall of light on the textured rock face – quite amazing. I could never create something as impressive as that.'

Dean pulls a face. 'Of course you could. The sketch I saw the other day has the potential to capture light on the water in a similar way. Remember what I told you: don't stop halfway . . . always complete each piece.'

'Phuh!' I shake my head and my cheeks colour. 'I'm tempted to invest in a set of watercolours and start again, though it's been decades since I last sat down with a brush and easel.'

'Seriously, you could complete a piece in no time using watercolours. Practice is all it takes. Believe me.'

I do believe him. I have no doubt that if I painted for twenty hours a week I would get better, decidedly better than the few days I can manage whilst on holiday. There's no point making endless promises to myself to continue once I'm home. I know the first thing I'll do after unpacking my pencils and sketchpad will be to push them aside before loading an economy wash. I'll have good intentions of joining an art class, but I won't. I know that life will resume as it was and I'll return to my usual routine.

'When will it be finished?'

'I haven't bought my watercolours or easel yet.'

'What are you waiting for, Ruth? The young lady in the art shop will sort you out. She's very talented, she knows her materials. And please let me view the finished piece when it's done. We can work on—' He's interrupted by the telephone ringing inside the gallery. 'I must dash, but please bring it in and we'll discuss your plans. Bye now.' He gives a nod before heading inside.

We'll discuss your plans. His words swim about my head as I traipse towards the art shop.

I baulk at the idea. It's one thing to paint for pleasure but an entirely different ball game to have a gallery display a finished piece for sale. The last composition I had displayed for an audience was a pasta creation way back in primary school that decorated the main corridor during parents' evening. I've honed my talents since then, but even so.

Benjamina

'For the love of God, will you please hurry up!' I squawk as Emma fiddles with the door lock. I have a tight grip of one of the ice cream tubs, which we've wrapped in newspaper to help insulation and prevent my warm hands from melting the product into a creamy goo during the ten-minute walk. 'Now is not the time to faff!'

'Look, I'm nervous, OK. It's been a long time since I've done something like this. I've taken it from an idea to reality in less than twenty-four hours and you're accusing me of faffing – seriously?'

I begin to walk. Even given the steep incline of the roads, I still believe we'll be cutting it fine. Why she wouldn't order a taxi to deliver us and the product in perfect condition, I don't know. Though I suppose she can't really afford the taxi fare; considering the quantity and quality of the ingredients she's used, she won't exactly be making a huge profit.

I can hear her pattering feet behind me. I don't wait for her to catch up but continue on my way. I'm on a mission to deliver the ice cream in the best possible state.

That's when I hear the rumble of tiny plastic wheels.

I turn and stare uphill. Emma is hot stepping as I imagined, but behind her snaking swiftly down the road, side to side, is Ziggy on his skateboard.

I wave, and he skids to a halt after safely passing Emma.

'Any chance you're going into town?' I ask, peering into his hazel eyes beneath the tumble of his dark fringe.

'Uh-huh.'

'I don't suppose you could take this …' I pass him my storage tub, 'and this …' I beckon to Emma, who hands her tub over as well, 'to the ice cream parlour on the quay? We'll make our own way there.'

'Am I to stay and wait?' he asks, looking from me to the two boxes he's now cradling.

'Of course,' I say, unsure where my sudden confidence has arisen from.

'Give them to Martin or Luca – either will do,' calls Emma, as Ziggy kicks off his skateboard, cradling her precious creation. Within seconds we've lost sight of him around the bend.

'And how do you know *that* young man?' asks Emma, her interest suddenly diverted.

'He popped up during an early morning walk, if you must know.'

'Did he now? I thought for a moment you had a secret agenda and he was the reason for holidaying solo in Brixham.'

'Oh no. I literally began chatting with him two mornings ago. He's the one who showed me round the fish market yesterday.'

'Romantic,' teases Emma, gently nudging my elbow as we stroll down the hill.

'Nah, nothing like that,' I say quickly. 'He's just a friendly guy, that's all.'

Out of the corner of my eye, I'm aware of Emma taking in my profile, studying me. I stare ahead, refusing to catch her eye. Ziggy's bright, full of life and seems very kind. Surely a girl can't make too many new friends whilst holidaying in Brixham, can she?

As soon as we enter the ice cream parlour, I know this should be my one and only visit: even the air is filled with calories. Ziggy is sitting at the nearest table, his skateboard propped across his lap, waiting patiently while Martin and Luca sample the ice cream with as much care and attention as I've seen dedicated to taste testing on *Bake Off*.

'And?' Emma doesn't wait for pleasantries, standing before the counter and scrutinising their expressions.

I make my way to Ziggy and sit at his table.

'Thank you,' I say to him, 'she's been like a cat on a hot tin roof all morning.'

'I thought I'd wait, watch the maestros at work. Look at the way Martin puckers up when tasting . . . how funny is that?'

I watch as a bottom lip protrudes, glistening with beige cream. I assume that's Martin.

'Is he the owner?' I ask, unsure who was who and what was what with regards to Emma's agreement.

Ziggy nods, his gaze still fixed on the tasting session.

'He takes it so seriously. You'd think he was judging a technical challenge the way he's contemplating his feedback.'

I laugh.

Emma's expression is one of sheer frustration as she watches Martin, unsure whether to burst into rapturous delight or apologise profusely for darkening their doorstep with her culinary disaster. The tension builds.

'Hurry up,' shouts Ziggy, repositioning the board across his lap. 'Some of us have lives we'd like to get on with.'

I glance at him, at his broad grin, sparkling eyes and an energy I am badly in need of.

'What are you doing after this?' he asks.

'Nothing.'

'Fancy a quick half along the front?'

And there it is. The second invite I've ever received from a male of my generation.

'Yeah, sure,' is all I can muster in reply. I'm not trying to act cool, just being realistic. The guy must have an empty afternoon, an hour to kill, or even be short of cash to have invited me for a drink but I don't care. I'm happy to accept.

'We'll nip out once the Paul and Prue of the ice cream world have finished their deliberations,' he jokes, shaking his head. 'It's ice cream, guys; you'd be better off asking us – your customers – what we think.'

'I love it,' I chime in, though I know my opinion counts for nothing.

Emma is dancing on the spot with pent-up nerves. Martin and Luca exchange the briefest of glances before Luca throws his tasting spoon into the sink.

'I sampled some yesterday, but is this the final product?' asks Martin, a coy smile on his lips.

Emma nods frantically.

I'm unsure if Martin's response is positive or negative. In the world of ice cream tasting, I am lost.

'Bloody hurry up,' grumbles Ziggy. 'The ice cream man from Brixham, he says ... what?'

'Yes!' exclaims Martin, bringing his fingertips to his mouth before kissing them in an exaggerated fashion. '*Bellissimo*! I love how you've scaled up the ingredients without losing the intensity of the flavours.'

Emma reacts like a child at Christmas opening an unexpected bike.

'So you'll take it?' she asks, looking from one to the other as if they are about to burst her bubble.

'Sure will, this is divine,' confirms Martin, glancing at Luca before disposing of his own tasting spoon.

'It's bloody gorgeous ... as good as my mamma makes!' says Luca, indicating that Emma should go into the back room. 'Martin will deal with the cash situation while I find a suitable container to put this lovely lot in.'

'Finally,' sighs Ziggy, standing and pushing his chair in. 'Are you coming?'

I didn't wish to presume, in case he'd changed his mind. I leap up as casually as a girl of my size can and shout my goodbyes towards Emma's disappearing figure. She doesn't even notice. So much for helping her out of a sticky situation.

'What's your poison?' asks Ziggy as we stand at the bar waiting to be served.

I glance at the optics, the chiller fridges and the shelves displaying every drink imaginable. Ziggy upends his skateboard to get it out of the way of passing customers.

'I haven't got one, to be honest. I usually just choose white wine.' My ambivalence towards alcohol is hardly surprising given the damage it's done to my family. How many school nights did I sit alone while my mum popped out to see her friends? How many birthday party invites did I refuse knowing there wasn't any money available for even the most modest present? I'll never know how much her drinking has affected my development, my choices, even my outlook on life.

Ziggy pulls a quizzical face. 'Seriously, you haven't got a favourite drink?'

'Nope. You?'

'Dry cider is always my first choice if I'm drinking ...' He stops and stares at me intently as if reading my thoughts. 'You don't do this sort of thing often, do you?'

I blush. He knows. It isn't difficult to work out – my awkwardness standing beside him screams self-conscious and naïve. 'Not really . . .' I stutter. I daren't say but, again, this is pretty much a first for me.

'What can I get you?' asks the barman.

'A large white wine, please, and a Coke,' says Ziggy, adding, 'A pint, no ice.'

'Large?' That isn't my usual choice.

'Relax, you can take your time. I'm free all afternoon.'

He's right. I should be relaxed, enjoying myself on holiday for the first time in years. And yet in the pit of my stomach my nerves are twitching at the prospect of sitting across a table from him and chatting.

How pathetic am I?

'Come on, follow me. I've got a favourite spot,' says Ziggy, collecting the drinks and leading the way towards the table beside the window, before returning to pick up his skateboard from beside the bar.

We settle ourselves at the table by the big window.

'Cheers, Ziggy.' I slowly lift the wine glass to my lips, watching the contents quiver. Can he see that I'm shaking?

'Cheers yourself. What's Benni short for?'

'Benjamina. I'm named after my father. He died before I was born, so my mum thought it was fitting,' I say, keeping my gaze low, focusing on the wooden tabletop. That's my usual ploy when explaining our family history. It's not because I get upset but rather to avoid the other person's reaction. The surprise. The shock. Sometimes the pity as they swiftly calculate the kind of upbringing I must have had. Though the reality of life with an alcoholic mother and a wayward older brother is hard for anyone to imagine.

'I'm sorry,' he says. I look up to witness genuine concern in his dark eyes. 'That can't have been easy for you.'

I give a nonchalant shrug, unsure how to proceed.

Ziggy's just proved that he's not like other guys. Which seems logical given that other guys don't ask me out for a drink in their local, don't invite me to sit at their favourite table by the window where passing friends might see, and don't focus on every word I say.

'I still have both my parents, yet I messed up at school and got into bother as a teenager. I depend on them when life goes wrong. I can't imagine either of them . . .' He stops, grabs his Coke, takes a long swig.

I nod. 'You can't miss what you've never had,' I say in a blasé tone, my standard attempt to jolly the conversation along.

Ziggy nods, eyeing me across the lip of his glass. It's obvious that he's seen straight through my remark. And for the first time in my life, that's OK by me.

Emma

I am on cloud nine. I carefully fold the three notes into a small wodge and hold it tightly in my palm.

This is the beginning of my new venture. I want to squeal with delight, dance along the cobbled streets and dash into the Co-op in search of more ingredients to create my next concoction.

This is divine. Martin's words roll about my mind, alongside the image of him glancing at Luca, the two of them nodding and smiling in agreement.

I wanted to tell him how much his words meant to me. The phrase sounds like a starting pistol in my head. It has given me the green light to go forth and experiment and explore my talent, but most of all it has provided me with a legitimate business proposition. The small bakery or coffee shop disappears from my future vision; I now have a clear idea to ponder whilst on holiday and implement once I arrive back home. A fully fledged plan that will pave the way as my first step towards freedom and a new life. A better life, a happier one, where *I* make the decisions and nobody questions my judgement. Where no one will add their suggestion, hint at their preferred choice or railroad my idea to fit their own agenda.

I stop walking and silently chastise myself. I've allowed my mood to change from sunny outlook to fog. I promised myself I wouldn't think like that for two whole weeks. My focus while I'm here is on ideas for a business that can support me; that in itself will be a giant step towards being where I want to be.

I set off again, silently repeating the mantra, 'You create the weather in your world, if only in your head.' Good girl, that's more like it.

If I quicken my pace, I might be able to buy more fresh

produce and create another batch of ice cream before I retire to bed. I might try blending the fresh lavender from the patio garden; there's plenty of flowering sprigs available.

As I walk the length of the quay, I squeeze my hand tight, feeling the corners of the wodge of notes digging into my palm. It feels good to have earned money from my talent. To have had recognition from those in the know. To have received a compliment from total strangers—

I stop dead.

In the window of the next pub, I can see Benni sitting opposite the skateboard guy. He's talking, she's laughing; their half-empty glasses sit between them.

So, she's not as solo as she makes out. It's only Tuesday and yet she's chatting and joking with this young man as if she's known him for a lifetime. I watch the warmth between them, the ease with which they interact. Why can't I have something like that? Why couldn't it be me seated opposite a man who is interested in my thoughts and ideas?

I watch as Benni picks up her wine glass and sips, her eyes remaining on him.

A voice in my head reminds me: *I know exactly why that can't be me.*

I turn and quickly stride in the opposite direction for fear of being spotted. I'll speak to her later, cut her a share of the takings, but she's obviously too busy to lend a helping hand with the next batch of ice cream.

Chapter Five

Wednesday 22 August

Benjamina

I tentatively finger the tourist information leaflet lying on the kitchen counter. I have no idea which of my housemates left it there, but suddenly I know how I want to spend my morning. It might be a good way to catch up on fun after spending yesterday helping Emma with her culinary delights.

I'm nervous, and I can't explain why, other than to blame it on the spontaneity of my decision. Before I know what I'm doing, I've rung for a taxi and am travelling the short distance to the local riding stables. The driver tries to conceal his look of surprise when I confirm my destination.

Cheeky sod, but what do I care about the likes of him? I can do as I please during this holiday.

Ziggy didn't bat an eyelid last night at my reply when he asked me if there was anything I wished I'd done as a kid. Some girls attended Girl Guides, others leapt about at gymnastics and tap dancing lessons. Me, I stayed at home and watched *Grange Hill*, *Blue Peter* and *Newsround*. That way I had no weekly subs to pay, no equipment to buy and no drop off/pick up time constraints on a lone parent. With a couple of packets of cheesy Wotsits, a can of Coke and a chocolate bar, I was set for the entire night, or at least until teatime. Horse riding was so far out of my reach, it might as well have been space travel.

The taxi stops beside a large wooden gate displaying a sign for Holly Lane Riding Stables. A painted black horse's head greets me with a toothy grin. I'm unsure if it's the right image given the symbolism for the *Godfather* films instantly flickers through my head.

I pay the driver and watch as the taxi leaves a billow of dust in its wake, smothering my black leggings and new trainers.

Too late now to back out: it's either go inside and enquire, or walk back to the cottage. I choose the former, though what exactly I'm going to say to the stable manager hasn't been established in my mind. I might simply ask for a tour. Or maybe, after they've taken one look at me and decided that none of their horses are suitable to carry the likes of me ... I'll slouch off hiding my embarrassment.

But at least I'll have tried. And that's what I'll tell Ziggy ... if I see him again.

I freeze as I close the gate behind me, the nerves finally kicking in in earnest.

What the hell am I doing here?

'Hello, can I help you?' calls a female voice.

I turn to see a young woman, probably no older than someone fresh out of school, striding towards me in skin-tight jodhpurs and a skinny-rib T-shirt, her mane of dark hair bouncing about her shoulders. She is the epitome of a horse rider: svelte, energetic and smiling.

I wish the ground would open up and swallow me whole.

'Hi,' she repeats more loudly. 'How can I help you?' She's standing before me in a matter of seconds, her clear, rosy complexion and her obvious fitness radiating like a summer morning.

'I was wondering if I could have a look around,' I say tentatively.

'Sure. Do you ride?'

I stare at her, wondering if her eyesight is intact.

'Er, no,' I say, glancing down at myself in order to check that some miraculous event hasn't occurred and I am still the proud owner of my plus-sized curves, with voluptuous thighs and hips.

'Are you interested in lessons?' she asks eagerly, her eyes wide and sparkling as she walks me across the yard. The area is surrounded by various fenced and grassed sections, and a covered passageway leads to the stables themselves.

I'm unsure whether to squeeze this girl tight and thank her from the bottom of my heart for her attitude towards the fuller figure, or reprimand her for taking the piss.

I choose to be polite instead.

'No, just interested in seeing the horses.'

'Oh great, that's so lovely to hear. Do you have much experience with horses?'

I want to say 'Yes, of course, I've ridden all my life'. Sadly, I haven't so I don't pretend – that could be dangerous. Instead I confess, 'I've always wanted to ride, so I thought I'd take a look.'

Her face is flushed with delight. I can't remember the last time I saw a human being with such a joyful expression. Her happy mood is infectious.

'I'm Maddie, by the way, and you are . . . ?'

'I'm Benjamina,' I say, surprising myself. Suddenly, for the first time in my life, I *feel* like a Benjamina. Racy and daring, the kind of woman who hangs out at riding stables and strokes beautiful horses all day. Or someone who sounds like she might wear a pair of jodhpurs and a skinny-rib T-shirt like Maddie, even if she can't in reality.

At the end of the covered passage we reach a double row of stable doors. Various people of all ages are coming and going, carrying brooms and forks and pushing wheelbarrows. They look like worker ants, busy but happy with their work.

At sporadic intervals along the rows a horse hangs its head over its door and neighs or noses at a passing person.

I fall in love at first sight.

Every sense is tingling and stimulated; the smell, the sight, the basic need to touch these majestic animals passes through me like a vibrant wave.

'Did you say you've ridden before?' asks Maddie as we pass along the line.

Do I lie or tell the truth? Benjamina would tell the truth.

'No, never, but I'd love to try one day.'

'Great! Ever mucked out before?'

'No.' A bubble of laughter lifts from my throat. I've never been to a stable yard before, so how could I possibly . . .

'Well, you can give me a hand if you want.'

I watch as Maddie strides along the central gangway, touching and stroking the horses' noses as she passes. A series of grateful noses, quivering lips and fleshy pink tongues return her kindness. Each stable door has a wooden plaque introducing its occupant. I clock the names with interest: Wispy, Herbie, Remy, Hobbit, Memphis, Shamrock and Rosie.

Such beautiful names.

I follow Maddie to the last stable on the right-hand side. It's empty, but the plaque informs me that Bruce lives here.

'Where's the horse?' I ask.

'In the paddock,' replies Maddie. She points at my pastel-coloured trainers. 'Are you OK in those?'

'Probably not the best choice, were they?'

'Nah, I can find you some wellies if you prefer. What size are you?'

'Six.'

'Stay here and I'll be back in a minute. If anyone pops by while I'm gone, say you're a friend of the family, OK?'

'OK.'

She darts off, and I'm left staring around the muck-ridden stable. Dirty straw is strewn across the ground, an overturned feeding bowl lies in one corner, and a distinct smell of urine is wafting at my nostrils.

*　　*　　*

108

'Here you go,' says Maddie, handing me a pair of funny-looking wellies.

'Have you cut them down?' I ask, staring at the small section of wellington which moulds up the leg.

'No, I picked ones that someone had already cut down into ankle boots – more comfortable if your calves are . . . well . . . you know.'

I smile. 'Yeah, I know.'

I wobble as I change into the boots. I must look a right bloody sight, but who cares? Once I've gone home they can talk all they want about Benjamina, the big girl, and her cut-down boots. I've heard worse!

'Here you go . . . scoop up the big bits of horse poo with that.' Maddie hands me a plastic rake with large slots. 'I'll grab a wheelbarrow.'

It feels funny to be scooping poo but it reminds me of the hook-a-duck fairground stall we once visited as young kids. I must have only been about five years old. I was pretty good at that, so I expect I'll be a natural at this.

Within three scoops, I realise I'm not.

Maddie returns with the wheelbarrow and instantly removes the scooper from my clutches.

'Like this . . .' She swiftly scoops and flicks, allowing the sawdust to fall away from the muck. When she does it, it looks so easy. 'Practice, you just need practice,' she says, busying herself unhooking a large net from the wall to reveal a large creamy lump hanging from the same hook.

'What's that for?' I ask as I continue to scoop and flick.

'That's a salt lick, and this is a hay net. I'll go and fill it ready for Bruce's overnight feed. The greedy bugger gets through a whole one every night. We've had to buy a new net recently because the holes were too big and he ate it too quickly.'

'Really?'

'Yeah, horses never stop eating.'

I nod. That story sounds all too familiar. I say nothing for fear of ridicule.

'There you go, that's perfect,' says Maddie, flicking the last of her sawdust up the wall to create a neat border of shavings against the painted brickwork.

'And that's to stop them damaging their legs as they lie down and move about?'

'Yep, a soft cushioning.'

I step back and admire her handiwork. Who'd have thought you could make sawdust look so appealing?

'Do you fancy meeting him?' she asks, collecting her shovel, rake and broom and leaning them against the outside wall of the stable.

I check my watch: it's getting late.

'Would you mind if I came back another day to meet Bruce?'

'Sure thing. Drop by any time you want.'

I like Maddie; she's honest, caring and kind – much like the feel of the stables and their four-legged occupants.

'I'll walk you to the gate,' she says.

I return my cut-off wellingtons and stride out through the narrow passageway in my trainers.

110

'Are you walking home?' Maddie asks.

'Yeah, I think I will. It's only a mile at the most.'

She opens the wooden gate and I nip through before she closes it tightly behind me. I turn back to her.

'Thank you. Would you mind if I came back tomorrow?'

'Of course not. You can meet Bruce and feed him a carrot or two.'

As I start my trek towards Rose Cottage, she calls my name and I turn round.

'Buy yourself some wellies for next time, OK?'

A smile spreads across my face; Maddie must be a mind reader. I wave cheerily. I can't wait to come back, to spend more time mucking out but more importantly to meet Bruce.

Ruth

I'm unpacking my newly acquired watercolours and art equipment after a busy morning painting when I hear a shriek from downstairs. Is that Emma, or a tourist passing the cottage? I tiptoe from my bedroom to the top of the staircase and listen before calling down.

'Emma ... are you OK?'

I hear a scurry of feet before Emma's startled face appears over the bottom banister.

'You will never guess what?'

'What?' I repeat idiotically.

'Martin wants another batch of ice cream and ...' She

pummels the bottom stair with her hands; I imagine it's supposed to mimic a drum roll. 'A quick drink tonight.'

I can see her bright expression and sense her joy, but I'm unsure which event she's celebrating.

'And you're jubilant because of which one?' I ask.

'The drink, of course! The ice cream too – Martin loved the lavender and honey flavour I made last night – but he's asked me out for a drink! How fantastic is that?'

'Great.'

Her face drops, her brow creases.

'You could at least get a little excited for me.'

'I am. But I'm a bit distracted by the fact that I've just delivered a finished watercolour to the gallery.' In fact, I'm numb with nerves and self-doubt. 'I don't know if Dean will even display it. He says he will, but . . .' It was the last thing I'd expected given that the composition was barely dry. But he was right yesterday when he said it would take a matter of hours to produce a composition in watercolour. The canvas – or rather the painting board, as Dean told me it was called – that the supplies lady directed me to was perfect. Huge compared to my sketchpad, but ideal, far better than the thick paper I used decades ago.

'Congratulations, sweetie. Seize the day and all that!'

'And you . . . you seem overly excited at the prospect of a date,' I say, leaning against the wall, my own achievement reigniting my nerves.

'Do you know how long it's been since a man asked me out for a drink?'

I have the urge to guess, but I don't want to get it wrong and annoy her. I shrug instead.

'Years, absolutely bloody ages . . . Woo-hoo!' Her face contorts like a wailing banshee before she disappears from view.

'Are you sure you should be mixing business with pleasure?' I yell, unsure if she's in the lounge or the back kitchen. Relationships aren't easy at the best of times, but to muddy the waters of her blending experiment seems idiotic.

Her face reappears at the bottom of the stairs.

'Mixing? My speciality is the blending of beautiful textures and flavours to create something superb. Have no fear, Ruth. This concoction will be bloody gorgeous.'

I'm confused.

'And the drinks date?'

She frowns again.

'I'm talking about the bloody drinks date – me and Martin getting to know each other better. You never know what might happen!'

Once again she disappears from view.

'Oh.' I lean against the landing wall and stare down at the empty hallway. I'm slightly confused. Is Emma's primary focus creating new and exciting ice creams or finding a love match? I could have sworn she said she needed a new career, nothing more.

I can hear her tuneful singing coming from the kitchen, so I return to my room. If I hurry, have a quick bite to eat, I could grab a pitch down by the lighthouse and see what I can achieve in an afternoon of painting.

'Ruth!' calls Emma.

'Yes,' I shout, returning to my banister position.

'Your mobile's ringing down here,' says Emma, appearing at the bottom stair holding my phone aloft.

I dash down to collect it, recognising the caller's details: Acorn Ridge.

'Hello?' Instant concern edges my voice. 'Ruth Elton here.' I hold my breath.

'Morning, Ms Elton ... Mrs Tedds here, from the Acorn Ridge Care Home. How are you?'

'What's wrong?' I blurt. I can't answer calmly. I understand the need for social pleasantries, but why would she be calling unless she had something important to tell me? I won't think her rude, just get straight to it!

'Ms Elton, I'm sure it's nothing to worry about, but we need to inform you of an incident that has occurred this morning. Your mother, Mrs Elton, can't be located in her room. Now, we are certain that the external gates are all locked and secure, which means she must be somewhere in the vicinity of the home, we just can't—'

'What?' My voice is a squeal; I can't help it.

'Please, Ms Elton, we understand how distressing this must be, but please be assured we are doing everything we can to locate your mother.'

'When was she last seen?' I ask as Emma comes to stand next to me.

'At breakfast this morning. She ate a hearty meal of—'

'I don't need to know what she ate, just where she is.'

'I can assure you we are doing everything in our power to find her. The police have been informed and our staff are currently searching each room hoping to locate her.'

'Police? If she's indoors, why are the police involved?'

'Ms Elton, it's a precaution, just in case. There's no need to worry.'

'Worry? Of course I'm going to worry. I'm two hundred miles away, I thought I'd left her in good hands and yet *this* has happened.'

'Ms Elton, I have no doubt that we'll be calling you very shortly to say we've located your mother. This is purely in the interest of openness; we wouldn't hide such an incident from a resident's family.'

'Mrs Tedds, I phoned this morning and was told she was fine and happy. Why would she have wandered off like this?' My voice cracks with emotion. I want to cry. I should never have left her; this is my own fault for being so damned selfish.

'Ms Elton, Mrs Elton has been the life and soul of the lounge since her arrival. I can assure you that she is as fit and well as can be expected given her condition. She's obviously taken herself off for a little walk. We will find her, Ms Elton. I promise.'

I have a wealth of questions but realise that time is of the essence, so I quickly ring off. I need to call Jack.

Emma stands close by, gently rubbing my back, as I speak to my son. Her face reflects my own concern. My mother is lost; she could be anywhere, facing untold dangers. Alone. Distressed. Frightened.

115

'Jack, your grandmother's gone missing. Can you get your-self over to the care home, please, to help find her? I'll never forgive myself if something happens to her.'

'She'll be fine, Mum. There's a standard protocol they have to follow when these things happen, but if it makes you feel better, I'll drive over and give them a hand,' says Jack, sounding unperturbed.

Benjamina

I sit beside the harbour wall, feeling pleased with myself. I didn't need a taxi to get back from the stables; instead I set a steady pace and walked. I should have continued straight home for a shower, but I needed a bench rest at some point. Here beside the harbour is as good as anywhere.

The sun is high, the crowds are growing and I can count on one hand, with a digit to spare, the number of times in my life I have felt this way.

1. The day I made hundreds of chocolate truffles.
2. The day I manned the charity stall and sold every bag for charity.
3. The day I left secondary school.
4. And now, the day I helped muck out a stable.

A voice inside my head mocks the decade gap between the first three events and the fourth. I silence it by reminding myself that I live a simple life. It's not a big life filled with complications and dramas, but a simple existence of sleeping, eating and working in which I care for those I love and look out for others in my daily routine. It isn't much; others possibly wouldn't want to change places, but it's my life.

But is it enough?

Today I want to be Maddie. I want to be like her more than I've wanted to be anything in my life.

I glance down at my podgy hands resting in the expanse of my lap. Ten puffy fingers, which earlier were wrapped around a shovel handle to flip horse poo and wood shavings. Not a task I'd have imagined would bring satisfaction, but I'm delighted knowing that Bruce has a clean bed on which to lie. It's no more thrilling than watching the vinegar bottles being systematically filled on the production line, and yet I have never left work with such a buzz in my chest.

And tomorrow I will be needed again to clean out tonight's muck. I can't contain my beaming smile.

How ridiculous must I look?

A twenty-five year old sitting on a bench contemplating the delight of returning to a stable for unpaid work of mucking out a horse, which belongs to someone else?

I look around at the crowds of holidaymakers passing my bench. Families carrying crying babies, toddlers clutching their crabbing buckets and elderly folk arm in arm saunter past. A group of young women strut by in fashionable high wedges and floaty hemlines, revealing tanned shoulders and thighs.

I'm mesmerised by them.

If I had legs like those, I'd never be out of shorts, morning, noon or night. Instead, I sit alone on a bench in my elasticated black leggings, a baggy T-shirt enveloping my upper half and, I suspect, a pair of red cheeks complete with a delightful glow due to the continuing sunshine. I've been told umpteen times that beauty is in the eye of the beholder, but sadly, very few people look past the outer packing to find my warm heart and good intentions.

I should be more like the girls striding up and down the quayside, eating candyfloss, queuing for a temporary tattoo or enjoying a cream tea at a posh café overlooking the harbour.

But do I want to do those things?

I can live without the candyfloss and the temporary tattoo, but I wouldn't mind their toned, slender thighs. I suspect that my inner beauty could tag alongside the trio, if released from this outer shell.

What else do I want?

I want to muck out horses.

I want to walk up and down hills without needing a bench as a pit stop.

I want to see a different pair of hands when I look down at my lap.

An ugly grey fluffy-headed herring gull waddles up and squawks at me. I assume it's this year's chick trying to fend for itself in this mad world. I have nothing to offer it. Ironic, given that we're at the same stage in life – I know how it feels.

I watch as it pecks unsuccessfully at a chewing gum blob on the pavement, then waddles towards a wooden lolly stick littering the gutter before skipping off towards a discarded chip wrapping.

The intense sun burns the base of my neck. I need to make a move unless I want to resemble a lobster. Not a look I'm aiming for, especially since my ponytail will leave a strange dividing line on the blistering skin.

I begin the slow walk towards Rose Cottage.

Funny how I've had my hair long for so many years and yet do nothing with it other than wash and dry it and wear it in a bobble. Emma says I've got a fine head of hair, so maybe I should start paying more time and attention to it; have it styled or learn how to create interesting plaits.

I stop walking and look down at my clothes. My wardrobe would benefit from an overhaul too, perhaps to include more floaty hemlines. That could be another goal once I've increased my daily activity.

Ruth

I don't move from the cottage all day. I pace the rooms and the garden with my mobile phone clutched to my side. I can't sit, eat or even drink the countless cups of coffee Emma makes for me.

I feel sick.

I feel sicker knowing that Jack is there and hasn't resolved matters.

'I've checked her room, Mum,' he told me earlier. 'There's

nothing out of place, nothing out of the ordinary. Her belong-ings are laid out on the dressing table – her brushes, her face cream – and that little teddy bear I had as a kid is on her bed. The only thing I couldn't find was her slippers; the carers think she was wearing those at breakfast time.' His words were meant to ease my mind, but they didn't. I'm simply more upset that I'm stuck down here when I'm needed back home. I knew I shouldn't have taken this bloody holiday.

'Ruth, come and sit down,' says Benni, who's returned to the cottage, and is sitting at the patio table with a plate of toast. 'You'll tire yourself out and be good for nothing.'

'I feel totally useless, Benni. I need to be doing something, anything.'

'I can see you've already packed your suitcases and plonked them in the hallway . . .'

'I shouldn't be here enjoying myself. I need to go home, I need to find my mother.'

'But if you do that, they're bound to call you while you're on the train to say she's safe and well.'

'Oh, I don't know. When Jack was tiny, he wandered off during a Christmas shopping trip. I took my eyes off him for a second and *puff* he was gone. The knot in my stomach was exactly like this.' I hold a clenched fist to the centre of my ribs. 'I couldn't think straight. I couldn't recall what he was wearing when a shop assistant asked me, and I'd dressed him that morning. I simply lost the plot, went blank, and now, with Mum . . . I couldn't tell you which slippers I packed for her stay.'

'Slippers don't matter, Ruth – you do!' She reaches for my arm and pulls me into the next seat. 'Please try and eat something.' She offers me the toast as if it holds magical nutritional powers.

I duly select a piece and take a bite. The butter is salty, the bread beautiful and doughy in the centre, but the morsel is claggy as I chew.

'Ruth, it isn't your fault. This is all part of her condition, you understand that, don't you? It might have happened if you were at home, returning from a day at the bank.'

I finally swallow the mouthful of toast and shake my head, because she's wrong.

'No. I phone her three times a day while I'm at work. I'd have known as soon as she didn't answer. I organise neighbours to nip in at specific times of the day to check on her. I would have been able to give an exact time to the police, whereas the care home haven't a clue – sometime after breakfast is all they can say.'

Benni nods reassuringly. Her kind blue eyes offer warmth and friendship.

'Thank you,' I say. 'I realise that you and Emma don't have to worry about me – this is your holiday – and yet both of you have been great today.'

'That's what friends do for each other. I can't imagine either of us simply heading out knowing that you've received such bad news. Emma told me what had happened as soon as I arrived back from the stables.'

'I've just never had friends outside of the family before.

Me and my mum were always reliant upon each other, such a tight little unit that we've excluded others from the circle. We should have invited people into our lives really – in hindsight, it would have made certain situations much easier – but you don't miss what you've never had, do you?' I say, picking at the triangle of bitten toast.

'Not until you're shown what you've been missing,' whispers Benni, sighing heavily.

'I suppose I shouldn't rely on our Jack,' I say. 'He has his own life to live. But I can't rely on Mum any more either; she's simply too frail.'

'Oh Ruth, it's never too late to have new people in your life.'

'I shouldn't be here, Benni – I should be at home looking after my mother like she looked after me. I'm down here pretending to be enjoying myself on holiday when the truth is, I have responsibilities. I've phoned the home every day just to ease my guilt, pretending to you and Emma that I'm fine and dandy when really I'm knotted with guilt inside, worried in case something happens. And now it has!'

'You can be honest with us, Ruth. We understand your concerns; we told you that the other night. I'd love a phone call from home to show they're missing me or want to know that I'm having a good time. And, after Monday night, I daren't call them in case the drama has increased and they demand I come home. I pretend I don't care, but deep down it hurts like crazy. I thought they'd miss me, but sadly it seems not.'

Benni's right: her mobile has been in the dining room for the majority of the holiday, and it hasn't rung since Monday night. It must be heartbreaking for a young woman to think her family don't care about her. I'm sure they do really – maybe they're just not affectionate towards each other. Some families aren't. Maybe my mother thinks I don't care about her, after I shipped her off to the care home.

'She's been missing for ten hours,' I say tearfully. 'If anything happens to her, I won't ever forgive myself.'

'Don't think like that. Nothing is going to happen to her. I'm sure that by this time tomorrow we'll be laughing about this. When she's safe and sound, you can continue with your holiday and focus on your painting again. You deserve some time for yourself.'

'I hope so.'

'I'm certain,' Benni says emphatically. 'Now, how about I give you a hand unpacking both your suitcases?'

Emma

'I promise, it's worth the walk,' says Martin as we ascend the steep incline towards Berry Head.

I was half expecting him to walk me back to the cottage after our quiet but quick drink in the Sprat and Mackerel. My stomach churns. I feel like a teenager who knows she'll be late for a parental curfew if she doesn't go home now. It's only eight o'clock, sunset is nearing but if I agree to stay our evening will lengthen – and my defences will be lowered. Deep down I know I should suggest we do this another night. Or even play the independent woman of mature years and tell him I have other plans with Ruth and Benni. Instead, I act like a naïve schoolgirl being led towards the unknown.

'Emma?'

I smile as he extends his arm for me to take. I don't hesitate, linking mine in his. I'm aware of the cheesy smile I'm wearing. I wish I had a little decorum and could refrain from expressing my delight, but what's life if we can't share how we feel whilst linking arms with a decent guy? I've spent too long being guarded about my emotions, hiding my feelings and pretending to be blasé. And in thirty-nine years, where's it got me? Childless and solo ... well, almost. So what's the harm in showing my pleasure? I'm hardly a slip of a thing being tempted down the wrong path in life.

We continue along Berry Head Road. My breathing is getting heavier and my legs are shaking, not entirely due to the steady climb but also because of Martin's proximity.

Earlier I noticed his neatly trimmed hair and freshly shaved faced. If he chances his luck and plays his cards right, I'll find him difficult to resist.

'Are you OK?' he asks, peering down at me.

I blush. How long has he been watching me? Can I feign a 'sure thing', or did my internal monologue register on my face as a coy smirk, giving the game away?

'Fine, never better,' I say, knowing I've never possessed a poker face.

'You muttered something. I didn't catch what you said ...'

I smile, afraid to utter a word. I fear the worst if my tongue and facial features have created a candid partnership to reveal the true workings of my mind. There'll be much embarrassment on my part.

'Anyway, as I was saying, the panoramic view from Berry Head is second to none. You can see for miles on a clear night. It's probably one of my favourite spots for an evening walk.'

We continue to stride arm in arm. The tarmac road wanes to a concrete pathway on which my kitten heels sound rhythmically. The row of large guest houses is replaced by the sumptuous grounds of a stately hotel, whose entrance drive we walk past.

'And how often do you take this walk?' I ask, feigning nonchalance.

'Several times a month, mainly . . . no, always on my own.' His words linger in the space between us as if connecting us shoulder to shoulder.

'How long have you been single?' I ask, unsure whether his remark was an invitation to ask.

'Five years. She wasn't happy, so we divorced.'

'And you wanted to remain married?'

'I was happy, I thought *we* were happy, so it came as a shock, but you can only do so much by yourself, can't you?' he says. 'A relationship is meant to be a two-way street, not just one-way traffic.'

I nod as flashbacks of my own heartache replay in my head. Simultaneously, a sudden pang seizes my heart. How can wounds be reopened in a millisecond, when time has passed and you imagined they were starting to heal?

'I know what you mean. It's painful when someone you want doesn't feel the same as you,' I say, giving his forearm a gentle squeeze. 'My last relationship was dictated by his insecurities; he simply wouldn't allow me to be myself. Always correcting me, trying to overrule my views and opinions – only to sulk and give me the silent treatment when his jealousy overflowed. It makes for such difficulties and ruins everything.'

Martin looks down at me, his eyes creasing as he gives a weak smile. His pain is clearly etched upon his brow; he's still coping, still hurting, working through each day.

'But hey, we have to look to the future, don't we? It doesn't do to dwell on the past.' He swallows hard, his Adam's apple moving rapidly.

'I agree. So tell me, what's so great about this place?' I clumsily change tack, hoping to lift his mood.

'Everything,' he declares as the walkway of aged walls leads us towards a bark-laden pathway surrounded by greenery. We continue until we reach a clearing overlooking the posh hotel and its sumptuous terraces scattered with relaxing guests enjoying the final moments of the day.

'Have you heard the church bells chiming during your stay?' Martin asks.

'I have, and we've been trying to identify the tune, but none of us can name it.'

He smiles, viewing the property through the foliage. 'I'm surprised you don't recognise it. It's "Abide With Me".'

Instantly I do. I'll share that snippet of enlightenment with Ruth and Benni later.

'That hotel used to be the vicarage where the Reverend Lyte wrote the words. It was originally a poem, and later became the hymn. His church honours him twice a day.'

'People ring that twice a day?' I say, imagining what a bind that must be to the parish volunteers.

'No, it's an automated system using tiny hammers on the church bells – like a giant music box really – but still, his work is recognised.'

I watch his brooding profile as he speaks. He's interesting, knowledgeable and passionate about his local area – so different from other men I've dated, who seem like empty vessels until they're alongside their drinking buddies. At which point I've been ignored or forgotten whilst a stream of infantile conversation unfolds like a childish game of Top Trumps, whether it be on world politics, motor racing or two raindrops running down a window pane.

My heart twinges again. Maybe such memories say more about me and my choice of men. At least they were enjoying their time amongst friends, unlike me. I should have had the self-esteem to collect my handbag and exit stage left. Sadly, I never did. Which I don't understand. I'm fairly confident, naturally outspoken and yet I stayed. Possibly for fear of upsetting and hurting others when all the time I was silently hurting myself.

Martin explains the importance of Torbay's nature reserve, and its historical significance due to the presence of a Napoleonic fort and the abundance of wildlife which needs protecting in this day and age.

'On winter mornings, standing on the main headland, you can watch a small pod of harbour porpoise swimming; they're beautiful.'

'I don't know what that is.'

'A porpoise?'

I nod. I'm so naïve, ignorant of most topics outside of catering. My education wasn't the best, but simply good enough.

'They look like small whales and are, I believe, related to dolphins,' he explains confidently.

I usually get flustered when I have to admit to my ignorance, but Martin isn't condescending; he simply explains things in a matter-of-fact manner.

'And do they play like dolphins?'

'Many people mistake them for dolphins when they see them tumbling through the waves, but they're incredibly rare nowadays – near extinction at one point.' He stops walking and turns to face me before continuing. 'Maybe you'll come back nearer Christmas and we can view them one morning?'

My face beams at the clear indication that he's enjoying my company as much as I am his.

'I'd like that.'

His arm unhooks from mine and he takes my hand. My palm tingles as our fingers wrap together and knot. Instantly a deep warmth flows like molten lava through my body.

I'd forgotten how good this simple act feels. How long has it been since a man lovingly took my hand in his? Five years? More? How can a marriage built on ridicule and reproach expect tenderness to survive? How ridiculous that I've shied away from a loving relationship for so long for the fear of being hurt. Surely moments like these outweigh the risk?

'Come on, if we hurry, we might be able to watch the sun going down,' says Martin, lengthening his stride. I'm pulled along for a pace or two until I catch up on the bark-strewn path.

Without warning, the overhanging foliage gives way to a vast area of grassy headlands, divided by a well-trodden gravel pathway. As we crunch along the path, signs on either side point us to the Northern Fort, a bird hide, the visitors' centre and a café. Martin ignores them all, continuing his pace straight ahead.

'A lighthouse?' I exclaim, releasing his hand and dashing forward towards the circular building. 'Why's it so short and squat?'

'It doesn't need to be tall and majestic like the one in the harbour. It's sitting at the highest vantage point in the county, so remarkably, it's the shortest and yet the highest lighthouse.'

'I love it!' I can't stand still, but pace around the green and white base, staring at the not-so-high circular eye. The roof is literally a few metres above my head.

How cute.

'I thought you'd be impressed, but not *this* impressed.' He laughs, watching as my face shows my delight. 'But that isn't what we're here to see. Look.'

He points out to sea. I stop pacing and turn as directed.

The sun lingers on the horizon, a fireball of red and orange, slowly sinking towards the waves.

'Come over here and watch.' Martin walks to the nearest bench and settles, his arm resting along the wooden backrest. I follow, sliding presumptuously into the space beside him. We sit. We watch. And we wait in silence.

As the sun slowly lowers, the sky comes alive in a blaze of warm tones, like a canvas masterfully touched by an artist.

I hold my breath as the final arc dips beneath the waves.

I turn to see Martin watching me, and not the horizon. Our faces draw near, his gaze lingers, and finally, our lips meet.

Ruth

My mobile rings at 3.05 in the morning. I leap from the sofa to answer as Benni and Emma both stir in their armchairs, pushing aside their duvets.

'Hello?' I say breathlessly.

'Hello, Ms Elton? It's Mrs Tedds here.'

'Yes, speaking . . . have you found her?'

'Yes, we have, Ms Elton. We located your mother a matter of minutes ago, safe and well, I'm glad to report.'

'And where was she?'

'Inside the care home, as we expected.'

'Where exactly?' I snap, impatient for details.

'Under the staircase in the lobby area. She's quite well despite being hungry and a little thirsty; nothing a good bath and an extra-long lie-in can't correct.'

Instantly an image of my mother sitting in a dusty cupboard springs to mind.

'And she was in there for how long?' I say, stunned by the details but calming by the second.

'Potentially seventeen hours, Ms Elton. The alarm was raised at ten o'clock this morning, and as I said, we located her a few minutes ago. It's quite common for people with this condition to hide things.'

'But to hide herself, for seventeen hours ... how is that even possible?'

'I can assure you we didn't stop looking all day. The other residents have been quite concerned that such a lovely lady was missing.'

'And my mother?'

'As I said, your mother is absolutely fine – none the worse for her ordeal.'

'Despite spending the day sitting alongside the spare Dyson!' I shriek, not caring for her blasé tone. 'I wish I could be as certain as you, Mrs Tedds.'

'I shall call you first thing in the morning with an update. I assure you, Ms Elton, your mother is in the best possible hands.'

I tap the screen to end the call. I don't want to hear her excuses for a second more.

'Safe and sound?' asks Emma.

I have enough time to nod before tears spill over my lashes.

'Oh come here,' says Benni, wrapping her arms around my quivering shoulders. My head sinks deep into her warm body and the fear of today is slowly released amongst friends.

131

Chapter Six

Thursday 23 August

Ruth

The three of us shield our bleary eyes from the morning sun and peer into the gallery window, looking past the shutter grille to admire my painting. The place may be closed, but glimpsing my own work displayed on the wall is the biggest thrill I have ever had. To the right, I can make out my framed piece. In my head the colours are fresh and vibrant, but in the darkened gallery it's as if each composition is sleeping, awaiting the spotlights to illuminate each highlight.

'I can't see it,' mutters Benni.

'The central painting on the right-hand side ... got it?' I say, not wanting to boast that once you're inside the gallery, my composition is in prime position on the main wall. Sadly, whilst peering from outside, the only prime position is starring at us centrally from the gallery's window. I can only dream of painting a composition to be exhibited in such a manner.

A pang of pride ignites inside my chest. After a lengthy absence from all things creative, I painted that!

I felt a little embarrassed asking the others to accompany me, grateful that both were delighted with the invite, despite the fact that it's only 7.30 in the morning and we endured a disturbed night. The painting is finished, framed and on display. Who knows how long I've got until it belongs to another person. Then I'll never see it again.

'Just think, someone else might admire your painting whilst sipping a gin and tonic in their favourite armchair,' says Benni. 'How weird is that?'

'It could travel anywhere in the world and Ruth's talent will be viewed by people she doesn't even know,' says Emma, moving her face nearer to the grille.

'I know, but at least I'll be left with memories like this,' I reply.

'It looks lovely, Ruth – I bet you're delighted.' Emma cups her hands around her eyes to view the painting more clearly.

'I am. I'm still a bit taken aback that Dean thinks so highly of it, but he must feel it's worthy.'

'Exactly. I don't think you can always judge your own work,' says Benni.

'Do you think every artist does this?' I ask nervously.

'I'm sure they do,' says Emma, her nose squashed to the grille.

'Really? I can't imagine that Monet would have walked

around Brixham at some ungodly hour to view his marina painting.'

'If he ever painted in Brixham he would have,' jokes Emma. 'Though the title would be *Marina in Midday Light* and not . . . what did you call it?'

'*Marina Mania*.'

'Fitting. What does the price label say?' asks Emma, stepping away.

'Two hundred and twenty pounds.' I blush at the thought. 'I didn't think he'd charge so much. I'd have happily sold it for a fraction of the price.'

'Hey, what do you know about selling art? Let him do his job and you do yours,' adds Benni.

'Are you happy with how you've arranged it financially?' asks Emma, turning to face me. 'I'm not asking how much, but I hope he's been fair with you.'

I give a slight nod, unsure what to say and slightly embarrassed that someone would care enough to want assurance that I'm not being fleeced. 'Thank you, that means a lot to me. Not everyone would care how much I'm receiving. I think he's been very fair regarding the percentage split.'

'As long as you're happy.'

I pause. 'The thing is, it's not about the money for me; it's more the opportunity to prove to myself that I can paint. For so long I've told myself that my opinion doesn't count. So until someone else appreciated my painting, deep down I thought I'd always doubt myself.'

'Oh Ruth,' says Benni, her hand gently rubbing my forearm.

'Seeing my work displayed like this is particularly special today,' I say, knowing I've gone too far to stop now. 'It's my birthday.'

Amidst a squealing chorus of 'Happy birthday!' I receive bear hugs from both Benni and Emma. It's been a long time since I celebrated my birthday, let alone shared it with friends, but already this one feels very special.

Benjamina

Apart from our early trek to the gallery, I've spent the entire morning at the stables. In four hours, I've helped Maddie muck out Bruce's stable, wheelbarrowed a load of dirty straw for the girl in the stable next door, and helped to sweep and hose down the yard with three other young women.

'Are you ready for some lunch?' asks Maddie, grabbing a rucksack and leading me outside.

'I am, but . . .' I didn't plan on being here come lunchtime. What I thought would be a quick visit kept me busy for far longer than I'd imagined.

'We can share,' she offers, striding across to an open barn homing each riders' allocation of hay bales. I watch as she climbs up with ease to settle on the top as if it were a large stage.

Please don't let me struggle up only to fall off unceremoniously and break both legs, I pray.

I take a big breath and lift my right leg. It's probably the highest it has been raised for many years. My left leg propels me up off the concrete with a huge push. It feels weird not being on the ground; the bales have a spongy, sturdy texture beneath my voluptuous frame.

Maddie politely looks away and pretends not to notice my struggle.

With some panting and much grasping at the hay, I finally make it to the top and settle beside Maddie, who has unpacked her lunch box. She offers me a sandwich.

'It's only ham and cheese,' she says, 'but the pickle is home-made by my mum.'

I give a nonchalant shrug, desperately trying to keep my face straight as it threatens to burst into an uncontrollable smile. I've accomplished something else new that if I'd thought about for too long I'd have refused to try. Go me!

'I'll provide lunch next time,' I say, taking her offering.

'Sure, it's what we do around here. There's none of this "that's mine and that's yours" kind of thing. We literally all muck in together . . .' She pauses. 'Unless you're Sonya, Gallop's owner, she never shares anything.'

'Gallop?'

'Yeah, stupid name for a horse if you ask me. It confuses the other horses if they're voice trained and she starts shouting, "Gallop!"'

I frown as I munch my sandwich.

'I never go out riding with her. I think it's dangerous if you're not ready and boom, your horse starts galloping. Sonya thinks it's funny. My mum asked me not to go hacking with her. Though I wouldn't anyway, we're not friends.'

'But still.'

'Yeah, but still. My mum trusts me to only go hacking with someone if I think I'm safe and they'll look after me and the horse.'

'Hacking?'

'It's another term for riding, but for light exercise rather than anything too strenuous – a gentle ride,' explains Maddie, chomping her sandwich between sentences. 'Bruce loves hacking with Rosie and my sister's horse Wispy, so I tend to go with them mostly. They don't do stupid stuff or dare each other.'

'Dare?'

'Oh yeah, some riders act stupidly on horseback. They seem to forget that they're responsible for what happens to their horse – they can easily get injured.'

'And the vets' fees?'

'Huge! What looks like a small hoof injury can cost loads. I daren't risk it, but anyway I wouldn't treat Bruce that way.'

Yet another reason why I couldn't have gone riding as a youngster. Where was a single mum from Burntwood going to find the cash for vet's bills, let alone all the other costs?

I notice that Maddie's face lights up every time she says Bruce's name.

'You love your horse, don't you?' I ask.

'Yeah! Slightly more than my sister,' says Maddie, without hesitation.

We both fall about laughing. There's no point trying to backtrack and pretend. Horse folk seem to tell it as it is.

*　　*　　*

I step backwards as Bruce gently nudges my hand with his white-striped muzzle. It's taken me several minutes to pluck up the courage to approach the sturdy black cob, as I'm in awe of his size and his dark shiny coat.

'He thinks you've got treats,' laughs Maddie, dipping a hand into her pocket for a handful of torpedo-shaped brown pellets.

'Can I?'

'Of course, here . . .'

I hold my hand flat, my thumb out of the way, and offer the treats to Bruce. He doesn't need asking twice; his lips nibble gently at my palm, removing the pellets. His dark gaze is transfixed, as if memorising my features, reading my thoughts and looking deep inside my soul.

An excited buzz runs along my spine. I can see the attraction of these majestic animals – like an invisible bonding that draws you in. I might be twenty-five, but I feel like an excited child feeding a horse on a walk in the country.

Emma

I've spent the morning on the phone trying to find something we can do at very short notice to celebrate Ruth's big day. Sadly, everything I try – whether it be a local spa day, a concert or an afternoon painting aboard a pretty boat – draws a blank at bookings for today. There's not much point taking up their offers for tomorrow; it's today or nothing.

I quickly rustle up a sponge cake and decorate it with iced

roses and a few green tendrils. Simple and classic is my intention. I nail both elements.

I daren't guess at her age so don't add any candles; best avoid offending when we're trying to be kind. If asked, I'd say early fifties, but there's no telling with some folk. I know women who look far older than their years, and others who haven't a wrinkle in sight and can pass for ten years younger. Fingers crossed it isn't a milestone birthday requiring something a little more elaborate than my classy sponge.

As I clean the kitchen countertops, I catch sight of the leaflet Ruth was reading a day or so ago. I could have sworn she'd thrown it in the bin. The front cover depicts the local riding stables – obviously this leaflet has done the rounds between all three of us during our stay. I flip through, uncertain what I'm actually seeking amongst the bar and restaurant adverts, local fish market and the Berry Head Hotel's menu. On page 6, though, I stop, ponder and breathe a sigh of relief.

I grab my mobile and after making a reservation for three, I dial Benni's number.

'Hello!' She answers immediately.

'Don't make any arrangements for tonight. I've found the perfect present for Ruth.'

Benjamina

'Who?' I ask, having never heard of the woman Ruth and Emma are eagerly discussing in the rear of the taxi.

139

'Oh dear, the young of today . . . I can't believe that you've never heard of her,' says Ruth condescendingly. I feel a bit miffed, especially given that I've paid for half of her birthday treat.

'She was known as the Queen of Crime,' says Emma. 'Seriously, half my teenage years were spent with my nose buried in one of her crime novels, trying to work out who'd done it and how.'

'Me too. I'm sure I've read every one written, some probably twice,' adds Ruth excitedly to Emma before turning to me in the back of the taxi. 'Maybe you should try one – I'd suggest Miss Marple to begin with.'

'No, it's Poirot for me,' says Emma. 'Though you're probably better off making up your own mind rather than us influencing your choice.'

I glance at the two of them, convinced that they've lost the plot somewhere between Brixham and here, a place called Greenway. I opt out and stare at the greying short back and sides of our taxi driver. I bet he's heard it all before, two excited women wittering on about something that belongs in an era long before my day. How am I supposed to know about things that happened before I was even born?

'It's a film, right?' I say, interrupting the conversation.

'No . . . well, a novel turned into a film, then a hosted dinner party,' explains Emma for the umpteenth time. Emma had relayed a half-garbled message whilst I was at the stables earlier in the day but still I haven't got my head around the last-minute arrangements. I was happy to chip in though.

'Has he got a moustache?' I ask.

'Yes!' they chorus.

'Is he the French detective with a middle-aged male side-kick?'

'Nooo!' wails Ruth. '*Belgian.*'

'That's pure sacrilege,' Emma says. 'I reckon we should kick you out and make you walk back to the cottage. You are not worthy to enter Christie's house having mentioned the F word.'

They begin to giggle. It's going to be a long evening if they keep up this ridiculous double act. I'll need the patience of a saint if the rest of the people at the dinner party have a similar attitude or there may well be a murder.

I give an unexpected snort at the very idea.

'What?' asks Ruth.

'Nothing . . . honestly, you've nothing to worry about on your birthday,' I retort, supressing the urge to giggle more.

Emma

'Seriously, give it a bloody rest, will you?' I hiss at Benni as discreetly as I can, as the waiter delivers lemon sorbet to the table of fifteen diners and one vacant chair. An additional sideways glare reinforces my meaning and pretty much confirms my mood too.

'I'm just saying, that's all,' snipes Benni between clenched teeth. 'They all look like extras from a drama. The colonel, the vicar, the obnoxious rich lady, the meek and mild companion, the mystery blonde and the lawyer type . . . Need I continue?'

'No, you've complained a million times in the last two hours, so please get over yourself and suck it up.'

'I'm by far the youngest here, surrounded by old people,' she mutters, digging crossly into her ball of frozen sorbet, causing it to slide and nearly escape over the upper edge of the glass dish.

She has a point, but she's managed fine for nearly a week with me and Ruth, so why the sudden concern about age?

I glance about the dining table, dressed in its finery with extravagant crystal candelabra, gleaming cutlery and fine porcelain. Benni's not wrong: each diner does define a certain element of Christie's society. I wonder if the people sitting opposite could say the same about us three.

Next to me, Ruth's in her element, happily chatting to an elderly chap on her right.

As I watch the waiter deliver sorbet to the far end, there's a touch on my forearm. I'm greeted by Ruth's smiling face.

'Are you OK?' she asks, peering at me.

'Just taking in the atmosphere really.'

'Me too. I can't believe we're dining in Agatha Christie's actual holiday home. She used to sit there,' Ruth points her tiny sorbet spoon towards the top chair, which remains empty out of respect to the great woman.

I nod, trying to hide my smugness.

I'm glad we've made the effort, though it wasn't a cheap present, but how can you put a price on guaranteeing someone

a birthday to remember? It's not as if Ruth has received anything from her son, and her mother wouldn't be capable of
sending a present even if she wanted to.

Ruth

I could cry with happiness. I can't remember the last time
someone went out of their way for me. I've only known Emma
and Benni for a matter of days, yet they've given me such a
wonderful birthday surprise. I enjoyed the cinema viewing of
Dead Man's Folly, especially as some of the scenes were filmed
here at Greenway. Even though I've seen it numerous times
before, it was still an indescribable treat to experience the
1950s-style cinema evening hosted in an airy marquee within
the spacious grounds.

This is simply the best birthday I have ever had. I'm a little
sad that Jack can't be here, but it's not his scene, possibly even
less so than Benni's, though at least he would know whose
house we're at, having been brought up with me watching the
various adaptations of each novel.

I have to pinch myself as Derek, sitting to my right, talks
knowledgeably about our absent hostess. He knows everything
there is to know, from her favourite tipple of fresh double
cream down to her collection of family board games stored
in the lounge. I listen in awe as he explains how she managed
to be so creative and produce such intriguing crime novels
whilst being a thoroughly good egg throughout her whole life.

Throughout the meal I keep glancing at the vacant seat at the head of the table, imagining her sitting there scrutinising us as potential characters. My spine tingles as the vacant seat also reminds me of her novel *Sparkling Cyanide*, in which a small party reminisce about their dearly departed friend. There are far too many of us here this evening to re-enact the scene precisely, but still, the very thought is thrilling.

I sit patiently as a waitress enters the room carrying a silver coffee pot and starts serving the far side of the dining table. I wish she'd begun with our side. I'm dying for a decent coffee: strong Arabian beans is my hope.

Suddenly the overhead lights go out, plunging the dining room into near darkness, apart from the table's candlelight. Women gasp, a door opens and a shuffling sound is heard. Then:

Boom!

The sound of gunfire ricochets around the dining room. I'm startled and hope the young waitress doesn't spill hot coffee on herself or a guest in the ensuing confusion.

The lights return momentarily, flicker and remain strong.

I grab at Emma, who is holding Benni's arm. All eyes are staring in my direction. I have no idea why. Slowly I follow their shocked expressions to where Derek is slumped, his head lolling towards my shoulder, his eyes wide. My gaze drops to the open wound that has appeared across his chest, an oozing red injury that wasn't present moments before.

I scream, my hands releasing Emma to clutch at my face in an attempt to cover my eyes from the murderous scene.

'Ladies and gentlemen, we would appreciate it if you would stand and step away from the dining table and make your way towards the lounge, where your coffee is awaiting you,' announces the waiter, his white serving cloth draped over his forearm.

I peer around the table, shocked that his announcement is so calm, so calculated, so cold.

'What the hell?' I say, clutching Emma's arm for support as she helps me from my seat.

'Oh Ruth, your face is a picture,' says Benni, struggling to speak through her laughter.

'What the bloody hell just happened?' I ask, looking frantically around the room as the other guests calmly depart for coffee.

I stare from Emma to Benni, then glance down again at the slumped body of Derek. I can do nothing but point in disbelief from one to the other, open mouthed and mute.

'Happy birthday, Ruth! Isn't this simply the best setting for a murder mystery night?' gushes Emma, her excitement overflowing.

Chapter Seven

Friday 24 August

Benjamina

We browse the shops on the busy street in a zigzag fashion, crossing the steep road as our interest is caught and snagged: craft shops with artful window displays, music shops selling every instrument imaginable, and gourmet food stores offering us samples of cheese, olives and chutney in tiny dishes from their countertops.

This wasn't my plan for today, but when Ziggy suggested a day out in Totnes during my early-morning walk along the harbour, I couldn't refuse him.

And now I've fallen in love with the town.

I want to browse inside each and every shop, but I know we have limited time given Ziggy's need for sleep before a busy night of fishing.

'There's a great music shop towards the top,' says Ziggy.

'It's retro stuff, a proper record shop where you stand and flip through the wooden boxes of vinyl albums. Do you fancy taking a look?'

I don't particularly – vinyl's not my thing – but I'll happily wait while he browses. He was kind enough to invite me, so I'll be patient.

It's a fair trek up the steep hill, but as soon as we near the shop, I can tell it's something special. Nestled amongst the other shop frontages, it looks entirely different; the window is dark and moody, with lots of collector's items and music paraphernalia. As we step through the doorway, we're greeted by a row of backs and lowered heads, each person quietly flipping through the boxes of records displayed alphabetically. Ziggy moves to the end of the alphabet, while I wander amongst the browsers. A calmness envelops me, the rhythmical flipping sound acting like a lullaby. Once in a while, an album cover is pulled from its home, inspected, turned over and the song list read, before being tucked carefully under an arm or returned to the box.

I like it in here. This is how a music shop should be.

The waistcoated woman behind the counter gives me a polite smile. She can see I'm a fish out of water filling time, but unless I disturb the tranquillity, I'm sure she'll allow me to pace.

The music overhead is by an artist I couldn't name, a song I've never heard before, and yet it feels right to be hearing new material in here.

That's when I see him.

I daren't move for fear of distracting other people.

He's quietly but carefully stacking album covers into a plastic carry case. His head is bent, his long, sinewy neck bare, as he replenishes stock amongst the vinyl-hunters.

And I know. It's instant. Instinctive. There's been one huge lie told within my family.

I stand and watch his mannerisms, his stance, his hands busily working. He is totally unaware that I am taking in every inch of him. His name dances upon my tongue but I hold it back, waiting for the right moment. The moment when my heart stops racing, my breathing returns to normal and an inner voice suggests the correct manner in which to handle this situation.

To everyone else in the store he is just a middle-aged man dressed in dark jeans and a baggy over-washed T-shirt; a man simply doing his job. Given the way he handles each record, it is a job he loves.

I'm frozen to the spot with fear. Fear about my reaction. His reaction. Definitely my mum's reaction.

I glance sideways in search of Ziggy, who has his back to me and is casually flicking through the wooden boxes like everyone else in the shop. There's no chance I can call or beckon to him without alerting everyone that I am having a major life crisis.

I'm on my own. Aren't I always?

I suddenly become aware that I'm standing stock still like everyone else but without a selection of vinyl to flip through. I need to move, seize my chance and introduce myself.

I take a deep breath.

Here goes.

He continues to stack the albums, neatening and aligning the edges, sporadically reading a back cover when his interest is caught. I take five steps towards him. Before me stands an older version of my brother.

'Dad?'

He casually glances up, looks away, then instantly returns his gaze to me, the 'dad' label obviously throwing his train of thought.

'Sorry?' He holds a Neil Young album in mid air and peers at me.

'Hi, Dad . . . I'm Benjamina Hammond.'

I watch as my words hit home. His blue eyes match Dan's, his mouth is uneven with a full bottom lip, again like my brother's. But his chin and his peering stare are definitely mine.

I don't need a second opinion, a DNA test – I simply know with every fibre of my body. Someone has some explaining to do.

'Hi . . .' I offer again, filling the lengthy silence, as I take the album from his hands and place it on top of the plastic case. Then I wait.

Emma

I open the front door expecting a charity collector or a house-mate pleading a forgotten key. What actually greets me is a six-foot youth with three days of stubble growth and an oversized kitbag.

'Can I help you?' I ask, peering at him.

'I'm looking for Ruth Elton.' His accent takes me straight back home to the Midlands. I stare past the rugby shirt and the masculine features to pinpoint those belonging to Ruth: her light brown hair, her delicate cheekbones and her green eyes.

'You must be Jack,' I say.

'Yes . . . Mentioned me, has she? Hello, nice to meet you . . .'

'Emma. I'm one of the others holidaying here. Would you like to come in?'

He doesn't answer, but steps inside as soon as I move backwards into the hallway, bringing the kitbag with him. I eye it and my heart sinks.

'Your mother's out painting at the moment – would you like tea, or are you heading out to find her?'

'Tea, please.' He kicks off his large shoes, and plods after me towards the kitchen.

Not the answer I was hoping for. I push aside the mountain of ingredients for a sumptuous batch of peanut butter and jam ice cream, then turn off the happy radio channel and switch on the kettle.

Jack leans against the fridge door and surveys the galley kitchen.

'And?' I ask, trying to sugar-coat my tone but failing miserably.

'It's not what I expected, that's all . . . It's more substantial than the kitsch cottage I imagined.'

I nod, taking on board his surprise.

'Sugar? Milk?'

'White with three sugars,' he says, adding, 'Has my mum settled in OK? No panic attacks about my nan?'

'Not since the seventeen-hour scare the other day. She's been a bit anxious since, but apart from that, she seems to be enjoying herself immensely.'

'Really? My mum?'

His remark hits the bull's-eye of my annoyance. What a cheek! He belongs to Benni's generation, yet she is years ahead of this youth in terms of life skills and attitude.

'Actually, you'll probably find it difficult to understand how much your mother needed a break, given the relentless stress she endures.' Arsey is my chosen tone whilst spooning sugar into a clean mug.

'I thought you guys were all strangers?'

'We are ... well, we were a week ago, but it only takes a matter of days to appreciate a person's true worth and morals.' I pause before continuing. 'We're friends, and I'm sure it'll continue that way once we return home to the Midlands.'

From the corner of my eye I see Jack shrug as if my comment lacks substance, much like the Rose Cottage he originally imagined.

Benjamina

I stare at the large bowl of carrot and coconut soup in front of me. I never choose vegetarian food and yet it smells gorgeous and tempting. But my spoon remains on my folded napkin. My stomach is spinning faster than a fairground waltzer; one mouthful and I'll be sick. In the busy café, where every table is filled with chattering diners, I sit in emotional turmoil, unsure whether to laugh or cry.

My gaze lifts to the familiar features of the stranger sitting opposite me.

I don't have a father. So what the hell am I doing sharing a bite to eat with him?

'Eat up, it's good,' he says, dipping his hunk of rye bread into his own soup before taking a bite.

'I'm not hungry.'

He nudges the bowl closer to my hands, a parental move that offers instruction rather than suggestion.

As I tentatively slurp the thick creamy soup and attempt to grasp a new set of family facts, my mind replays the highlights of the last thirty minutes of my life, much like a cinema trailer of forthcoming attractions.

After I announced who I was, my father froze, much like I had earlier. Eventually he began to breathe again, and I watched the cogs in his head whirring as his gaze scanned my features. He stopped when he reached my chin – protruding somewhat whilst pinched on either side. An exact double of his.

'Benjamina?'

'I think we need to talk,' I said, conscious that we were drawing attention in this intimate setting.

He nodded, whispered a hasty instruction to the waistcoated woman serving and grabbed his wallet from behind the counter.

Ziggy was wide-eyed on hearing my brief but rushed explanation, as I interrupted his browsing. 'I'll catch you in an hour,' I told him. 'OK?'

Then Ben and I left the music shop, heading towards this quiet café a little further up the steep hill.

'So she said I was dead?' he asks me now.

I nod, unsure whether I'm supposed to justify my mother's actions.

'Didn't you think it weird that she didn't take you to a grave to lay flowers on my birthday or Father's Day?'

I slowly shake my head. I feel so stupid. It must have been easy for her to string such a tale. I didn't question anything. I simply believed everything I was told.

'And no one else in the family has ever commented or hinted at the true facts?'

'No.'

Ben sits back, deflated and yet very much alive compared to the father I've spent years yearning for.

'And Dan?'

'I guess he knows as much as me, unless she's taken him into her confidence and I was the only one who didn't know. Which wouldn't surprise me, actually.'

'You'd think he'd have slipped up if he'd known all these years.'

'You'd think *she'd* have slipped up, but she never has.' Even after a late night with her mates, after one too many brandies.

Or when we were short of money when school trips needed to be paid for or Christmas was nearing. Or when she lost her temper with me for being me . . . which was probably too much like him.

'I simply couldn't stay,' he says. 'It was killing me inside.' He hesitates before continuing. 'Look, Benni, I didn't even know she was pregnant with you, but I was there for Dan. I stayed for his sake, not your mum's. He was only a little boy, a toddler, and she was simply . . .'

I'm not going to make this difficult for him. I understand exactly what he means. My mum is demanding. Suffocating. Wanting to know everything about everybody whilst not truly caring about anyone or anything other than where her next drink is coming from.

'Does she still drink?' His voice is soft, his eyes sympathetic.

I give a sharp nod. There's no point denying what she is.

'An alcoholic in the true sense of the word,' I say. 'Semi-functioning is how I describe her.'

'And Dan?'

'Now there's a question.' I pause, trying to find the words to describe Dan and his wayward behaviour. 'Dan's Dan. The product of an alcoholic mother, a whining younger sister and a social system that probably doesn't take kindly to young men like him. Especially when he can't be bothered to help himself by working, or studying, or doing the right thing. If you get my drift.'

Ben grimaces.

'He's a waste of space, in my opinion. He's been lucky to

get some well-paid jobs labouring on motorway maintenance, but at twenty-eight he should have established himself in life: a home of his own, a partner, a steady job. Instead, he's gambled it all away. I love him to bits, but he doesn't help himself. It wouldn't surprise me if history doesn't repeat itself – heavy drinking often goes hand in hand with gambling.'

'I see . . . And you?'

I give a heavy sigh. 'To tell you the truth, I've got little more than Dan. I haven't had his opportunities when it comes to employment and have never earned decent money, but I'm nothing like those two, as strange as it might sound having been raised in the same house as Dan, by the same mother, with the same attitude to schooling and her issues regarding money and alcohol. I'm a fish out of water when I'm with them.' I stare up into his kind blue eyes. 'Maybe I'm more like you.'

Ben nods slowly, his gaze never leaving mine.

'Maybe you are your father's daughter . . . in which case, I understand why you escaped down here for a holiday on your own. What else do you do back home?'

I explain about the agency and the factory; about the solo holiday advert I spied online and the two friends I've made in just seven days.

'And you . . . any family down here?' I eventually ask the burning question.

'I have two teenage lads with a previous partner,' he says. 'Look, lass, this is quite a shock for me and it will be more so for them. They know all about Dan, but you . . . Well, she

155

never even told me you were on the way. I'm not the kind of guy that leaves a woman when she's . . .'

I can hear the struggle in his voice.

'I have to be honest with you. You're probably not worldly-wise enough to understand how I felt back then, but I simply needed a new beginning. I'd become someone I didn't like, or even recognise. I wanted to reinvent myself, be the man I'd once planned to be.'

'I get that,' I whisper. I know exactly how it feels.

'Everything with your mum happened so fast. We went from first date to parenthood in a matter of months. I thought I was doing the right thing by going with the flow. The relationship wasn't built on love or attraction . . . it simply happened and then it all got too much for me. I'm not proud of my actions. It looks like I skipped out, but I didn't, honestly. It was a sad situation. I couldn't cope with her or her drinking, and I had nowhere to take Dan. I thought they were both better off without me. I told her it was over, explained why and even where I was heading. She was amicable at first, but within weeks she'd stopped me seeing Dan, then she started ignoring my calls. One thing led to another, and I lost touch when they moved house.' He pauses. 'It sounds pathetic, I know. I never intended not to see my son. We could have made it work, if only things had been amicable.'

I can't judge him. I know how it feels to live in that situation. Suspecting there's more to life but knowing I'm not getting a sniff of it because of my mum's lifestyle.

'But there comes a moment when we make our own choices,' I say as cheerily as I can in an effort to lift the mood.

'That's true, lass.'

At last I've found someone like me. He'll understand how I feel.

I reach across the table for his hand. It's scaly and dry, yet comforting nestled in mine. He's calm, I'm content. I can't argue with his explanation; I know it couldn't have been an easy decision to make. Though Mum's life couldn't have been easy either. Which comes first, loneliness or drunkenness? I wouldn't have wanted to be in either of their shoes, but still, she shouldn't have lied. Who knows what she'll say when I get home and explain?

'I think you're right, Ben . . . Dad,' I tell him. 'New beginnings are important, but you have to be brave enough to take a chance in life.'

'Too right, lass.'

Ruth

'I don't know what you expect me to do,' I say, as Emma tries to ignore my efforts to reason with her. 'He's my son.'

I watch as she wipes the worktop for the umpteenth time, avoiding my gaze when she turns to the sink to rinse the cloth of crumbs. Jack sits at the dining table, cradling his tea, listening to my muted apology to a woman who was a total stranger not more than a few days ago.

Once again, I'm piggy in the middle.

I step forward and gently touch Emma's arm in a futile attempt to stop her robotic motions of wiping and clearing.

'Can't he check into a hotel?' she asks.

'He's my son ... I'm not going to see him without somewhere to stay, am I?'

Emma finally stops cleaning, glances up at me and sighs.

'If it's a big deal, we'll both find somewhere else to stay,' I say. 'What's it to be?'

'Ruth ...'

'No. I'm not asking my son to leave.' My 'no' is defiant and strong. It sounds like a 'no' that means 'no', and not a soft, flimsy 'no' that ought to grow a backbone.

'OK, when you put it like that.'

I squeeze her arm and mouth, 'Thank you.'

'Jack, let's go and fetch the rest of your stuff from the car. Where did you say you'd parked?' I keep him talking as Emma resumes cleaning the kitchen and we make our escape from the cottage.

'What's her problem?' asks Jack as we cross the playing fields where every inch of parking space has a car bumper wedged into it.

'It's not you. It's the situation. We've got on so well for a week, and now, when we're genuinely having a great holiday, things have changed. I think she's irritated by your arrival but not by you.'

'Thanks for being so bloody honest, it's just what I need:

more women telling me what I should be doing – I hear enough complaints at home.'

'She doesn't mean it, and I'm sure Megan doesn't either.'

'Believe me, Megan means every word. In the month we've been living together, she's changed big time.'

'Oh Jack, I'm sure she hasn't.'

'Mum, she has. Now she doesn't want to go out at all at the weekend; she just wants us to stay home and save money. She's cutting out discount coupons from magazines, saving up for a dishwasher. She expects me to say no to every boys' night out. As if!'

'She's trying to build a home with you . . . she's nesting.'

'Nesting? Mum, we're far from nesting, believe me . . . Why can't we just carry on having fun, enjoy ourselves with the added bonus of living together? Megan's moved the goalposts.'

When we arrive at his car, I instantly see that it contains not only a couple of suitcases, but also football boots, a gym holdall and a skateboard I thought he'd flogged on eBay years ago.

'Have you moved out?' I ask, shocked by the contents of his car.

'You could say that.'

He depresses the key fob, lights flicker and die before he lifts the tailgate, his hand pushing the contents back into place as they attempt to spill on to the tarmac.

'Jack—'

'Mum, don't give me a lecture. I'm big enough and ugly

enough to choose my own path in life. I've got my reasons so what's it to be – are you going to help or hinder me?'

'Jack!'

'Mum, please!' his voice is whiney, he knows how to get on my good side. 'I need some space; I thought a night or two here might be the answer.'

'You can't simply run out on a relationship because things aren't going your way.'

He pauses, his hand resting on the open tailgate, and eyes me.

'I'm not running out on her, Mum. If you must know, the real truth is she's maxed out on my credit card in just four weeks and hasn't the money to pay her share of the rent.'

'No!'

'Yes. Now do you get my drift? I was embarrassed to tell you – I feel like a total mug, Mum. I know I deserve better than that from a partner.'

'I can't believe she'd do something as calculated as that. She's never caused you a moment's trouble in two years. Are you sure?'

'Believe me, I'm sure. We've a fully furnished house all bought online with my credit cards so now she's trying to claw back every penny to meet next month's minimum payments.'

I fall silent. A mother shouldn't meddle in her son's affairs, but surely he's got the wrong end of the stick here.

'Here, can you carry this, and maybe this?' Jack piles several bulging carrier bags into my arms. 'They're not too heavy for you?'

'I'm fine,' I struggle to say under the bulky weight. 'I can manage.'

Within a few minutes, we're making the return journey to the cottage. I have no doubt that Benni won't complain about Jack staying over; young people are good at accepting whatever is thrown at them, unlike us older folk. In fact, she could be the solution to talking Emma round. I pray that Benni has returned to the cottage in our absence and that Emma has given her the lowdown on Jack's arrival. If so, I'm expecting a very different atmosphere on our return.

'Mum?'

'Yeah,' I say, struggling under the weight of his belongings.

'Happy birthday for yesterday.'

'Thanks, Jack.' In a blink of an eye my maternal instinct forgives him. There's always next year.

Emma

Where the hell is Benni when I need her support?

I uncork a cheeky Merlot and pour a large glass before sauntering into the garden to sit alone amongst the sweet-smelling lavender. I'm not peeved that Jack's here as such; it's the fact that I'm expected to welcome him with open arms into our holiday cottage for the remaining week without a please, thank you or kiss my arse! The three of us were having a jolly nice time, and now everything will change. And while he's lying on the sofa, shoes off, remote in hand, flicking through the channels, his mother's upstairs changing the sheets in order to give up her room and sleep on the sodding sofa. It's Jack who should be kipping on the sofa. Bloody typical; it's taken her days to stop worrying about her mother, and now this.

Give me strength: the kids of today don't know they're bloody born!

Instantly I feel guilty for condemning an entire generation. Benni is an exception to the rule.

I sip my wine, and smile. Benni does make me laugh. First impressions suggest a young woman who appears physically robust but nothing else. She can't cook, she doesn't drive, she hasn't even secured a permanent job yet. But despite all this, she's fearless. She accepts whatever happens and gets on with it. Creatively finding solutions to whatever situation she's faced with – now that's a skill worth having in life.

If only I'd had some of her gumption as a youngster, I wouldn't be here on my own, childless and wasting my talents at thirty-nine, would I? No way, José! I should have taken more chances in life, seized the day more often. Instead, I kept hoping things would change for the better, without actually doing anything about it.

I prop my feet on to the seat of the chair opposite and sip my wine.

What I wouldn't give to turn the clock back. To relive moments when I held back from saying what I truly thought, doing what I wanted and taking the risks that others advised me not to take.

'Hello, who's that hogging the sofa?'

I jump as Benni appears from the dining room to stand beside my chair.

'Hi, I was just thinking about you. That's Jack. He appears to be staying with us for a few days because he needs his mum.'

Benni's eyebrows lift comically into her blonde fringe.

'Do I sound like a bitch?' I ask, aware of my tone.

'Yep, but you might have a valid reason.'

'Listen to you, all deep and meaningful. Go on then, tell me my reason and ease my conscience.' Her phrase intrigues me.

Benni points to the open bottle of Merlot.

'Yeah, sure, grab a glass then you can explain yourself.'

I watch as she returns inside. I see her pass the first kitchen window, then the second, to stand before the glasses cabinet.

I silently urge her to reach for the top shelf and grab one of the large wine glasses, not the titchy tumblers lined up like soldiers with easy access.

I smile as she stretches up to the high shelf.

That's the spirit, girl.

She returns to the patio, puts her glass on the table and waits. I know why.

'You're such a sweetie, you know that, don't you?' I lean forward to pour the wine, understanding her manners and her appreciation of my invitation.

She shrugs off my compliment.

'And you need to stop doing that too.'

'Doing what?'

'Rejecting every compliment you're given. It gets you nowhere in life. Be bold; accept and acknowledge praise. All you have to say is "thank you", regardless of how embarrassed you are.'

'I can't.'

'You can. Let's try.'

'Emma!'

'You have a lovely smile.'

She turns away, hastily sipping her wine. The evening shadows hide her intense blush, which I know is burning her cheeks.

'Just say it. Lift your chin and say it with pride.'

'Thank you, Emma,' she mutters into her chest.

'Useless . . . bloody useless. You can't go through life shying away from people; it doesn't bring you happiness and it doesn't get you anywhere fast.' I stop as the church bells begin to chime, and point to the twilight sky, signalling for Benni to listen. 'I forgot to say, it's "Abide With Me". Martin told me the other night.'

'Oh . . . the football anthem,' she says, listening appreciatively and nodding in recognition.

'No,' I correct her, as if offended by her modern association and lack of knowledge, despite my own shortcomings. 'It's a hymn, actually, written here in Brixham.'

'But it's played at some football finals too,' insists Benni. 'I've heard it.'

The tuneful chiming ceases.

'Anyway, game over, we've named that tune. So why might I have a valid reason?' I ask.

She turns to face me, and I can see excitement bubbling

from within. Suddenly her stature changes, her eyes sparkle and she leans forward, eager to share.

'Because today I realised there's always a reason for our actions. We might not want to be totally honest with others about the root of an issue, but there is always a reason.'

'Wow, and that's your thought of the day?'

'I've never realised until today—' A smile of contentment spreads across her features.

'You *do* have a beautiful smile,' I interrupt, admiring her happy expression.

After the slightest hesitation, Benni says, 'Thank you. I appreciate you noticing.'

'Good girl . . . but continue. I'm intrigued.'

'Sometimes we simply need to explain ourselves for others to be OK with our choices.'

'But what if they're hurt by our choices?'

'Explain why you're doing it, why it's important, and it'll ease their pain in the long run.'

'Does it?'

'Yeah, because they'll have the knowledge that it isn't them causing your pain.'

'But what if it is?'

'What if it's what?' asks Benni, frowning.

'If it *is* them causing your pain . . . shouldn't they know?'

Benni pauses and sips her wine before continuing. I do likewise.

'I met my dad today for the first time, and after hearing him talk, I'm fine with his actions. He had a valid reason.'

I splutter my wine across my lap in shock.

'I thought your dad was dead!'

'Mmm, so did I, but I'm OK that he's not.'

Ruth

I can hear Emma frantically calling me from downstairs as I plump up the pillows on Jack's bed. If she's about to continue her lecture about my son, I'll pretend I can't hear and stay up here a little longer. I have no objection to sleeping on the sofa for a few nights; at six foot two, there's no chance Jack will even fit.

'Ruth!' The bedroom door bursts open, revealing Emma, red-faced and panting for breath. 'Seriously, woman, you need to answer when called. You've got to come downstairs. Benni has had one hell of a day, and boy, you're never going to believe who she's met.'

'Excuse me, I'm busy,' I huff, determined not to give in to the demands of a woman who less than an hour ago was making me feel embarrassed about my protective nature.

'Don't get all sulky. You and Jack can please yourselves. I put my two penn'orth in purely to make you realise how quickly you snap back into the mummy role. He's an adult; old enough to make decisions and cope with the consequences.'

I shake my head. She has absolutely no understanding of motherhood or nurturing, and yet she stands there offering me a lesson on how best to support my son.

I straighten the duvet, purely to busy my hands.

'OK. I'm sorry, Ruth,' she says. 'I'm sorry for commenting, sorry for interfering and sorry for making you feel self-conscious about your mothering instinct, but ... but I have a valid reason for doing so.' I watch as she leans against the door jamb and chuckles at her own speech.

How much has she had to drink?

'Ruth, come downstairs and hear the whole story from Benni. Seriously, she'll explain about her thought of the day based on her chance meeting with ... a very important person.'

She peels herself from my doorway and returns downstairs. I can still hear her giggling out on the patio.

'Hi, Benni, how are you?' I ask when I eventually decide to join the pair sitting outside. There was no fear I'd rush; I'm my own person and I'll decide for myself what I do and when. Boy, have I undergone a reflective week.

'Good, thanks. I've had the most amazing day,' explains Benni, her face a picture of joy. 'You'll never guess who I met while I was in Totnes!'

As I listen to Benni, I'm sure I hear Emma mutter, 'Took your time.'

I ignore Emma and focus upon Benni. The young woman seems like a different person this evening. She's wearing the same clothes, the same ponytail, the same soap-and-water face, and yet something about her has changed. She's alive with energy.

I shrug, unable to name anyone famous who might be in Totnes.

'My dad!' she squeals, her hands lifting in excitement to flap about her face.

I glance at Emma and back to Benni.

'I thought he was dead,' I say carefully.

'And me.' Benni bursts out laughing. 'It turns out he left my mum when my brother was little. First he lived in Torquay, then he ended up buying a place in Totnes.' She spills forth information about his previous partner, his two teenage sons and his music shop. I stand and nod, overwhelmed by her enthusiasm and positive attitude.

'Wow, catch your breath, love,' says Emma, topping up Benni's wine glass when she pauses. 'Ruth, do you want to grab a glass?'

'I will, but . . . I can't believe what I'm hearing. You're telling me that your mother has lied for all these years about your dad being dead and you're OK with it?'

'I'm upset with her for denying me access to him, for not even telling him that I exist, but – and this is where I had my epiphany moment – the moment Ben – he's my dad – explained why he left, I stopped being angry with her for hiding the truth. She was embarrassed, and so she lied. If anything, I feel sorry for her carrying the burden of a lie for all these years. She might have been much happier if she'd been honest. Does she drink so heavily because of that pain, or was she always destined to be the drinker she is? And the strangest thing is, when my dad explained why it had happened, I got it. Instantly. I understood what he meant about new beginnings, how he needed to get away, erase the route life had taken him on and start again. That makes sense to me . . . it's what I want too. Which is why we've arranged a dad and daughter date for next Wednesday. I'm finally going to get to know my father.'

Chapter Eight

Saturday 25 August

Benjamina

I pull the luminous yellow banding over my head and secure it around my middle. It's tight, but I'm not going to complain. Maddie has a matching tunic, which is possibly a tad more flattering, but it wouldn't fit me.

'Are you happy to lead him, or do you want me to?' she asks, holding Bruce's long rein looped in one hand. Her free hand holds his head bridle.

I shrug. I have no idea what she's planning to do, or why.

'I don't mind, what do you think?'

'How about I lead to start with until we meet up with the others and then you can take over when you feel like it?' she suggests. I agree. I'm happy to be invited to join their morning hack. There's no chance I'll be complaining about this chance to enjoy the fresh air and the company of the horses.

'Are you ready, Maddie?' calls a young woman, appearing at the open end of the stables, her chestnut horse clip-clopping behind her.

'Yes, on our way, Summer,' cries Maddie, passing me the coiled rein in order to secure her riding hat. I have no intention of riding, but she's already fitted and secured my hat for me.

Maddie leads Bruce out into the yard, where we join three other riders, all on foot, leading their horses towards the far end of the yard.

'The bay at the back is my sister Marla's horse,' says Maddie. 'She's at work, so Jenny's exercising Wispy for her.'

'Marla from the Queen's Arms is your sister?'

Maddie gives a quick nod.

'I'm staying over the road from the pub – Marla's doing my friend a favour,' I explain.

'Yep, that's my sister,' says Maddie, following my gaze as I stare at the other three horses.

'What's a bay?' I ask.

'Sorry, I keep forgetting . . . a rich brown.'

'Is everyone's mobile charged?' asks the lady at the front, her jodhpurs splattered with dried mud and her frizzy hair sprouting from beneath a riding hat. I know she isn't asking me. My phone is safely at the cottage, supposedly being ignored, though I do check it each time I walk past, hoping for a missed call.

A chorus of 'yes' rings out above the clopping of hooves and the jingling of tack. It sounds like heaven.

How strange that a specific sound can speak to your soul.

If only I were leading my own horse across the stable yard, I think wistfully.

My calves are throbbing, my heart is pounding and I fear I may have the biggest blister on my right heel, but it's all irrelevant given that I've walked two miles in the company of four beautiful horses and their owners.

The sun is shining, the hills are lushly painted in every shade of green and the blue sky is near perfect, without a single cloud.

I've struggled – I won't pretend I haven't – but not in the way I imagined. My pace isn't as quick as theirs, and my stride is small, due to the bulk I need to move, and I'm sweating like I never have before, but it feels great. As we return to the stable, I don't look it but I feel like a million dollars. Alive, and very grateful for the chance to spend time at the stables.

Ruth

'Did Nan come with us?' asks Jack, as we walk the length of the harbour wall arm in arm.

'No, just me and you. It was a rare moment for us to spend some time alone.'

'I bet she wasn't happy about that arrangement.'

'Mmm, I remember it well. Her attachment to you was so strong, Jack – I wonder if she felt a connection to my father through you.'

172

'It's possible, I suppose, given that I was the only male in the household.'

Jack's right; maybe his presence helped her to cope with her grief at losing her husband. I suddenly feel sorry for my mother, struggling alone whilst responsible for others.

'I'll always be grateful for her help,' I say, 'but I had every right to make my own choices regarding my own son, Jack.'

'Much like me now, hey?'

I stop walking, pulling my arm from his. He's over six foot, a strapping man in jeans and a rugby shirt, but I can't help but see him as the little lad who always ran to me to solve his problems, if his grandmother wasn't around.

'Oh Jack.' Is that really how he feels? Where do I find the strength to put my opinions aside, enabling him to make his own decisions?

'It's simple. I'm not happy, Mum. This isn't the outcome Megan and I planned for, but I have to do what's right for me. I'm moving out.'

'Jack—'

'Mum, please.'

I want to say 'Hear me out, then decide' but I mustn't do that. I know the pressure of hearing someone else's views, solutions and desires for your life. But how do you reject their opinion and still stay true to your own? I've never found a way.

'I know,' I say. 'You must do what you feel is right. It's your life, Jack.'

'Thank you. The last twenty-four hours has given me a fresh

outlook. I'll drive back tonight and stay at a friend's house for a few nights.'

Deep inside, something shifts as my maternal fear dissolves. I did it. I managed to hold back, unlike my own mother. It's what Jack needs from me, to provide the green light to live his life as he wishes.

'In the meantime, be kind to her. Break-ups aren't easy,' I add, as if I have a wealth of experience.

His arm wraps around my shoulders and squeezes tight.

'And you?' he asks, looking down into my face.

'Me? I think this holiday might be the making of me . . . in one way or another.'

Emma

I arrive back to find a full cottage, Ruth, Benni and Jack lounging around the garden enjoying a lunchtime tipple.

'So, anyone ready for an al fresco lunch?' I ask, trying to maintain a cool composure after a busy morning.

'Have you been to the posh deli?' asks Ruth, sipping a large glass of wine.

'I have. I picked up a selection of cheeses and olives that were on promotion in the chiller, plus a huge quantity of goat's cheese for a new ice cream.'

Benni pulls a face overflowing with disgust.

'Goat's cheese and beetroot will be a perfect addition to our menu.' I let the words settle before hastily returning to the kitchen. Through the open window I watch as Ruth and Benni stare at each other; their confused expressions confirm that they heard my hint. I rapidly turn from the window as both of them leap up and dash inside, heading my way.

'Emma, what have you done?' asks Ruth, rushing into the galley kitchen.

'*Our* menu?' asks Benni impatiently, filling the doorway. I notice that Jack remains outside in the sunshine with his beer glass; that's how grateful he is for us putting him up overnight.

I carry on unpacking my shopping bag. I'm not expecting them to approve. All morning I've known they'll pass judgement on my decision.

The silence grows; the weight of expectation is uncomfortable.

'Emma?' mutters Benni, squeezing past Ruth's slender frame. 'What's going on?'

I wish I could rewind the last three minutes. I want to ignore their presence and simply plate up a selection of cheese and olives as I've planned. I turn away and begin searching the drawers for a sharp knife.

They continue to stare and the atmosphere thickens.

I don't have to share my personal business with Benni and Ruth; there's no rule against retaining your independence whilst holidaying at Rose Cottage.

I slam the drawer shut and turn to confront my audience.

'I'm now the proud investor in a local ice cream parlour; it's all signed, sealed and delivered. So now I need to earn my corn by creating an exciting new menu.'

They glance at each other before either speaks.

'Are you serious?' asks Ruth, her eyebrows knitting together.

'It's a bit hasty, isn't it?' adds Benni.

'Absolutely not. I have a talent with flavours, Martin has the business and the premises; what's more logical than us combining our interests?'

'How much of your interests?' asks Benni.

'Ten thousand,' I mumble.

'How much?' shrieks Ruth, her hands flying to her mouth in shock.

'Did you say *ten thousand*?' asks Benni faintly.

'Yep, a round ten thousand . . . it's a fair price for a share of the business and a decent return on my money. I wouldn't get nearly as much interest if it was sitting in a bank account, so I've put it to work.'

'Have you spoken to your bank, sought legal advice from anyone?' asks Benni, shaking her head.

'I've done my homework, if that's what you mean. I'm satisfied with the business accounts, the contracts and the scope of my involvement. I can do as much or as little as I please.'

'It sounds too good to be true,' says Ruth. 'At the bank, we'd advise customers to seek independent advice, and suggest a cooling-off period too.'

'I don't need that. I'm seizing the day with both hands. And I'd appreciate it if the two of you would stop ruining my glorious moment by raining on my parade. We've spent all morning with a solicitor, so I'd like some down-time this afternoon.'

I resume my search for a knife and find a suitable one for slicing and begin arranging the cheese board.

'Emma, if you're happy then we're happy, but please be careful. You've known this man for how long?' says Ruth, her voice soft and low.

I start to unwrap blocks of cheese from the confines of greaseproof paper.

'You might still be able to get legal advice if—'

I cut Benni short with a laugh.

'How ridiculous are you two? If the boot were on the other foot, I'd be delighted for either of you, genuinely delighted. I'm proud of my decision. I should be singing it from the rooftops, in fact, not having to defend it.'

'We're not criticising you, Emma. We simply want what's best for you, given the circumstances,' says Benni, reaching forward to rub my forearm as if I need a sympathetic touch.

'Well, don't. Focus on yourselves, because from what I've been hearing over the last few days, neither one of you knows what you're doing when this holiday finishes. Me, I've got myself a future, so I'll be busy moving forward.'

Benni's plump hand retracts as if burnt, and the two of them silently retreat to the patio. I stand stock still at the counter and peer through the window. Jack watches them quizzically as they seat themselves and receives a sharp look from Ruth warning him not to ask. Benni settles in her seat before picking up her wine glass and resuming her lunchtime drink.

It might sound harsh, but it's true: they both need to wake up and smell the bloody coffee before it's too late. They'll be on the train heading back to the Midlands in no time, and to what? A bank job and factory work.

Benjamina

'If you're not happy, then don't go back.' Ziggy's eyebrows lift as I stare across the pub table. My hands absently play with the cardboard beer mat as I ponder Emma's new venture. I'm cautious about her swift decision, but deep down I wish something similar would happen to me.

'You make it sound so simple,' I mumble.

'It is. You don't like the job and you're not happy with the prospect of agency work. They can't even promise a full week of shifts next week. It seems to me they're using you to feather their own nest.'

The situation sounds much worse when Ziggy summarises it.

'So what have you got to lose?'

'Nothing,' I say, grabbing my wine glass and sipping. We've spent the afternoon drinking and chatting at the window table of the Sprat and Mackerel, watching the world and his wife walk along the quayside enjoying the sunshine while we enjoy each other's company.

'What about my family?'

'Surely your mum will help you out to start with, until you get on your feet down here?'

'Phuh!' I spit my mouthful of wine across the table, quickly wiping it up with a paper napkin from the table's cutlery box. 'You must be bloody joking. If it's a choice between me and a bottle of vodka, believe me, there's no decision to be made. I'd lose every time.'

'Really?'

'Really. She loves me, there's no doubt about that, but she loves her drink just as much. As far as she's concerned, I'm old enough to look after myself. I pay my keep each month, I do my routine jobs around the home and I never bring trouble to her door – I do all I can to please them both. But my mum's long past the parenting stage.'

Ziggy takes a swig from his beer bottle. 'Fair do. You can't rely on her support then; what about your brother?'

'Same attitude as my mum. Dan needs every penny for his own bad habits.'

'Drink?'

'Gambling.'

'Horses?'

'Cards mainly.'

'Back to square one then, my lovely, as home obviously won't cloud your decision.'

'Nope, and given the surprise arrival of my dad, who knows how they'll react? Especially when I keep in touch with him.'

'What qualifications have you got?'

I squirm. This is the precise reason why I work in a factory.

'Stop worrying. You can't have any less than I have,' says Ziggy, reaching across the table to clasp my hand. I release the beer mat.

'I have nothing of use.' There, I've admitted it. 'They're not worth the paper they are written on, so I'm starting from scratch in every sense. Twenty-five years old and yet no further on than when I was sixteen.'

Ziggy squeezes my hand in his giant paw.

'Any chance you've a hidden talent for hauling fishing nets on to a rusty trawler?'

I burst out laughing and Ziggy rocks his head back to empty his beer bottle in one deep swig. His hair falls back and then forward, covering his healthy glow; his dark eyes peer through his fringe.

'I haven't a clue,' I say. 'I've never tried.'

'Well, maybe you should.'

Emma

'Forget them, they're jealous,' says Martin as I explain my housemates' reaction to my fabulous news.

'Don't say that. We've had such a fun time. I'll put it down to their insecurities about their own futures. Neither of them is happy and so it's difficult for them to accept that some of us are slightly bolder and I've accepted an unforeseen opportunity.'

'Hear, hear,' says Martin, holding his pint glass aloft as if making a toast.

'They'll know how good it feels when it happens to them,' I say, tapping the rim of my wine glass against his.

'Or will they? From what you've said, they'll both end up

slipping back into the usual routine once they're home and then – probably this time next year when they are booking their summer holiday – they'll think about missed opportunities and end up wishing they'd had the courage to follow their own dreams.'

I nod in agreement. I'm slightly uncomfortable talking negatively about Ruth and Benni, as we've enjoyed a good week together, but still, I can't understand why they couldn't be happy for me. If I can take the plunge and be bold, why can't they? You only get one chance to live a purposeful life, so why not go for it?

'Live each day as if it were your last!' says Martin cheerily, squeezing my hand in his.

'I agree. Here's to us.' I raise my glass and take a sip before continuing. 'Let's not focus on them any more. I think you'll be impressed by the smoothness of the goat's cheese and beetroot sample I made this afternoon. I've surprised myself, given that my initial idea was to accompany it with caramelised onion, but at the last minute I changed my mind when I spotted fresh beetroots on sale. Tomorrow I'm planning to blend sweetcorn and salted butter to create a chunky rather than a smooth texture.'

'It sounds so tempting. I can't wait for you to begin production on a larger scale – we sold out of everything you produced within a few hours. Our customers can't get enough of your unique flavours.'

We chat eagerly, making plans for the next few months. Now that my decision is made, it's full steam ahead for a refurbishment of the seating area and a rebranding before next spring.

'Did you tell them about the flat?' asks Martin, finishing his pint of Guinness.

'Not once I'd seen their faces. I'll mention it in the next few days.'

'It's unfurnished, bijou by anyone's standards, but it's above the parlour and it'll be perfect for you over the coming months. I'm sure you'll make it feel like home with a fresh lick of paint and a few pieces of furniture.'

'And I'll wake to such a gorgeous view, with the herring gulls gliding past my window,' I say dreamily. 'I can't wait. Who'd have thought that on the back of one summer holiday my life could change so dramatically?'

'This world favours the brave. Don't ever forget that, my love.' He gives my hand a squeeze.

This is what I love about spending time with Martin. He's warm, tactile and open. How many times have I wished that I could share my life with a man who knows instantly what he wants when he sees it? My experience of dating is a string of men who show some interest at first; they enjoy the chase and the flirtation, only for their affections to fade over time.

'Come on, let's split from here. A change of scenery will help to lift your mood,' he says, breaking into my thoughts.

I don't really mind if we remain here all evening or take a walk to view the setting sun. The only place I don't want to be this evening is Rose Cottage, especially if Ruth and Benni are still wittering on about my new venture.

I drink up and we leave the Sprat and Mackerel.

The sun is almost lost from view, but its warm golden tones linger for a final few minutes as we stand in an embrace at the lighthouse railings, looking out across the sea.

I sense that Martin loves the fact that his favourite view has suddenly become special to me too. It sounds childish, but I want to recapture the essence of our first visit a few nights ago.

'I can't wait for you to visit the Midlands and meet my family and friends,' I say, my back nestling into his chest, his chin resting on my shoulder, his breath tickling my right ear.

'Nor me. I hope I don't disappoint anyone by being just an ice cream seller.'

'Hey, don't put yourself down. You've worked day and night to build your empire. From what you've said it hasn't been easy, but you've made it work, and now, together, we'll build on the foundation that you started.'

'It's been tough at times, but you're right – together we can do so much to improve the parlour. The business will go from strength to strength,' he whispers, before his mouth lowers to my neck and begins touching my skin in the gentlest way.

A tingle runs the length of my spine. My chin lowers, lengthening and tilting my neck, as I enjoy the sensation of being held tightly and kissed so tenderly. I have no intention of resisting him, no thought of pulling away; instead I'll revel in these delights in such a beautiful setting. This is proving to

183

be the best holiday I have ever experienced in my life. Martin continues to cover my neck in tiny kisses, and nuzzles his nose behind my right ear. His touch is intoxicating and difficult to resist when it's all I truly want. I feel like a schoolgirl again; I want to giggle with the excitement of a new love, the prospect of sharing and exploring together. When you're older, new relationships progress so quickly. There's more honesty, more understanding; you appreciate life for what it is.

'Just be careful, you've known him less than a week,' warns a voice inside my head that sounds remarkably like Ruth.

Seriously, how can that be?

Chapter Nine

Sunday 26 August

Ruth

'La, la, la, la, laaaaaaa,' sings Emma, as I enter the kitchen a little after seven o'clock, to find her in full production mode. Every surface is covered, with ingredients, mixing bowls and cooking utensils scattered far and wide. There's no point asking what she's doing; it's bloody obvious.

'When did you buy new catering whites?' I ask.

'Yesterday. They're only cheap ones from the local kitchen store, but still, they'll do.'

I want to ask about health and hygiene certificates, but daren't; she doesn't need me raining on her parade again. I'll mention them another time.

'Tea?' I ask, attempting to grab for the kettle amongst her debris.

'Nope.' Her reply is curt but pleasant as she peers at her

weighing scales to read a measurement. She's a woman on a mission and obviously hasn't a moment to lose given the manner in which her hands snatch and grab at various items within arm's reach.

'Coffee?'

'Nope.'

'Gin? Wine? Ice cream?'

'Nope, nah, and yes please!' she laughs, squinting to view the tiny LED display before spooning a minuscule amount of sugar out of the bowl. She stands straight, nodding at her own accuracy. 'Any chance you can make your tea in the dining room? I'm a tad busy in here.'

'You don't say!' I accidentally-on-purpose slam the cupboard door, having taken a tea bag from the box. 'Would you like me to make my toast outside on the patio too?'

'Ha, ha, so bloody funny. I'll be finished in an hour, so if you want to wait, then please yourself ... Oh great!' Emma shakes her head as Benni appears in the doorway in search of her breakfast.

'Thanks for the warm welcome, Emma. I'll "oh great" you one of these mornings and see how you like it,' says Benni, her blonde eyebrows high, blue eyes wide in surprise. 'Morning, Ruth, this one's dishing out the compliments, is she?'

'Can't you see how busy I am?' growls Emma, her eyebrows knitting tight.

'It would be easier if you moved production to the parlour, given that you now own part of the sodding business,' retorts

Benni. 'They'll have a catering freezer too, which might prove handy.'

'No can do, sweetie. Martin's ordering a whole new set-up so we can infuse and blend flavours on a much bigger scale, so there's no point moving production until after its arrival and installation.'

'In the meantime, you're going to continue with your cottage industry here?'

'Yep, there's no strength without a struggle.'

'A true entrepreneur, too busy for the likes of us, given the ground-breaking work that's being undertaken,' I say, avoiding Emma's glare. 'So the kitchen is out of bounds.'

'That's very considerate, given that we're supposed to be sharing,' mutters Benni, before turning to me. 'Has Jack left?'

Emma ceases her measuring to turn and stare at me, a look of surprise on her face.

'Yes, Benni, he left about ten minutes ago, though some people probably didn't notice,' I say, swallowing hard to suppress a wave of emotion.

'He didn't say goodbye to me!' spits Emma, looking quite indignant.

'I wonder why?' I retort. 'Benni, we thought you might be asleep and didn't want to disturb you.'

'That's fine. I hope he sorts things out one way or the other,' she says, watching my reaction.

I agree, though deep down I know what his decision will

be. I need a cup of tea more than ever now, as my composure begins to wane. I held it together as I waved from the doorstep, but now, with Benni's kindness, I fear I might cry.

'Ruth, do you fancy joining me on the harbour front for breakfast?' Benni says, her sassy attitude reawakening in an instant.

Emma sucks in her cheeks and returns to weighing sugar.

'Don't mind if I do. Something a little fancy and out of the ordinary, perhaps.'

'Great idea. I might even treat you to a glass of bubbles as a holiday treat – I've always fancied finding out how the other half live,' jokes Benni.

'Count me in.' I throw down my tea bag, push aside my waiting mug and flick the kettle off. 'Excuse me, can I get past?' I say, nudging Emma's backside out of my way. I can see the excitement bubbling behind Benni's gaze, and irritation in Emma's, though she refrains from commenting.

Benni grabs my arm and quickly links it through hers. 'Come on, Ruth, we know when we're not wanted,' she says. As we turn and walk towards the doorway, where we need to separate in order to go through the architrave, Benni suddenly stops and turns and addresses Emma, who is watching our departure. 'I expect you're too busy to join the likes of us. Ciao!'

I want to laugh at the expression on Emma's face; she is utterly shocked by Benni's outspokenness.

We grab our handbags from the lounge, stifling our giggles

until the front door is firmly closed behind us. Then we let them spill loud and proud as we go through the garden gate.

'We shouldn't laugh,' I say eventually. 'But she's almost manic at times about this ice cream idea.'

'The ice cream industry will be awash with her unique flavours,' says Benni, cupping a hand to her ear. 'If you listen carefully you can hear Ben and Jerry quaking in their boots whilst sobbing in fear.'

'You're too cruel,' I say, playfully slapping her wrist like a naughty child.

'Cruel, but honest.'

Benjamina

I have no idea where we're heading or where we might find a champagne breakfast in Brixham; I haven't seen any advertised whilst I've been here. But surely any chic café with a bar licence isn't going to say no to two ladies ordering a full English and requesting two glasses of bubbles. Their manager needs firing if they do.

'Come on, best foot forward,' I say. 'We'll need to work off the calories before we arrive to enjoy this as a guilt-free treat!' I'm feeling ridiculously proud of myself for having the gall to do exactly as I please. On waking, I never dreamt that within thirty minutes I'd be leading Ruth towards the quayside in search of alcoholic beverages.

We find the perfect establishment without any trouble,

situated on the quayside. Just two other customers are sitting on the oversized cream leather padded seats, enjoying plates of waffles, surrounded by stylish décor.

'Good morning, ladies, table for two?' asks the young waitress, flipping to the next page of her serving pad.

We follow the slender young woman, her spritely step leading us across the polished floor towards a window table with a stunning view of the harbour. She pulls out our chairs and invites us to sit, then offers us each a small leather-bound breakfast menu. 'Can I fetch you any drinks?'

'A pot of tea for two, and two glasses of champagne, please,' I announce for the first time in my life. It's naughty, but the impulsiveness of our decision simply adds to the enjoyment.

'Benni!' exclaims Ruth, glancing up from her menu.

I wave a hand in her direction, dismissing her reservations.

'Isn't this what holidays are about? Doing the things we're not supposed to do every other day of the year? Anyway, we're celebrating your success. It's not every week that you get your artwork displayed in a gallery!'

Ruth smiles and visibly relaxes into her plush seat.

I stare at the breakfast delights listed on the menu.

'You have the devil in you today,' says Ruth, reading her menu.

'Possibly. And do you know what ... I don't care.'

Her eyebrows lift.

'Seriously, Ruth, I can't explain it, but I feel as if I've been released into a brand-new life. I don't know if it's the location, the people or even just spending time with the horses. Something deep inside me has changed and I love it.'

Ruth lowers her menu.

'Wow, that is a huge statement to make.'

'It sounds like something a life coach would say, doesn't it? But it's as if blinkers have been removed from my eyes, and I'm seeing the world in a new light for the first time. I want a fitter, healthier me who welcomes interesting people into my life whilst doing all the things I've shied away from in the past. I'm sick of sitting on the subs bench . . . I want my slice of happiness.'

'I know how you feel,' Ruth says. 'I've realised my path too. I have an urge to quit my job as soon as I arrive home and do as I please with my life. It sounds ridiculous, but I've found a renewed energy. I feel like one of those Icelandic geysers that simply bubble and gush with energy at random moments. I want to paint everything I see, to capture the light, that precise moment in time and the essence of an emotion.'

'Here we are, ladies,' says the waitress, carefully delivering two glasses of champagne on to our table. She swiftly departs after taking our order for two full English breakfasts, with fried bread and additional black pudding.

'I've never done this before,' says Ruth, a slight blush rushing to her cheeks as she lifts her glass.

'Me neither,' I say, raising my elegant glass towards hers. 'Cheers, and here's to new beginnings.' The bubbles dance upon my tongue; it feels wonderful and slightly naughty given the time of day.

'Cheers, Benni . . . Absolutely, new beginnings.'

*   *   *

'Can you believe Emma's signed a contract already?' I ask as Ruth cuts energetically into her crispy bacon. 'She hardly knows the guy.'

'Mmm, it's a bit quick for my liking. How does an impromptu drink to discuss ice cream blending turn into a dreamy sunset walk and a hasty appointment with a solicitor? There's more to this than she's letting on.'

'I agree. She walks down to the quayside each night to meet him; why won't he pick her up or send a taxi if he's paving the way for something more personal than business?'

'I wouldn't want a stake in a business venture that I wasn't actively involved in each day, would you?'

'It certainly isn't a viable arrangement with her living in Rugeley; surely she's taking a huge risk by investing in the business.'

Ruth nods whilst chewing her bacon, before answering.

'Exactly. She's making out they'd been flirting before the business deal, but when? I thought her main focus was to experiment with fabulous flavours, using this opportunity in Brixham like a taste test to benefit her own venture once she's home.'

I feel Ruth's missing my point, so I spit it out.

'She must have mentioned her redundancy money pretty early on in their discussions. I think he's feathering his own nest with her cash.'

'Do you think?' Ruth's emerald eyes are wide with shock.

'She told us about it on our first evening in the Queen's Arms, don't you remember? She didn't hold back about her redundancy money. If she said the same to him . . . well, bingo!'

'Funny how people's heads are turned at the mention of money,' says Ruth wryly.

We both sigh heavily before exchanging a thousand words in a single glance.

'If Emma wants a summer fling, then all well and good, but that wasn't her plan when we talked at the barbecue on our second night,' I remind her, knowing we'd all made vows that night.

'If her focus has changed purely because of his sudden interest in her redundancy money . . . well, there's the issue,' sighs Ruth, putting her cutlery down to sip her cup of tea.

'Which Emma may well be blind to,' I add, finishing my toast.

'Sadly she'll only see what she wants to see.'

'Especially if he's got under her skin with sunset walks and a few carefully chosen promises. But her friends aren't so smitten, are we? We won't allow him to blindside our new buddy.' I hold my glass aloft as Ruth exchanges her teacup for her champagne glass.

'We'll watch her back, and if needs be, we'll fight her corner too,' she says, gently clinking her glass against mine.

'Despite her bossiness over the kitchen space to blend weird and wonderful flavours of ice cream.'

'Exactly!' says Ruth, sipping her bubbles. 'And I'm grateful that we've no such complications threatening to sideline our future dreams.'

Emma

I couldn't possibly suggest or change anything regarding Benni's clothes, but her hair and make-up, well, I can certainly offer a helping hand.

It might make up for my crabbiness this morning.

'What's wrong with my ponytail?' she asks, flinching as I rake my hands through her tethered mane.

I hesitate, deciding whether to be honest.

'Well, if this is your daytime look, you need to try a little harder for your date look, that's all I'm saying.'

Silently I praise my own tact. There's no need to upset her. But given the rushed manner in which she's got ready, this ponytail looks exactly like that of a stable-bound nag. Bushy, frizzy and shapeless.

'Look, if you'll let me, I could put this up in a messy bun complete with twisted tendrils in a matter of minutes.'

Benni eyes me cautiously.

'Seriously, the transformation will be amazing. Ziggy will think you've spent hours getting ready for your night out.'

'He said it's nothing special. I don't want to make too big a deal of it.'

'That's fine. A messy bun can be dressed up or down depending on the occasion.'

'I never wear my hair up. I've thought about learning how to do a fancy fishtail plait, but I haven't got round to it.'

'You never wear it down either; you simply pull it back into

194

that damned bobble,' I say, hoping my advice isn't falling on deaf ears. 'Look, make an effort for the man. He'll appreciate the sentiment and you'll feel more confident.'

'Emma, we're only friends, you know. There's nothing going on between us. If anything, I think he feels sorry for me.'

'Are you serious? If he's asked you to go out with him, you need to pay a little attention to how you look.' Clearly Benni understands nothing about men. I'd never dream of going out on a date looking the same as I do in ordinary life. Surely she's not that naïve? Though given her chosen outfit of an elasticated skirt and yet another baggy T-shirt, I can't imagine she's had much experience.

Finally she agrees, and I race to it, knowing she is running out of time. I grab my wide-tooth comb, drag that damned awful plastic bobble from her hair and get to work.

It'll take a matter of minutes. And I will hairspray it thoroughly to ensure it stays in place, whatever they get up to.

'And what does madam think?' I say, offering her the mirror once I've finished.

Her face says it all. Her mouth is open, her gaze staring.

'You like?'

'Oh Emma . . . is that really me?'

'Beautiful, eh? How about I add a little colour to your eyes and define those brows just a touch?'

Benni is speechless, so I have to assume she trusts me when she closes her eyes. I fetch my make-up bag. I know perfectly well that you shouldn't share make-up, but in these circumstances I have no choice. I doubt Benni even knows what a make-up bag looks like. From what I've seen this holiday, she's a soap, water and talcum powder kind of girl.

Benjamina

'Stop worrying, will you,' says Ziggy. 'You look fine. It's a beach barbecue, not a fashion show.'

He's attempting to reassure me as I tug and pull at my clothing, feeling anything but satisfied with my appearance. It took me an hour to select an outfit from the five nondescript ensembles I've brought with me. Each consists of a cotton skirt with an elasticated waistband, ballet pumps, and a batwing baggy top covered with a slouchy cardigan. Not an ideal look, I think, remembering the trio of tanned, svelte beauties striding along the quay, but a look that I can afford and that covers every inch of my flesh. I'm grateful that Emma has styled my hair and make-up, adding flair to my usual look. I owe her one. I'll have to ask her for a lesson sometime during our remaining days.

I attempt a smile, knowing that Ziggy's being kind. I'm certain he'd much prefer to be taking a fashionable, slender woman to meet his mates; instead he's called at Rose Cottage to collect me. As we begin our trek towards the cove, I imagine him holding hands with a woman dressed in tight-fitting jeans, knee-high boots and a figure-hugging top that highlights her assets whilst maintaining her modesty. The kind of outfit I saw earlier on a mannequin in the high street. The chances of me morphing into such an image are slim.

'Benni?' His voice jerks me back from the daydream. 'Give me your hand.'

I do as I'm told, uncertain of his intention, which only becomes clear as he wraps his fingers tightly around mine. Our clasped hands are all I can focus on as we walk along the cliff edge.

At the signpost, we follow the path towards Churston Cove. It descends through a densely wooded path, and my ballet pumps slip and slide on the dried mud. Sporadically the uneven track dips and drops as it twists between the trees, leading us through an enchanted wood.

All I can think about is my hand in his.

'The guys are all great,' Ziggy says. 'Mainly lads I went to school with and their girlfriends ... and some ex-girlfriends too, which sounds weird, doesn't it? But it's how the crowd are: we hang together and have a laugh.'

I nod, as if used to such a situation. The reality is, I'm not. I'm used to whispered remarks, snide comments about my size, loud piggy noises and contemptuous looks from girls who should know better and young men who'd never speak to me.

I'm trying my best to hide it, but inside I'm dreading this. I have been all day. I'm only here because Ziggy was kind enough to invite me. I've never been given the opportunity to attend a beach barbecue before, and I doubt I ever will again. I want to embrace tonight; ... I need to join in on occasions such as these, find ways to relax, and make the most of chatting with people of my own age. I can't afford to keep shying away from social situations. That was the old Benni; this holiday is meant to be a new beginning for me.

'Mind your step,' says Ziggy as the dirt track descends swiftly. He releases my hand and I clutch at his shoulder to steady myself as my gaze fixes upon the sight below. The natural cove, with a shale beach sloping down towards the lapping water, is picture perfect. In the centre of the beach, midway between the cliff and the water's edge, is a sprawling group of young people mingling around the beginnings of a campfire. In the twilight hue, the scene looks intriguing; as a meeting point it certainly beats the graffiti-covered bench in Burntwood's local park around which our youths congregate, swearing and swigging cheap cider. I reckon that about fifteen bodies are lounging around, unpacking bags or larking around as we descend into the cove.

Ziggy takes my hand for the final few steps as we clamber over boulders towards the shale.

'Ziggy, my man!' calls a voice from the sprawling crowd.

'Smudge, you lazy mucker ... you call in sick then come out to party!' hollers Ziggy, helping me over the final rock before we hit the shale.

'Doctor's note signed and sealed, my man; that'll keep your father happy!' replies Smudge, jumping up from his supine position to back-slap Ziggy in an affectionate welcome.

'Skiving more like!' replies Ziggy, dropping my hand to return the manly gesture. 'Smudge, this is Benni.'

I watch as Smudge withdraws from his male bonding to deliver a warm, welcoming smile and extend a hand in my direction.

'Nice to meet you, Benni. Come and meet the crew … but first, what's your poison?' I turn to look at Ziggy, who is smiling broadly.

'See, I told you,' he says. 'They're just like me.'

'What have I said wrong?' asks Smudge.

'Nothing, Benni here had never heard anyone say that phrase before me and now … well, it says it all really.'

I laugh, grateful for the immediate acceptance, which chases away my self-conscious nerves.

'Come on, Benni,' Ziggy says encouragingly. 'No one here cares a jot.'

'I do,' I mumble, my harsh refusal softened into a stern whisper.

'Please.'

'No!'

'But—'

'Just go … you're embarrassing me,' I say curtly, gesturing for him to leave me alone. I'm aware that three girls sitting to my right are watching and listening intently.

Ziggy stands and momentarily pauses, looking out towards the lapping water where numerous bodies are jumping and splashing as their limbs meet the water, before staring down at me. In the distance, despite twilight falling, I can make out the majestic lighthouse on the far side of the harbour.

'I'll ask one more time before I head in . . . are you coming?'

'No!'

'Fine.' He hastily peels off his jacket and T-shirt and drops his trousers in a pile before running full pelt towards the water. I stare at the discarded clothes by my feet.

Is he out of his tiny mind? Or simply blind? The chances of me ever taking off my clothes in public are close to zero. I feel angered by his persistence. How insensitive can a guy be?

I fix my stare towards the open water as my mind swirls with rushing thoughts and annoyance. Alongside me the blazing campfire offers warmth and much-needed light to view the proceedings.

'Are you not joining them?' asks a girl sitting to my left.

'Nah, it's not my scene,' I lie. I don't wish to strike up a conversation with anyone at this precise moment.

'You can go in wearing your underwear; no one cares around here. It's the same as a bikini, isn't it?' she adds, flicking her mane of chestnut hair as she speaks.

'I suppose I could, but I don't really feel like it.'

'Well, if you change your mind, I've got a spare towel.'

'Cheers, but I'm happy sitting here,' I say firmly.

'If you're sure . . . I'll be heading in then . . . see ya.'

I watch as she jumps up, strips as quickly as Ziggy did and dashes down the shale beach before screaming as her feet meet the water. I watch her move elegantly into the water. If I had a figure like hers I'd be showing it off too, but Christ, can you imagine it . . . me in my undies wobbling after her trim silhouette. Lord, it's one image I can save this crowd from. I imagine most of these young men wouldn't give a girl like me a second look fully clothed, let alone partially naked in my sensible knickers and sturdy bra.

The trio of girls sitting to my right jump up and follow suit, de-robing down to their lacy undies in seconds and joining the crowd splashing in the sea. I glance around. I'm sitting alone on a shale beach, cradling an empty wine glass and disliking intensely the only person who is holding me back in life: me.

It brings back memories of primary school sports day, when I would sit on a bench feigning a twisted ankle because I didn't want to take part in the egg and spoon, wheelbarrow race or skipping competition. In secondary school, I successfully avoided swimming lessons for four entire years, feigning an allergy to chlorine. My refusal to attend netball practice, cross-country runs and Duke of Edinburgh expeditions floods my mind. Obviously I've made a hobby of avoiding anything and everything relating to exercise or public participation where others can view me alongside other people. Not because of any lack of skill or my straitened circumstances, but simply due to my size.

My usual excuses of being big-boned, having a slow metabolism or an inherited family trait have become my comfort blanket . . . that and a second helping of rice pudding.

I watch as a slim silhouette emerges from the water and walks steadily up the beach towards me. When she's a few feet away, I realise that it's Marla, from the Queen's Arms.

'Hello, it's nice to recognise a familiar face amongst the

crowd,' I say, delighted to see her. 'I hope my friend Emma isn't driving you potty with her tubs of ice cream. I thought she'd have moved premises by now and started using the parlour's equipment rather than continuing to pester you guys.'

'Not at all,' Marla says cheerfully. 'She's slipped me a few quid to thank me, and my boss isn't fussed, so there's no worries. Are you coming in, Benni?' she asks, crouching on to her haunches beside me. I'm certain she's wearing only underwear but it could be a black bikini for all I can tell. Her damp skin glistens as she leans closer. 'The water is lovely and warm . . . warmer than out here.'

'I don't think so . . .' My words trail off. I can't feign an excuse. She's female; she understands.

'Ziggy'll take care of you; nothing bad will happen,' adds Marla, pushing her damp hair back from her delicate features. Why would anyone this beautiful be bothered about me joining them? I'm sure she's saying it just to be kind. Or I bet Ziggy sent her.

'Honestly, I'm fine. I don't like water anyway.' Even my lie sounds heavy and clunky.

'I think you know my younger sister from the stables,' she says, sitting down on the shale, drawing her knees to her chest and wrapping her arms tightly around her legs, possibly a poor attempt to keep warm.

'Maddie? Yes, she's been great. She's shown me so much and taken me out when she's exercised Bruce. I saw your horse Wispy too.'

'Yeah, Maddie's horse mad, stable mad and Bruce mad . . .

or that's what my dad says, anyway. She mentioned over dinner that you'd been helping out in the yard for most of the week.'

'I have. I've loved it. I always wanted to ride, but . . .' I don't need to explain. 'I'm hoping to visit each day for the remainder of my holiday, if they'll put up with me.'

'They'll welcome the extra pair of hands; there's always work to do in the yard. Maddie's enjoyed your company.'

'I've learnt that there's something very special about being around horses. They look at you and . . .' Words fail me. How can I explain what I feel when I look into those dark eyes?

'They hold your gaze and almost read you from the inside out,' says Marla, giving me a knowing glance. 'That's how it feels to me, anyway.'

'Exactly. You get what I mean.'

Silence descends. Marla begins to shiver, and goose bumps appear on her porcelain skin. She begins to rub frantically at her slim legs.

'Are you sure you aren't coming in? I'll wait for you and we can head down together,' she says, looking from me back to the water, where the crowd continue to splash and play.

'Nah, it's really not my thing.'

Secretly I'd love to. But I'm not going to say yes, so I'll continue to say no until everyone is fed up or distracted. I have my pride, and it won't allow me to uncover this body before strangers – correction, before *anyone* – in its current size and shape.

*   *   *

A little later, I look up to find a woman offering me a fresh glass of wine, which I take gratefully as she settles beside me. She's like me, big-boned.

'Reckless is what I think it is,' she says, staring out to sea as heads and shoulders bob about in the dark water. 'A total disrespect for health and safety. I keep telling them alcohol and night swimming don't mix. They'll pay the price one of these nights and then who will they blame? Not me. It'll be the likes of me that's left to raise the alarm with the lifeguard when one of them gets into difficulties.'

I hear what she's saying; she's not wrong but I can also detect the lie. It's the same lie I could imagine myself repeating week after week if I were a regular in this crowd.

'I'm Helen, by the way.'

'Benni . . . nice to meet you, Helen.'

'Foolish behaviour, don't you think?'

I imagine I'm about to hear round two of the lie.

'It must feel good, though . . . they look like they're having fun, despite the danger,' I say.

'Yeah, maybe, but still . . .'

Mmm, but still, we won't be joining in because we're embarrassed by our bodies. Not our big bones, slow metabolism or family genes. My excuses have dissolved. I'm more concerned with the size of my thighs, the flesh circling my abdomen and the pendulous movement of my unbridled chest.

*   *   *

'The water is beautiful, you should have come in,' says Ziggy as we sit beside the campfire cradling our drinks, the crowd singing songs as one guy strums a guitar nearby.

'Nah.'

'Seriously, what's the issue?' Ziggy's hand reaches for my arm; his gentle touch feels too tender to belong to a man.

The truth sounds ridiculous, even inside my head; there is no way I will allow the words to spill from my lips. He'll laugh. Fancy having to admit that your dress size determines how you enjoy yourself, or not as the case may be.

'I'm waiting,' he jokes, nudging me. 'I wanted you to join me.'

He's staring intently, his gaze direct and piercing. He sounds genuinely miffed that I stayed on the shale. No, that can't be the case. Surely he's joking; he can't possibly mean that he wouldn't have minded me undressing and joining him in the water.

I blush.

His eyes haven't left my face for this entire thought.

How stupid am I? If I wait a few seconds longer, he's bound to start laughing, he'll say the trick is on me, roll around in fits of belly laughter at the very thought of me swallowing every cheesy line.

And yet he remains silent and solemn, staring intently into my eyes as if he means every word.

Yeah, right, who does he think he's kidding?

Erin Green

Ruth

I empty the contents of the box on to the bathroom floor. The various bottles and plastic gloves fill me with dread; ridiculous as it seems, I'm nervous. This is entirely out of my comfort zone.

I sit on the closed lid of the toilet and slowly read the accompanying instruction leaflet. The diagrams make it look so simple, but a number of 'what ifs' deter me from dividing my hair into three large sections. Surely if fourteen-year-old schoolgirls can manage this, so can I.

I stand, collect the plastic bottles from the floor and arrange them along the sink unit. I pull on the foul-smelling rubber gloves finger by finger, then stare at my reflection. My mother's face from two decades ago gazes back. The same mass of grey-brown hair, unkempt eyebrows, deep ridges around the mouth and a dull finish to once rosy cheeks. I recognise my own eyes, but the once twinkling glimmer seems to have faded too. When and how did that happen?

'Stop kidding yourself, Ruth,' I whisper to the woman in the mirror. 'It's been years since you took an interest in your appearance. Why start now?' She fails to answer me; in fact she refuses to meet my gaze, as though she can't bear to acknowledge my existence. 'Boy, I can't look myself in the eye let alone others.'

My hands act before my brain triggers the idea. I sweep up the collection of plastic bottles lined up like soldiers and

206

drop them in the bin, then wrench the rubber gloves from my hands, tearing one in the process, and stuff them in on top.

What the hell was I thinking? Who the hell am I trying to kid?

Chapter Ten

Monday 27 August

Benjamina

'Benni, what're your plans for today?' calls Emma, rapping sharply on my bedroom door.

I pull the duvet over my head and inhale deeply. Today the world and his wife are on holiday; somehow this fact negates my own fortnight away. If the entire country is on holiday, I can't possibly be. I envisage the bottling machinery of the vinegar factory standing still and silent. On rare occasions I've seen the production line pause – on Armistice Day, for example, when we honour the fallen soldiers – but never for the entire day.

'Come on,' Emma says. 'The sun is shining, and judging by the amount of traffic snaking past the lounge window the harbour will already be busy.'

'So I'll spend the day at the cottage, avoiding the crowds,' I reply, hearing my own grumpiness.

I hear the bedroom door open, and Emma's voice gets louder.

'Don't be narky. They're only enjoying what we've been doing for days.' She tugs at the bedclothes, but I hold tight, aware of the awful sight of my pyjama-clad body lying beneath.

'Benni, come on . . . let's go and do the tourist thing amongst the tourists.'

'We *are* tourists!'

'Nah, not really. We've established our own little home in a matter of days. Let's go and be *true* tourists for the day!'

I pull back the duvet and peer into her eager face.

'Seriously?'

'Yeah, come on . . . I'll go and wake Ruth.' She dashes from the room and I hear her running down the stairs. But when she bangs on Ruth's door, there's no reply.

Ruth

As I watch the families streaming along the concrete walkway towards the lighthouse, I feel awful, selfish, even as I instantly will them to go away and leave me alone. Can't they see I'm painting? I need peace and quiet, not a crowd of critics standing behind me commenting on my composition and colour palette, as if I'm a contestant on a landscape painting programme and they are the experts: 'Mmm, the foreground's not quite detailed enough for my liking'; 'She hasn't captured those clouds quite right'; and even 'A lighthouse – hardly original, is it?'

If only they knew that it's taking every ounce of courage I have to sit here painting in public while they mill round me critiquing my work. I bit my tongue when an elderly lady said she'd seen better on the wall of a primary school.

I take a break and watch as two young boys tussle and play while their parents walk behind them hand in hand. They look happy with their lot. Content with their world of crabbing buckets and rucksacks.

My Jack would have loved a brother. Younger, obviously.

I'm drawn to their relaxed manner, their togetherness, their happiness as a unit. No shouting, no arguing; just a healthy family unit.

Could I ever have had that? Me and a husband, with Jack and perhaps one other child? That togetherness strolling along a pathway in the sunshine?

I swallow and look away.

I was so naïve, even at twenty-seven. Mum knew that, of course, and took full advantage of it. I'd disappointed her, so she took charge of the situation and told me exactly how it would be. I'd return to work, she'd look after my baby and we'd simply make the best of it. It was a different era – society had moved on – but she thought people would still talk and pass comment like they had in the sixties. Mum knew best. We were to remain respectable and maintain our reputation as a family of three. We'd focus on us and remain just us. There was no place for others, gossips or otherwise. Mum, me and Jack. That's all I ever knew. And yet somewhere along the line there must have been others who were interested in knowing us, in sharing our lives. A stranger, perhaps, whose gaze lingered a fraction too long; a warm smile as I entered a room. How different life would be now if I had noticed, smiled back, welcomed someone else into my world.

My innards feel like lead, and I sigh, exhaling deep regret.

It does no good to ponder on what might have been. I did as I was told. I provided for our family thanks to my full-time job at the bank, and Mum stayed at home and cared for Jack. My son, who I shared with my mother. And, in a strange kind of way, who almost became *her* son.

'There you are! We've been looking for you all over!' cries Emma, appearing from nowhere.

'I've been here all morning; I wasn't lost,' I retort, fiddling with a brush.

'We're having a tourist day; are you coming or staying here?' asks Benni, sidling up behind Emma and peering at my watercolour. 'This is very good, Ruth – you've captured that bit perfectly.'

I nod, staring as she points to a part of the painting criticised earlier by a passing expert.

'I suppose I've done two and a bit hours. I could call it a day,' I add, worried that my nosedive towards the past will linger if I remain on my own.

'We'll help you pack up. We can stash your equipment at the ice cream parlour – Martin won't mind – and then head out along the front: fish and chips, candyfloss ... we could even visit the *Golden Hind* and see what it's like inside,' says Emma, her expression brightening with each suggestion.

Emma

We walk the length of the harbour defence and deliver Ruth's belongings to the storeroom at the ice cream parlour.

I feel cheeky asking, but needs must.

'It would take thirty minutes or more to walk to the cottage just to return her equipment,' I explain to Luca, who nods understandingly as we quickly retreat towards the parlour's exit.

'You can't afford to waste precious time, not on a bank holiday,' he says, as he fills a waffle cone for a child at the counter.

'Too true. Catch you later,' shouts Benni as we step outside.

'So, what's it to be?' I ask, surprised that we've convinced Ruth to join us.

'The *Golden Hind*,' suggests Benni, staring across to the ship moored a short distance away.

'Are you sure?' I say, adding, 'I didn't have you down as a pirate kind of gal!' I'm not sure I want a guided tour of a replica ship.

'We're tourists! It's got to be done!' says Benni, leading the way without waiting for an alternative suggestion.

'Can I choose the next activity then?' asks Ruth, trotting to keep up with Benni.

'Sure, as long as it involves food,' I agree, following them.

I tag along, never quite catching them up as they reach the harbour ticket office, and I join Ruth waiting at the side while Benni queues, unsure how she is working the transaction. Individual tickets, or one person pays for all three? I do the obligatory grabbing of my purse to show willing, when she returns, as does Ruth. I don't know what there is to see inside, but if the other two truly want to do the tour, I'll tag along without complaining.

'Put your cash away – I've paid for three. Here,' says Benni, pushing one ticket into Ruth's palm and another into mine.

Ruth stares at the ticket with a puzzled expression. I'm not sure she's used to such generosity.

She's truly flummoxed by Benni's action. Bless her. Obviously her responsibilities mean she doesn't get out much.

She opens her purse and offers Benni the money.

'No thanks, Ruth – it'll be your shout later. It'll work out fairly by the end of the day, trust me.'

The penny drops. Finally, Ruth puts her purse away and accepts Benni's kindness.

Benni takes the lead, striding along the ship's gangplank towards a pirate dressed in frills and a tricorn and waving a large cutlass beneath a spider's web of rigging and crow's nests.

The plank decking is sturdy and new-looking, but the flimsy side barriers made of knotted rope make me feel slightly queasy. I glance dubiously at the rippling water below and am grateful that the ship is securely moored and sailing nowhere soon.

Benjamina

'Ruth, I'm so sorry … I didn't realise how nasty seasickness could be,' says Emma, rubbing Ruth's back while she vomits over the side of the ferry from Torquay.

I stand the other side of the pair, clutching the rail, trying to avoid the spray from Ruth's noisy retching. I'm grateful that the railing is a solid barrier and not slatted, otherwise everyone could witness what she had for breakfast.

I stare around the other passengers, who sit in neat rows attempting to ignore Ruth's plight. Each time she retches, numerous people lift tissues to their mouths as if in sympathy.

'Emma, here …' I pass her a packet of tissues gratefully received from a woman with a baby a few seconds ago. Emma takes the offering and quickly opens the cellophane, passing Ruth a fresh tissue to wipe her mouth.

I'm glad this ferry trip wasn't my suggestion. I can see from Emma's concerned expression that she wishes she'd kept her mouth shut. We could easily have nipped to the nearest pub for scampi in a basket; instead, Ruth was sick as soon as we sailed. And the return journey has proved to be no better.

'We should have got a taxi,' says Emma.

I shake my head. 'Ruth was pretty adamant that we should come back by ferry.'

'I know, but …' Emma points to Ruth's heaving shoulders, bent double over the railings, 'this is bad.'

I shrug. I've no idea what's bad or normal regarding sea-sickness, having never witnessed it before. I don't know how long it will take Ruth to recover or whether this is the end of our bank holiday jollies and a taxi ride back to the cottage is in order.

'We're nearly there, Ruth,' says Emma reassuringly as the ferry draws into the harbour.

'We'll find a bench and have a sit-down before doing anything else,' I say, collecting my bag and Ruth's ready to disembark at the first opportunity. 'I'll nip to a chemist if you need anything.'

'The chemist won't be open,' mumbles Ruth, the first thing she has said in thirty minutes.

'OK, a double rum then – that might make you feel better,' I joke, grimacing at Emma over Ruth's head. 'Pirates relied on a belly full of rum to settle their stomachs.'

Emma gives me a quick glance before turning away. At least I'm trying to help the situation, which is more than she's done.

We walk Ruth along the gangplank and towards solid ground.

'Sorry if I was sick on you,' she whimpers as we walk either side of her, clutching beneath her underarms and holding her upright between us.

'Don't be daft, you couldn't help it. I should have listened,' says Emma in a jovial tone.

'Yep, that you should,' I mutter.

'How was I to know?' retorts Emma, glaring at me.

'She did say . . .'

'Not quite. What she actually said was "I'm not too good on boats",' snaps Emma, as if Ruth isn't present.

'I wonder what that might mean?' I snap back.

'Ladies, ladies . . . I'll be fine, honestly. I just need a sit-down and a cold drink. I'll be right as rain afterwards. I'm not used to boats, that's all.'

I look at her greying complexion and doubt that she will be fine. I'm starting to think Ruth isn't used to much in life other than working full-time and returning home to care for her mother and Jack. I have a strong suspicion that we'll be returning to the cottage and tucking her into bed before too long.

Ruth

Benni and Emma buy fish and chips – I didn't fancy anything to eat after being so ill – and we make our way towards the harbour to settle upon a bench. A steady stream of tourists saunter past as they tear open their paper parcels and spear chips with tiny wooden forks.

I am not used to days out with anyone other than my family. My last outing might have been our local WI group's coach trip to see the Blackpool illuminations, or was it the tour of the *Coronation Street* studio set? Jack refused to come with us, leaving me with Mum as my partner for the day. She never left my side, even when we were encouraged to change seats to talk to other ladies. That's how life has been: my mother always linked to my arm, demanding I stay near. I'd never have strayed far, but a quick chat with new acquaintances wouldn't have harmed either of us. Family can't live exclusively in each other's pockets. It would have been nice to have a wider social group in which to enjoy myself. I'd have been happier as a rounded individual rather than being restrained by the narrow social band of just the three of us.

I sigh, causing Emma to glance up.

'Are you OK?' she asks.

I'm not sure if sharing is caring in these circumstances.

'Ruth?'

'I'm fine.'

'But?'

I glance at Benni a short distance away, throwing chips to the seagulls circling the harbour.

'I've wasted so many years, Emma. It's dawning on me how long I've spent dedicating my life to raising our Jack and now caring for my mum. I've gone from nurturing one to the other and somewhere along the way I've become lost in between their needs. Does that sound selfish?'

'No. Not at all, Ruth.'

I watch as she continues to eat, her gaze not leaving mine.

'I should be grateful, I know I should . . . but I'm not.'

Emma nods, her jaw chomping rhythmically.

'Surely there was room for other acquaintances, friends . . . even relationships. And yet I've shied away from everything to focus on Jack and Mum.'

Emma's listening intently, but I'm not sure she'll understand my burdens given her solo status.

'It's as if I excluded myself from life, kowtowed to Mum's beliefs and opinions in order to make amends for disappointing her. I did everything she demanded, brought home the bacon while she raised my son. Yet now, when I should be gaining a little independence, I'm being tied down yet again.'

'That's not how it should be,' Emma says. 'You need to enjoy a purposeful life too. You can't just devote yourself to caring for others until the day arrives when Jack has a family of his own and your mother passes away.'

'I know, but I actually feel guilty for wanting a life of my own, and that can't be right, can it?'

'It certainly can't. You deserve something for yourself, Ruth. It can't be all give, give, give – we each deserve something for ourselves from this life.'

She's right.

'But how can I change things?' I ask.

'You need to start putting yourself first. Make some changes and decide what you want for the coming decade or two! That's what I've done.'

'What if I haven't got a decade or two remaining?'

'Even more reason to get yourself into gear! Stop wasting time and start living the life you want.' Her voice is strong, confident and energetic. I wish I had the same zest for life.

I nod.

'Good. But don't just nod, do it. You deserve a little bit of fun before it's too late,' she adds.

'I know. It's been so long, I've forgotten what it feels like.'

Emma's eyes widen as a cheeky grin spreads across her features.

'Maybe we need to remind you then.'

'Behave yourself,' I say, before my deep-seated shyness over-whelms me, as always.

Emma

It's gone dusk as Martin unlocks the door to the ice cream parlour. We enter without a word, the only sound the Yale lock catching behind us.

The parlour is in near darkness, apart from a shimmer of illumination from the refrigerator lights. The chairs are upturned on top of cleaned tables – everything is spick and span ready for tomorrow's trade.

Despite her recovery, Ruth and Benni called it a day much earlier than I'd expected, enabling me to make arrangements with Martin.

'This way, though mind you don't trip on the first stair, the treads a little uneven,' he says, grabbing my hand and leading me across the tiled floor.

His fingers interlock in mine, pulling me urgently towards the back section of the parlour where a door leads to the private quarters above.

My heartbeat matches his urgency as we fly up the staircase in the darkness. I feel like a teenager on her first date with the school hunk.

'Please don't feel obliged, but if it's suitable then it provides a solution for us both,' explains Martin as we reach the top stair and enter a small apartment.

Bijou is an over-exaggeration. Lilliputian is a more fitting description of the tiny space illuminated when Martin flicks on the overhead light.

'Are the other rooms any bigger?' I ask, judging that five strides in any direction will end up with my nose touching a wall. It's much smaller than any room in my Rugeley home; in fact my bathroom is larger than this.

I attempt to open the sash window overlooking the harbour, but fail miserably, despite heaving at it forcefully given the layers of aged paint.

'I'll get a handyman to sort it out,' says Martin. 'Well, what do you think?'

He follows me as I view the other rooms, each one getting smaller in size like a set of Russian dolls.

'The floorboards need sanding or carpeting, every wall needs painting and those cobwebs need professional handling given the size of them,' I joke, trying to envisage the place without the towering piles of cardboard boxes and remnants of shop junk. Could I make it my home and wake after a restful night's sleep amidst the idyllic sounds of the harbour?

'Fair comment, but with a little elbow grease and plenty of hot water you'll have it shipshape in no time, I'm sure.'

'True. I suppose it'll be cheaper to rent than any other property round here – which would all definitely dent my bank account.'

'And remember, it'll only be for a short time while I get myself together financially, then maybe we might find a place together.' His coy smile draws me in, his words a soothing balm to my beating heart.

'Martin, I'm not sure . . . Doesn't this feel rushed to you? We only met a few days ago and yet . . .' My voice trails off, unable to vocalise my thoughts.

He nods. 'I know things are happening fast, but surely we have to embrace what we've found in each other rather than judging or questioning our feelings? If it helps, I'm as nervous as you are at the pace at which this is progressing, but still . . . I'm loving it.'

His features glow as he speaks, his words coming without hesitation. Surely, if he can be this brave, then so can I. Can't I?

'Come here,' he says, his arms opening wide, reaching for me.

I nestle into his strong frame, his arms wrapped about my shoulders while my eyes rove around the room, taking in every detail. I feel as though I'm living in a fairy tale; isn't this everything I've wanted from a relationship since I swooned over my first Mills & Boon book?

'It definitely has potential, I suppose. I could put some of my furniture into storage, downsize for a while.'

'It's certainly an option if you don't want to sell anything.'

'OK, let's do it. I can live here while I settle into a new routine in the parlour. It'll mean no commuting, and I'll get to enjoy the beauty of the harbour view when I'm not working.'

I break free from his hold and wander around, visualising

221

my furniture filling the place. I have to be realistic; I will need to sell certain pieces as not everything will fit, but still, what's a few bits of furniture in comparison to finding your life partner? How weird that in a matter of days I have accepted this man, even without full knowledge of his flaws, his history, his intentions . . .

I start to choose from an imaginary paint chart: a warm, cosy colour for the lounge, a fresh, positive shade for the kitchen and a relaxing tone for my bedroom to encourage sleep and happy dreams. As I stand at the bedroom window looking out across the harbour, I can see my potential happiness in the grimy reflection.

'Emma?' Martin's voice draws me near, like a command. I cross the room and fall into his arms, craning my neck to lift my face to his. My eyes close as our mouths passionately convey our silent feelings for each other.

Our breathing increases, our lips merge into a melting pot of passion as our hands frantically reach for each other's body. Eventually, my hands find his belt buckle; his slip under my T-shirt.

It's been a long time since I wanted a man as much as this. My inhibitions disappear, along with the remnants of my solo holiday.

'Emma, are you OK?' whispers Martin.

'I'm fine, honestly . . . and you?' I ask, unsure of protocol or sexual etiquette as we lie naked amongst discarded junk and dusty cardboard boxes.

Martin gives a throaty chuckle that builds into a rapturous belly laugh.

'We sound like strangers meeting on a train, and yet we've just ... well, crossed a boundary,' I say, slightly embarrassed that my naked flesh is on full display in the muted light from the street lamp outside the window.

'I take it you'll be moving in as soon as it suits,' whispers Martin, as he nuzzles into my left shoulder.

'I believe I will be.'

We fall silent amid a renewed surge of passion as our flesh entwines for a second time.

Chapter Eleven

Tuesday 28 August

Ruth

I cup my hands to the glass as I have every morning this week. It's my daily fix of admiring my own composition. Which probably appears very narcissistic and explains why I haven't insisted the others accompany me after the first time on my birthday.

I find myself staring at a painting of a beach complete with early-morning dog walkers.

It takes a second to register. I should be staring directly at my watercolour of the *Marina Mania*. It's not there.

I scour the surrounding paintings. Maybe Dean's had a switch around? But he promised me the prime position on the wall, so where's he moved it to!

I feel stupid when I actually glance at the painting in prime position – as if mine would ever be there! I cringe, relieved I'm entirely alone to absorb this; my ego obviously has ideas above her station. The usual large lighthouse composition remains in situ. Granted it isn't centre stage in the window but, still, yesterday my composition was prime position on the wall as you entered the gallery.

I check each section of gallery wall visible through the closed shutters.

I can't see it.

Benjamina

'Here, Benni, take the leading rein,' says Maddie, offering me the length of rope attached to Bruce's bridle. 'Hold it like I showed you, looped in your palm and not around your hand.'

I take the length of rope, folding it as instructed before my free hand takes a tight hold nearer his mouth. It feels good to be trusted to lead him from his stable into the yard amidst brilliant sunshine.

'Happy?' asks Maddie, her eyes scanning my face and then both of my hands to ensure I am following her strict orders.

'Yep, this feels lovely . . . but why aren't you riding him?'

'Today we're just going for a walk like you would with a dog, so you can lead him round the whole way if you want.'

I do want. I'm wishing for so much right now. I wish my holiday was just starting. I wish my train ticket wasn't booked for Saturday. I wish I'd spent my youth around horses at the local stables even if I only ever bagged a ride as a 'thank you' for mucking out. Right now, Maddie has no idea how much I wish for. Even a genie, a magic lamp and a tin of Brasso couldn't possibly grant all my wishes.

Under Maddie's watchful gaze, I lead Bruce across the stable yard through the rear gates leading on to the bridle path that winds through a woodland area.

'I can see why you would walk here rather than ride,' I say, looking around at the low-hanging branches and the luscious foliage growing either side of the footpath.

'Exactly. You need to plan what you're doing with your horse, otherwise you end up running into trouble without realising it. Some riders walk a pathway first then return for their horse, because it can change from one day to the next.'

'I imagine it can. I've never thought of walking a horse like this, but I suppose it's still exercise for their muscles.'

'And it stimulates their brain. Can you imagine being locked inside a stable all day, staring at blank walls?'

'They're exactly like humans,' I say. 'I know how mind-numbing it is to stare at a conveyor belt filled with empty vinegar bottles. After an eight-hour shift, everything looks intriguing, even the labelling machine.'

Maddie laughs. 'I couldn't do that. When I leave school, I want to work with horses.'

'Here at the stables?'

'Not necessarily. More like equine sports massage and remedial therapies. I'll need to go to uni, so I'd best get my grades.'

'And leave Bruce?' His dark ears rotate and flicker on hearing his name.

'Never. I'll be moving him to a stable close by. I couldn't leave him.'

'Do your parents know that?' I ask, the giggle in my voice suggesting I know the answer.

Maddie laughs again. 'Not yet, but they'll cope.'

'Too much information is dangerous for parents, is that your train of thought?'

'Certainly is.' Maddie suddenly stops and listens intently. 'Can you hear that?'

I stop too, and listen whilst stroking Bruce's brushed mane.

'I can't hear anything,' I say.

'I swear I heard the pounding of hooves,' says Maddie as we resume our walk. 'Anyway, as I was saying—'

From nowhere, a large grey horse suddenly appears on our left-hand side. The rider is leaning forward, her body low and flat against the horse's lengthening neck, her hands frantically pulling at his reins.

'Oh great!' spits Maddie, as the grey horse dashes past.

'Faster, Gallop! Faster!' cries the rider, her features con-torted in a scream as she shoots past us.

I don't need telling who the rider is.

I feel an urgent tug on my left hand and in an instant the coil of rope is gone. I turn to see Bruce's rear end disappearing after the galloping horse, his leading rope trailing behind him.

'Bruce!' shouts Maddie, running after him, without a word of criticism to me.

Should I have held the leading rein tighter? Could I have grabbed the end of it as it flew from my hand? I don't know, but I'm certain I can't run fast enough to catch the figures disappearing into the dense woodland.

So without my mobile to hand, I do the only helpful thing that comes to mind, and start back towards the stable yard as fast as I can to raise the alarm.

Ruth

'It's gone!' says Dean the second I enter the gallery, curiosity having finally got the better of me.

'What?' I drop my art equipment at my feet.

'Sold!' His face lights up as he explains. 'It was my last sale before closing yesterday . . . I was going to phone you later today with the good news. I wouldn't want you to pass by and wonder if I'd moved it.'

'Oh no . . . of course . . . I would have wondered if I couldn't see it,' I say, feigning understanding while knowing exactly how I reacted this morning when I couldn't see it. 'Am I allowed to ask who bought it?'

'A nice young couple from Glasgow – they said it reminded them of their very first holiday to Brixham during their university days. I believe she said it would be hung in their dining room back home.'

'Lovely.' I squirrel the information away. I, Ruth Elton, will have a watercolour hanging in a dining room in Glasgow. I silently thank the young couple and hope my composition survives the journey back home without a scratch. I want it to be perfect for ever. A little piece of me decorating someone else's life.

'So congratulations, that's the first one sold,' Dean says, drawing near and planting a decorous kiss on my cheek.

I'm taken aback that he's so tactile with a stranger. Never in my life have I offered a congratulatory kiss to someone I hardly know. Watercolour sold or not!

'Are there any other paintings nearing completion?' he asks, stepping back. I'm certain that my body language – rabbit frozen in headlights – speaks volumes to this warm and affectionate man. I'm grateful when he glances at the wall clock, giving me a moment to recover.

'I'm just heading to the lighthouse to finish a watercolour I started the other day,' I say. 'I've chosen a different perspective from the painting displayed in the window, so fingers crossed it will sell too.'

'Excellent, it doesn't do to have artists producing the same goods,' says Dean with a smile. 'You must bring it in to the gallery when it's finished. Actually, I was just closing for lunch . . . any chance you'd care to join me?'

I hesitate and blush profusely.

'I'd love to,' I say before common sense can butt in to refuse the invite.

'I'll stash that behind the counter,' he says, indicating my equipment bag plonked at my feet, 'and shut up shop for an hour.'

I feel like a spare part as Dean busies himself with security alarms and door signage. He's definitely older than me, but from the way he strides around the gallery I can tell that he has far more energy and vigour. Part of me wishes he'd hurry up, as the waiting is enabling my mind to conjure up all sorts of reasons why this might be a bad idea.

I was planning to paint all afternoon; the light will have changed in an hour or two.

I'd arranged to have lunch at the cottage with Benni.

I haven't sat opposite a male who isn't biologically related to me since my younger days.

'All done. Are you ready?' he asks, leading me from the gallery.

We walk the length of the quayside and I nervously rattle off plausible painting ideas I've had this week. I must sound like an overexcited child listing all the scenic spots around Brixham, alongside my desire to visit the stables and Berry Head, which Benni and Emma have recommended. Dean listens carefully, providing suggestions and outlining possible pitfalls regarding my suggested composition. For once, it feels as if someone is listening to my ideas without diluting my passion.

Eventually he indicates left and we arrive outside the chic café where Benni and I had breakfast on Sunday.

'Oh, I like it here,' I say.

'I'm glad to hear it. I can recommend their champagne . . . especially after a first sale!'

Dean holds the door wide, enabling me to pass.

'Thank you,' I say.

'My pleasure.'

Benjamina

Finally, I make it back to the stable yard. As I stumble through the gate, my breath is laboured and my heart feels as though it's about to burst from my chest. My right knee is aching and I have a painful stabbing sensation under my ribs, but I've made it. I've never been so grateful to see a wooden gatepost.

'Summer! Help!' I holler as I see a jodhpur-clad figure striding across the stable yard. She stops, turns and comes running.

'Benni, are you OK?'

'Bruce legged it,' I gasp. 'Gallop girl was screaming ... Maddie running ... chasing him ... lead rope gone ... the woods ...' I'm doubled over, leaning against the gate, panting for breath.

'Calm down,' Summer says. 'Stay here while I fetch some of the others ... OK?'

I nod, speechless, and she jogs briskly in the direction of the office.

I close my eyes and wait, my mouth agape, snatching warm summer air with each pant. My forehead is burning; a trail of sweat runs along my back. I think I'm about to die if my heart doesn't slow any time soon. Can you have a heart attack at twenty-five? I never thought my final moments would be spent hanging on to a gatepost in Brixham.

A clatter of boots draws near and I open my eyes to see Summer and two women heading my way.

'She said the woods, Maddie gave chase but you know what he's like – he'll keep running until he's done,' says Summer, as the trio near.

'Benni, did you enter the woods via the bridle path or by the road?' asks the older woman, her hand reaching for my forehead.

'Bridle path . . . we left through this gate,' I pant. 'Maddie's got her mobile.'

She beckons to the other woman. 'You stay here and make sure Benni's OK; call an ambulance if she's not,' she says, adding, 'Summer, phone Maddie. Find out exactly where they are and if she or Bruce are injured. We'll head out to meet them.'

Summer pulls her mobile from her pocket and the pair leave me with my first-aider.

'Do you feel faint?' asks the woman, crouching down to peer up at me.

I shake my head. I feel a lot of things – guilt is pretty high on the list – but faint isn't one of them.

Within twenty minutes, Summer calls to say they've located Maddie and together they've cornered and recaptured Bruce and are heading back towards the stables.

In the meantime, I've been helped into a hard-backed chair and given a damp compress to wear about my neck, my pulse monitored constantly by the first-aider.

'Is Bruce OK?' I ask as soon as she ends the call.

'He's sustained a nasty gash along his flank that'll need

looking at by a vet – Maddie's parents won't be happy given the circumstances,' she says. 'But nothing too serious.'

'And Gallop's rider?'

'Well, she'll have some explaining to do when she returns. This isn't the first time she's caused an incident like this,' she says, releasing my wrist. 'I think you're probably feeling a lot better now. You had me worried for a moment back there.'

'And me,' I say with a muted laugh. 'That's probably the furthest I've run in my life.'

'Well, you did the right thing, if that's any consolation, despite nearly killing yourself in the process.'

'Will he be OK?' I ask, feeling slightly foolish at my feeble-ness.

'Bruce will be fine – but Sonya and Gallop might find them-selves moving stable yards.'

Emma

I'm pretending to stare at the TV set, but the reality is I'm watching Ruth from the corner of my eye as she sits on the sofa. Benni's out enjoying herself and we've hardly said two words in the last hour.

I could chance my luck and tell her about viewing the flat, which might go some way towards breaking the ice. Though given that she wasn't terribly supportive about me signing the business contract, what's the chance she'll understand this decision?

'Ruth ... would you like me to put a treatment on your hair?' I ask gingerly, not wishing to offend her.

Her face lights up.

'Funny you should say that. I did buy a hair dye a few days ago then threw it away as a bad idea.'

'I know. I found it in the bathroom bin. I assumed it wasn't Benni's, given the colour. I'm happy to do it for you.'

Ruth doesn't answer, but her eyes are suddenly alive.

'Go and change into an old T-shirt and I'll fetch a couple of bath towels to cover your shoulders and the carpet.'

'You're doing it down here?' she asks, swirling her index finger around the lounge.

'Yep, I might as well. Benni's out and we're not expecting guests, are we?'

'Not to my knowledge.'

Ruth is up and out of her seat in one leap, heading for the staircase. I follow in order to retrieve the box of hair dye from the bathroom cupboard and fetch the necessary towels. Seeing her reaction, I'm pleased I asked. I doubt she gets much pampering at home caring for an elderly mother.

'I think it's strange how life follows a particular path. At Benni's age, I had the world at my feet, and yet I found myself pregnant, so certain opportunities were closed to me.' Ruth clutches the draped towel beneath her chin as I vigorously shake the application bottle.

'Same here. I left school full of ideas for opening my own

restaurant, and yet I accepted the first job I was offered and have let my life slip by ever since.'

'Odd, isn't it, how one or two simple choices determine so much.'

'Jack wasn't planned then?' I ask. I don't mean to be nosy; I'm genuinely interested.

Ruth shakes her head, despite me asking her not to move. As a result, I accidentally cover the top of her right ear with brown hair dye.

'I'm still unsure how it happened. One minute we were flirting across the bank tills, then one thing led to another and ... well, Jack was on the way. My mother went mental. She accused me of being a trollop, the village bike, everything you can think of. She said I'd ruined my life. Back then I believed her, but now I'm not so sure. If I'd been strong enough to stand my ground, I could have supported Jack and still had a life outside of motherhood. It wouldn't have been easy, but I'd have coped. I'd have had the company of other young mums, and when Jack was old enough I could have regained a proper social life. Who knows where I'd be by now if I'd followed that path.'

'And Jack's father ... you said he wasn't interested?' I ask.

'He just couldn't commit. He was honest about it.'

'So your mum stepped in as a surrogate parent?'

'Oh yeah, in a big way. She took over, really, from the moment I returned to work. I suppose I felt grateful for her support so didn't question my role in Jack's life until she had firmly established herself at the centre of his world. I was the breadwinner and she was his primary carer.'

'Which is why it meant so much when he came looking for you the other night,' I say, sheepishly remembering my annoyance at Jack's intrusion.

'It's the first time he's ever done that. My mum has always been his first choice, given their closeness. Of course, now, with her condition, there's no way he'd upset her. Who knows, he might need my support over the coming months once he and Megan split up.'

'It's definitely over then?' I ask, a sudden pang recalling my own hurt. Who am I to question others when my situation needs finalising?

As we've been talking, I've been sectioning her hair and smearing dye on each strand. I feel sorry for her. If only it was as easy to refresh and re-colour our lives once we realise our errors.

'It's never too late, Ruth,' I say. 'You're still young enough to find love or a companion in life ... especially once I've worked my magic on your hair.'

'I hope so.' She pauses. 'Funnily enough, I accepted an unexpected luncheon invite today,' she says, half twisting round to view my reaction. 'He was very charming.'

'Who was it?' I ask, trying desperately to rein in my surprise.

Ruth spends the next fifteen minutes reliving her day: the empty wall space, selling *Marina Mania*, and the cash payment due from Dean. I can't help but notice that her delight overflows when she recalls his kind offer and generosity during lunch.

'He sounds like a suave devil to me,' I offer, enjoying her pleasure each time she mentions his name. Her stream of chat has saved me from spilling the beans about the flat viewing and my liaison, which I'm sure she won't approve of. I'm glad I offered to colour her hair; we're back to being friends without the negative undercurrent of the previous few days.

In no time, I've reached the final section and am attempting to twist her mass of hair into a self-holding bun on top of her head.

'There you go, all done,' I say. 'I suggest you stay put while I make us both a cuppa.' I wipe my hands on a towel before setting a thirty-minute timer on my phone.

Ruth

As Emma is making our tea, I hear a sharp rap on the front door. Clutching the bath towel beneath my chin, I go to answer it. I flick the catch and immediately step aside half expecting Benni to dash in full of apologies for not taking a key. She doesn't. Instead, as I turn about to re-enter the lounge, I realise the figure remains on the doorstep. I double back, self-conscious that I appear as I do, but curious to learn who's there.

A man stands there, his green eyes taking in the sight before him, his broad frame filling the doorway. It isn't Martin, nor Ziggy, or Dean.

'Is Emma Grund staying here?' he asks, his gentle voice

not matching his towering presence against a backdrop of twilight sky.

'Yes, can I ask who's calling?' I'm confused beyond belief. Emma hasn't said a word about a new friend or acquaintance. She's let me prattle on about Dean and our beautiful lunch, but said nothing about her own day.

'I'm Rob, her husband.'

I freeze, stunned to the core. My manners are forgotten as I instinctively look down at his left hand, as if to confirm his status.

'Is she in?'

I don't know what to say for fear of doing the wrong thing. He's neither aggressive, threatening or abrupt so should I call Emma from the kitchen? Ask him to step inside? Or demand formal identification? In the end, I don't have to choose as the kitchen door swings wide and Emma enters the hallway clutching two mugs in one hand and a plate of biscuits in the other.

'I've opened a packet of those—' For a second she simply stares at our guest before there is a clatter of china, and tea and biscuits crash to the tiled floor. 'Rob!'

I step aside, avoiding the puddle of mess seeping along the grouting groves.

'You forgot this,' he says, offering her his upturned palm, in which sits a gold wedding band.

'You have no right to come here!' hisses Emma, her brown eyes seething as she stares at him.

'I have every right,' says Rob, closing his fist around the ring before calmly turning to me. 'Do you mind if I come in?'

I'm unsure if I should be answering, or even whether my presence is welcome.

He steps inside without waiting, strides over the puddle of tea and glances into the lounge.

'May I?'

I look at Emma, who is raking her hands through her auburn hair, giving me no feedback or clue on how to proceed. I want to support her; she looks like she needs a friend. Do I call the police? Shout for a neighbour?

Someone needs to take charge, and it feels like it should be me.

'Rude of me, I know, but can I ask why you're here?' I say, reaching for Emma's right hand as Rob hovers by the lounge door.

'I take it she's failed to mention she's married, then,' he says, looking from Emma to me and back again. 'You lied to me, Emma. You said you'd be back in a few days . . . sending daily texts to delay that happening isn't on. What am I supposed to do: just wait until you choose to return? How bloody selfish is that!'

'You're supposed to respect my decision, that's what you're supposed to do!' says Emma through gritted teeth, as I squeeze her hand tightly to reassure her that I am here for her. 'It's over, Rob; it's been over for a long time, but you won't accept my decision.'

'I'll accept it when you do it in the proper manner. Who in

their right mind books a singles holiday with strangers when they are married? I take it you're one of the house share?' he says, turning to me.

'Solo holiday, actually,' I correct him, before realising how daft I sound. 'But yes, there's three of us sharing.'

'Though Emma forgot to mention any of those details to her husband.'

'Rob, don't,' whispers Emma, lowering her chin and releasing my hand. 'Ruth, I'm so sorry ... you shouldn't be dragged into this. Can we shut the front door?'

I immediately respond, not sure if I'm doing the right thing by either of them.

'Can you give us a few minutes ... alone, please?' she asks, indicating for Rob to go through to the empty lounge.

'Sure, but I'm staying right here in case you need me,' I say, plonking myself down on the bottom stair.

'Thank you,' she says, mouthing 'sorry' to me as she follows him into the lounge.

My heart is racing, my mind spinning. I can't believe what has happened in the space of ten minutes. I wonder what, if anything, will happen in the next ten.

I'm in two minds whether to call Benni and disturb her evening. Or simply sit and wait.

I can hear their voices, raised and urgent behind the closed door; 'you lied' and 'it's over' keep being repeated, but neither of them is shouting during the exchange. Rob's tone doesn't sound angry or aggressive, but demanding and forceful in a controlled manner.

I stare at the puddle of tea spreading across the tiled floor, the fragments of china marooned in the middle.

Emma isn't a solo holidaymaker. She's lied from the moment she met us. Lied about her past, lied about her plans. Simply lied.

Benjamina

We sit on a bench, gazing out at the harbour lights spread wide before us, eating steaming hot chips from an open bag.

I don't want to go home. Correction, back to Rose Cottage. I've had a lovely afternoon with Ziggy, chatting and joking around. I've learnt that he has two sisters, hates mustard, had one steady girlfriend from age fifteen, but no one since she hurt him when they were twenty-one, and he can't ever see himself living anywhere but Brixham.

Likewise, I've disclosed my love of food, my fears about my mum's drinking and my desire to be like other women. I've even mentioned my goals for the future following this holiday.

'So there's no one special back in the Midlands?' Ziggy asks.

I stare at him, speechless.

'Er, no,' I say at last, swallowing the urge to burst out laughing.

'What's so funny?'

Does the man need his eyes testing?

'Because ...' I mutter, gesturing the length of my seated body as if the reason isn't blindingly obvious.

'Because what?' He looks confused, his brow creased and his eyes screwed up. His wooden fork complete with chip hovers a short distance from his mouth.

'Just because,' I say, not wanting to explain further. He's got two sisters; surely he's heard about the whole body-image thing, even if he doesn't understand it.

'What are you on about, Benni?' he asks, discarding his chip fork and shifting around on the bench to face me.

'My size . . . It puts guys off.'

He draws back as if my words have burnt him.

'Are you serious?'

'Yeah, I see it all the time. Young guys only want slim, svelte women, size six or eight, whereas I'm a size . . . well, the exact size doesn't matter. I'm not petite, nowhere near, so I don't get asked on dates. I've never been sent flowers. It might sound utterly wrong to some women, but I wouldn't even be offended if I received a wolf whistle whilst walking past a building site. In fact, it would probably make my day that some red-blooded male actually thought I was attractive rather than looking at me and wondering . . .'

My words trail off. Ziggy's mouth is open, his eyes wide. I can see he's shocked by my outburst and I realise that now is probably the time to say goodbye, thank him for a lovely afternoon of chatting and chips.

I clamber to my feet, adjusting my waistband.

'Well, it's been good knowing you. I've enjoyed our chats and maybe I'll see you around,' I say to his stunned, upturned face.

I'll make my way back to the cottage and repeat my disastrous rant to the other two, who will no doubt cringe, then offer me a very large drink to make me feel better about having aired my dirty laundry – my big-girl knickers – in public to a near stranger.

As I step away from the bench, Ziggy moves. His bag of chips hits the pavement as he stands up; then his hand reaches for my cheek and his mouth, hot and salty, is pressed heavily to mine.

We stand united on the quayside, in full view of passers-by, and continue to kiss. I can feel the heat and urgency of his hands as my body absorbs this sensation for the very first time.

My senses are working overtime.

My eyes are firmly closed.

My hands slowly find the courage to lift and wrap around his waist and back.

My hearing is alert to every sound in the universe. Herring gulls dive-bombing the scattered chips, passing traffic, and the voices of passers-by.

But there's not a single snigger, passing remark or crude comment to be heard.

Nothing.

There is only Ziggy's mouth on mine, our noses softly bumping and my internal monologue self-consciously reminding me that moments like this don't happen in my world.

Chapter Twelve

Wednesday 29 August

Emma

The force with which Benni bursts through the kitchen door makes both Ruth and me jump out of our skins. We've been sitting in silence at the dining table cradling our morning cups of tea. Ruth's wrapped in her pink quilted dressing gown with matching slippers. I'm still in my pyjamas, having spent a sleepless night replaying the events of last night.

Benni stands in the open doorway, both hands clutching the door jamb, her mouth working frantically but nothing spilling forth.

'In the Lord's name, what's wrong with her?' says Ruth.

Sheer panic races through my veins. Given my current emotional state, I'm not fit to support anyone else this morning. I'm just about holding my own shite together.

'Benni, are you hurt, injured, ill?' I ask, my tone razor sharp.

244

My gaze roves about her body in search of a wound that might need stemming or dressing. There's nothing.

'He kissed me!'

'He what?' screams Ruth, her hands flying up to her face in excitement.

Benni's words don't register at first. I'm expecting to hear her say: argued, dumped, cheated. All feasible options race around my fug-filled mind before the actual verb calms my racing neurons much like calamine lotion applied to chicken-pox.

'Ziggy kissed me . . . last night in the open air in front of everyone passing by the harbour. He didn't try to hide it. He didn't care what anyone thought. He did it.'

Benni flops into the vacant seat beside Ruth, whilst I slump in my post-traumatic state and stare across the table. Her face is glowing, her body alive. She's transformed from the woman who left the cottage yesterday afternoon for a quiet drink on the quayside.

'And you?' asks Ruth, leaning forward into Benni's personal space.

'I kissed him back.'

'You didn't!'

'I did.'

I watch the quick-fire exchange as though it's a verbal tennis match.

'And who pulled away first?'

'I can't remember,' beams Benni.

'What did he say then?'

'He didn't say anything. He gazed into my eyes, then leant forward and gently kissed my forehead before finally stepping back and releasing me.'

'He kissed your forehead?' I ask, frowning.

'Yeah, so tenderly.'

'Oh how nice,' whispers Ruth.

'I know,' swoons Benni, her head lolling sideways.

'Umm,' I sigh, in a dubious tone.

'Emma, don't ruin it,' says Ruth.

'In my book, I want a man to kiss with passion, not tenderness.'

'By the sounds of it, nothing much is happening in *your* book, Emma,' mutters Benni with her newly acquired spark. 'It seems to be all work and no play. Whereas me ... well, boy oh boy.'

I open my mouth to reply, but decide not to utter another word. Let her enjoy her kiss.

'Please don't burst my bubble,' she pleads. 'By the way, Ruth, I like your hair colour. It makes you look sassy.'

I agree. Despite the timings going adrift when Rob arrived, the colour suits her.

Ruth acknowledges the compliment before challenging me.

'Are you trying to convince me you wouldn't switch places with Benni right now?' she says, staring across the table as our lovesick friend gazes dreamily into space.

'Mwah!' I squawk sarcastically, more to convince myself than Ruth.

'*Especially* after last night?' she adds quietly.

Benni sits tall, her gaze bouncing inquisitively between the two of us.

'Thanks, Ruth,' I say.

I stand, collect my empty teacup and bolt towards the kitchen to busy myself.

Ruth

'He's a good-looking chap, I can tell you that. And boy, did Emma jump when she spied him on the doorstep,' I say as Benni settles on the edge of my bed to hear about last night's drama. 'She dropped the tea and biscuits all over the floor – I eventually cleaned them up once he'd left, which was gone midnight.'

'So this is the guy who's been jealous and controlling?'

'Yep, the very one. She reckons he suffocates her with his constant need to know everything, making all the decisions in their life and even refusing to accept that the marriage is over. She says she's been forced to act like this to escape the relationship.'

'We were sitting on the quayside watching the harbour lights,' Benni says dreamily, 'so I got back much later than I was expecting. But I'd never have guessed she'd had a visitor. Nothing's out of place.'

'I stayed on the bottom stair in case she needed me. I heard it all. Every single word. I felt awful listening while they argued back and forth, but what choice did I have?'

'So she lied about being single?'

'Yep. It turns out they've been living separate lives for ages but within the same house, like a marriage on autopilot. Emma felt she had to get away for a bit to make plans that she could implement on arriving back home. From what I can gather, she'd told him she was staying with friends in Kent for a few days, but he searched her emails and found the booking confirmation for Rose Cottage. He went mad at the "solo" reference, given that they're still married. She obviously hadn't bargained for the opportunity at the ice cream parlour nor the added complication with Martin. She'd told Rob that she was planning to spend her redundancy money on opening a coffee shop or a bakery in Rugeley.'

'Which is what she told us too,' interrupts Benni caustically.

'Absolutely. Anyway, her original plans changed as the days went by, which I understand because mine have too, and you've said pretty much the same about wanting new beginnings. But surely she should have been upfront with him rather than sneaking off behind his back like that.'

'Bloody hell . . . Still, who knows what either of us would do if we were that unhappy,' says Benni, the voice of reason.

'Perhaps . . .'

'What a night! What's she going to do now?'

'I've no idea. She's ploughed her redundancy money into this guy's business, and I've no doubt the deal is signed and sealed by now.'

'What a minx. I'd hate to think what else she's been getting up to but hasn't mentioned,' says Benni with a twinkle in her eye.

248

'Benni, don't joke. This couldn't be any worse. I really thought I'd found a new friend for life, but after last night, I'm not so sure.'

Emma

I don't really want to leave the cottage, knowing that Ruth and Benni are bound to have a tête-à-tête regarding my antics. As I close the wrought-iron gate, I'm tempted to dash back inside and catch them in the act, proving they lack decency and manners.

I don't but my urge to be proved right is nearly overwhelming. Instead, I straighten my shoulders, lift my chin and set off towards the ice cream parlour.

Three teenagers are sitting at one of the tables as I enter, though none of them have an ice cream. Luca is cleaning the display counter's glass cover with a cloth and soapy water.

'Hi, Luca, is Martin about?' I automatically head around the counter, but halt on seeing his reaction. His eyes widen, his mouth gapes open but nothing comes forth. 'Luca?'

'He's not here . . . Wednesday is his day off,' he stammers, wringing the cloth in his hands. He looks nervously over his shoulder before continuing. 'You might do better calling him if it's urgent.'

'OK, thanks, I will. Is it all right if I nip upstairs and take a look at the windows? I don't want to waste money on blinds if it's easier to have a curtail rail.'

Luca gives a fleeting nod, quickly returning to his task.

I open the door leading to the private staircase and bound up the steps. I might as well get one job done before explaining to Martin about Rob's fleeting visit last night. He's divorced; he'll understand exactly how the ground lies when a marriage fades and emotions unravel. He's lived it, breathed it and survived the legalities.

I insert the Yale key that Martin gave me. It feels great to be entering my own little place, regardless of how grubby and junk-filled it is at the moment. In the lounge area, streams of brilliant sunlight illuminate the space, making it more appealing. I watch the dust motes drift and dance around the room.

A coy smile creeps on to my face when I spy the scuff marks on the dusty floorboards where our naked bodies cavorted only two nights ago.

I can't afford to waste time reminiscing about that night; I need to speak to Martin. I dart to the main window and begin inspecting the surround to decide on blinds or a curtain rail.

'Excuse me . . .' The woman's voice has an edge. I imagine her confused expression before I turn around to face her.

'Yes, can I help?'

She's older than me, nearer Ruth's age, and incredibly thin. Her collarbones poke forward like wire coat hangers and her sinewy neck gives her a harsh appearance that her messy greying bun doesn't soften.

'I was about to ask you the same thing,' she retorts. 'Can I ask why you have a key?'

'Martin gave it to me. I'm just checking the windows ready for moving in . . . you know, deciding whether to have blinds or curtains. I'm not sure which I'd prefer.'

'Excuse me, this place isn't for rent. I don't understand how this little arrangement has come about, but I think you need to speak to my husband about it.'

'Your husband?' I physically reel backwards as the words punch home.

'Yes. My husband,' she repeats emphatically.

I stare at her blankly, questions forming in my mind, then point idiotically at the clean area of floor by her right foot. She turns, glances down, then looks back at me bemused.

'Floorboards?'

I haven't the heart to explain.

'You're married to Martin?' I manage.

Her nod of confirmation shatters my new beginning like shards of glass dropped from a great height. I drop the Yale key and run from the apartment, down the stairs and out through the door leading into the ice cream parlour. Luca is standing stock still in the middle of the floor, waiting.

'You knew! Why didn't you say?' I scream, unleashing my fury.

'He didn't say a word about giving you a key to upstairs . . . I had no idea anything was going on apart from the ice cream you've created and delivered.'

'He's screwed me over for ten thousand pounds and you're telling me you don't know about it?'

Luca's gaze shifts from my contorted features to something

behind me. I turn and find Martin's wife standing in the doorway, hands on hips.

'Yeah, that's right,' I spit. 'I've ploughed ten thousand pounds into this business . . . I signed the paperwork on Saturday morning. Ask him, check if you want. I'm not lying.'

The atmosphere becomes heavy as Luca and the woman glare at each other.

'I promise you, Liz, he hasn't said a word to me,' Luca says eventually.

'The conniving bastard!' she hisses, storming forward and roughly grabbing my arm. 'And you, you can get out of my sight!' She drags me unceremoniously towards the parlour door, wrenching it open and pushing me out on to the quayside. As I stagger upright, she locks the door with a defiant flourish. I stare open-mouthed at Luca, who's pacing the tiled floor and shrugging as she rants.

I grab my mobile phone and call Martin. Surely he'll have an explanation.

Benjamina

We sit at Ziggy's favourite table in the Sprat and Mackerel, ignoring the picturesque view of the harbour and sipping our drinks.

I have my dad's chin, and I can't stop staring as he speaks.

No one has ever told me that I look like him. Has Mum secretly compared me to him whilst speaking to me? She must have. She might not have liked his decision but she once loved his face. Looked forward to seeing him when he came home from work, waking up beside his smiling eyes. Maybe not at the end of their relationship, but certainly when they first met. Am I a painful reminder of him?

'Are you OK, sweet?' Ben's question breaks into my thoughts.

'Sorry, yes, I'm fine. I just can't believe this is happening. Given Mum's explanation, I never thought about seeing you, and now . . . well, here we are, and it has truly blown my mind. I don't know what to think or say. But I'm grateful that it's happened.'

'Me too,' he says. 'I realise it's a shock for both of us, and I don't want to rush you, but I did mention our meeting at home. I told my boys on the night we met.'

'No way!' I squeal in delight. A wave of acceptance rushes through my veins like malt vinegar into an empty pickling jar.

'Yeah, I did. I've no intention of keeping you a secret. I sat the lads down and explained what had happened in the shop. When I dropped them back home, I even mentioned it to their mum, Jess. She's always known about Dan, but I told her about you and your holiday, and they're all chuffed to bits.'

'Is everything amicable between the two of you?'

'Oh sure. Jess is great – we've stayed friends despite the relationship ending. It would be wrong for the lads to have us at war.'

'Great stuff. And your sons, they want to meet me?'

'Ben always wanted a sister; he was dead upset when Will was born.'

253

'Ben?'

'Yep, another Ben.'

I'm transfixed hearing about my teenage half-brothers – it's weird, and yet I'm ready to accept whatever they bring to my world. I can't wait to meet them. I want to be their big sister. Fingers crossed, we'll get along slightly better than me and Dan have in the past.

'This feels like a new beginning,' I say eagerly.

'It is, Benni, but we can't rush things, can we? I wouldn't want to rock the boat for you back home. We need to be open with everyone.'

He's right. I need to plan how I'll deliver the news to Mum; then, depending on Dan's reaction, he might want a share of the excitement too. Deep down, I'm hoping he doesn't know about Ben. Hoping he hasn't kept a dark secret from me.

'Absolutely,' I say. 'But their reaction is their problem, not mine. I can't worry about what's out of my control, can I?'

'Nope. But for the record, if Dan wants to make contact, I'll happily welcome him into our family too.'

I'm chuffed to bits. I couldn't ask for more. I'd say exactly the same if I were in his shoes. Obviously we have more in common than bone structure.

'That's very fair of you, Ben.'

'He's still my lad despite his lifestyle – and your mother's opinion. The choice is his.'

I have no idea how I'll broach the subject with Dan, or even when, but given the sincerity with which Ben's words are spoken, I have no doubt about what I'll be suggesting to him.

Who knows, over time he might venture down here himself and meet our dad face to face.

'Does that sound fair?' asks Ben, finishing his cider.

'I'd say so. You've put the ball in his court.'

'Good. I realise you've only a few days of your holiday remaining, so please don't feel you're being pressured, but what's your plan for the rest of the day?'

'Nothing really. Ruth and Emma are both busy, and Ziggy will be sleeping ready for his night shift at sea. So I can do as I please for the rest of the day. This holiday has made me realise that I should be more proactive in life.'

'It sounds ridiculous, but I think of life like this: that every day, we each pave our own yellow brick road,' laughs Ben. 'Mine won't have the same destination as yours, but it's what I've created for myself. Does that make sense?'

'Absolutely,' I say, adding, 'And today my yellow brick road travels towards an extended family, who I can't wait to meet.'

'That's good, because they're desperate to meet you too. In fact, they're wandering around the harbour right now, hoping I'll call them in to join us.'

'Do it, ask them to drop by,' I say, excitement bubbling deep inside.

Ben grabs his mobile and quickly texts his sons. Within a second, there's a speedy reply and, couple of minutes later, the pub door opens, revealing two eager faces peering in our direction.

I squeal with delight as two lanky teenagers with identical chins to mine enter and head for our table.

Emma

I feel ridiculous. Dashing from room to room grabbing my scattered belongings: underwear drying on radiators, bathroom toiletries from shelves, sandy pumps from the porch, then back upstairs to my bedroom like a fugitive who's spied a flashing blue light nearing his hideout. It's the fastest I've moved in years.

I stuff the items into my suitcase any old how, my hands frantically working on the bulges until the case can close securely.

I have five minutes before my taxi arrives, so if I've forgotten anything, then so be it. I'm prepared to lose it purely to be out of here, away and gone. I heave the suitcase from the bed, bumping it against my legs as I manoeuvre it along the landing and down the narrow staircase.

I have one last dash around the ground-floor rooms. I could leave a note on the kitchen worktop – the first place they'll look – but I won't. I'll text them later from the train. If I text too early, they'll try and talk me out of it, I know they will. This way, they'll read my message and understand without trying to persuade me to stay, especially after Rob's visit last night.

If I walked in on Benni skulking off like this with days remaining of her holiday, I would try to talk her around. I'd make her tea, give her a big hug and tell her there are plenty more fish in the sea, and that she should take these extra days to straighten out her thoughts and get herself together before deciding on her future. But I can't follow my own advice. Which makes me doubly determined not to be here when they arrive back full of the joys of Brixham sunshine and harbour talk. I'll only bring them down with my pathetic tale of woe.

I'm thankful that I didn't confide in them about viewing the apartment, or our little rendezvous. I could die with embarrassment when I think about us romping on bare floorboards amongst the junk.

What a silly bint I am!

Why was I even surprised when the git didn't answer his phone?

I'm suckered in the moment anyone shows me the slightest bit of attention or kindness. Hook, line and sinker like a bloody crab on a line simply waiting to be reeled in and then thrown back into the mire once I've provided some entertainment. I'm nothing but a glorified bloody crab scrabbling for the titbits of life.

I hear the sound of a car drawing up by the cottage gate, and stride into the lounge to see a red taxi waiting outside the large bay window.

I lock the back door, grab my jacket from the peg and haul my suitcase over the doorstep before giving Rose Cottage's front door a mighty slam.

'Hello, love, Paignton station, is it?' says the elderly driver, opening the boot and lifting my suitcase inside.

'Please.' I have to resist the urge to tell him to hurry. I don't want the other two to arrive in these final moments. I simply want to leave. Be gone. Forget I was ever here.

Ruth

The main Berry Head road, leading to the newly built accommodation, is steep and winding. I use the excuse of the beautiful scenery to pause and take a breather, looking out across the harbour view. I feel exhausted, which surely isn't right whilst on holiday.

This morning has been hectic. First Emma's emotional state over breakfast, then Benni's delightful news followed by my bringing her up to date about Emma's drama. Then finally my own joy at delivering my second completed watercolour to the gallery.

I stare into the distance and see the lighthouse proudly positioned at the end of the harbour's defence barrier. It feels amazing to think that only a few days ago I was sitting at the base sketching its outline. Today Dean will frame my composition before displaying it on his gallery wall. Amazing what you can achieve when you put your mind to it.

I watch the waves crashing against the concrete defence barrier, the herring gulls ducking and diving overhead and the billowing clouds drifting gently by.

How peaceful, to stand and watch the world go by. How idyllic.

But who am I kidding? I can't take such a leap of faith

at my age . . . or hers. Though the estate agents don't know that. As far as they're concerned, I'm an independent woman looking to escape to the seaside. I bet they show hundreds of eager holidaymakers around their apartments in hope of a sale.

I lean against the stone wall, its gnarly texture comforting beneath my palms.

How many people have stood here over the years and dreamt of spending their remaining days looking out across this stretch of water? Thousands, I should imagine. And how many have been brave enough to take a step towards making their dream a reality?

Well, there's no chance of that for us. I'm purely being nosy whilst I'm here. Seeing how the other half live, so to speak. Though given the way my stomach is lurching at the prospect of telling a few white lies, I won't be doing this again.

I breathe in the dream moment as a memory, before turning and heading for my three o'clock appointment. I'll take any literature they offer. I'll ask a load of questions and throw in some 'oohs' and 'ahs', like they do on those property programme on the TV. Those couples rarely purchase the viewed properties, so what am I worried about?

How difficult can it be?

As I continue the steady climb, pretending it might become my daily walk, I look up and see a taxi approaching. The woman in the back is staring absently through the window, a look of deep sadness etched upon her face. I wonder if others have ever viewed me in such a manner. All at once, I recognise the woman. It's Emma. Simultaneously, she awakens from her thoughts and notices me.

Our eyes meet for the briefest of seconds.

Sadness.

The emotion overwhelms me.

Then she's gone.

I swiftly turn, watching the taxi grow smaller and smaller as it weaves its way down the hill.

Where is Emma going?

'Hello,' says a female voice beside me. 'Is it Ms Elton?'

I turn to see a young woman with blonde highlights and red-painted lips staring enquiringly at me, hand outstretched. Her company badge identifies her as Ms West of Next Move: Sell, Rent or Buy.

'Yes . . . Ruth, please,' I stammer, shooting one final look over my shoulder at the taxi.

'Perfect timing . . . Shall we?' Ms West doesn't wait for an answer but strides towards the nearest residence. I follow, lingering two steps behind and wondering whether I should phone Emma. I watch the estate agent's nimble fingers produce keys and swiftly gain entrance, talking as she does.

I'm torn.

I must focus, take an interest and ask as many questions as I can.

I'll phone Emma as soon as I've finished viewing the apartment.

Benjamina

'Hi!' I call, bursting happily through the doors of the ice cream parlour. I'm halfway across the tiled floor when I realise that my warm greeting has been met by a gloomy face. 'What's up, Luca? Have you had a power cut and all the stock's melted?'

My joke falls flat. Much like a power cut in an ice cream parlour on the hottest day of the year.

Instantly I feel an inner panic.

'Luca?'

He slowly shakes his head, his lips rolling together as if wanting to form words, his hands twisting a tea towel into a rope. To watch a grown man be lost for words takes me by surprise. He looks really upset.

'Luca ... what's happened?'

He throws down his twisted tea towel and steps from behind the counter, beckoning me towards the nearest table.

'She came in when I was cleaning and went up to the apartment,' he says, sinking on to a chair. I sit opposite.

'Who? Emma?'

He nods. 'Liz didn't ask, she didn't say a word; she simply followed Emma up the stairs. I should have stopped her, I should have known he'd pull a stunt like this sooner or later. When they came back downstairs, Emma was shouting about ten thousand pounds and signing paperwork. She was distraught ... totally shocked. Then Liz kicked her

261

out. I should have done something, but I just couldn't think straight.'

I watch as he covers his face, distraught.

What the hell am I to say now?

'I should have helped her and now she's gone! She's gone, hasn't she?'

'Luca, who is Liz?' I say slowly.

He removes his hands and looks at me.

'She's Martin's wife.'

My mouth is agape; I haven't a clue what to say. I reach for my mobile and look at the screen. There's no message from Emma.

'Where's Martin now?'

'I don't know. He's forever playing with fire and messing about behind Liz's back, but I honestly didn't think he'd try it with Emma.' He slumps in his chair, deflated.

I'm in shock. I don't know what to do. Should I dash back to the cottage? Call Ruth? Or perhaps I should hunt down Martin.

'From the moment she walked in here, I thought she was lovely, and now he's ruined everything.' Luca gives a deep sigh. 'Typical Martin, always chasing his tail simply to please the bank manager. He doesn't care a jot about anyone but himself.'

'Does Emma know how you feel about her?'

'Nah, I only really saw her when she delivered the samples . . . I never got the chance to get to know her better. And how can I continue working here now knowing how my boss has treated her?'

I stand up. I need to do something. I can't sit and wait for a tear-stained Emma to find me.

'Look, Luca, I think she's been blinded by his charm and the chance of starting afresh thanks to her tasting talents, but honestly, if she realised how you felt, I know she'd be flattered.'

I see a spark in his eyes; at least he's listening.

'I can let you have her mobile number if you want it. Give it a day or so, but seriously, think about telling her. It might not be too late for you and her.'

I grab a paper napkin from the dispenser and begin searching through my contacts for Emma's number, relieved that I've started carrying my mobile since the horse-riding emergency. I'll write it down for Luca, then I'll attempt to call Emma myself.

Emma

I sit on the station platform and wait, my ticket home in my hand. I'd done the usual, bought a coffee and attempted to snack on a soggy tortilla wrap promising the delights of the orient. I binned it, opting for crisps instead.

I shouldn't have gone to Berry Head. I should have made him drive straight to Paignton station, but oh no . . . soppy old me had to take one last look, enjoy one last moment of a lingering memory of good times. And now look what I've done.

I have no doubt that Ruth recognised me as we drove past. Her features went from relaxed to wide-eyed and staring in the shortest of seconds.

263

Why oh why didn't I simply come straight to the station?

The quick walk around Berry Head was hardly the same in the middle of the day, with screaming children demanding ice cream and parents hushing them in irritation. There was no moonlight walk, no tender kiss, not even a reminder of the time we shared staring out to sea. Lord knows what I was thinking. It was all an act; Martin must be laughing his socks off. It's one thing to fall for the smooth talk, the warm embrace, but to actually ... do it on a dusty wooden floor after a few throwaway comments about our future makes my skin crawl.

I switch on my mobile. Seven missed calls: Ruth and Benni. Great, so now they both know.

I gulp down a wave of guilt. They've been so kind, so caring and friendly these past ten days, and now this. They'll think I've walked out on them too. They won't understand what a prat I've made of myself; I didn't share half of it with them. They'll think I didn't trust them.

What a bloody mess!

And now I'm to return home, tail between my legs, ten grand lighter and weighed down by the prospect of a business venture with a sodding crook some two hundred miles away.

What a fool!

I watch travellers hauling suitcases from train carriages. Whether they're coming home or arriving for a holiday, I hope they find a better outcome than I did. I correct myself, instantly. I hope they're not taken in as a mug, a desperate, lonely mug seeking new beginnings.

My internal monologue has gone too far. Angry tears spill

over my lashes and down my face. I hastily wipe my hand across each cheek for fear that the world will see my distress. Though on second thoughts, who cares nowadays – no one ever stops when they see a stranger cry in public.

To think I trusted him. Trusted him with my money. With my future. With my . . .

I stop. The final thought snags in my mind; I hadn't got as far as admitting it to myself, let alone him.

With my heart.

Bastard.

I go with the flow of emotion, turning to hide my sorrow and wait for it to subside.

I'll be home in a few hours, washed, changed and unpacked, and then I'll put the wheels in motion. I'll phone Ruth and Benni, explain the reason for my sudden departure. Though no doubt Ruth has already spoken to Benni, given the number of missed calls.

Then I'll . . .

I pause. What is it I want to do?

I'll sit down and write a list of options, before methodically working through the feasibility of each one. I'll be like Benni. Benni, who has never had secure employment. Young Benni with her gung-ho attitude towards life and the bravery to face whatever comes at her.

If she can survive, why can't I? I'll ignore the fear and do what I need to do . . . who knows, I might even find the answer I'm looking for.

Just like Benni.

My renewed vigour dries my tears.

Suddenly a wealth of feasible ideas pop into my mind. I grab my phone and begin making my list.

Apply to every restaurant and hotel back home
regardless of whether they are advertising or not.
Start up a cookery-for-beginners course.
Write a cookbook based on unique tastes.
A change of career????

I type the final line and sit back.

Am I too old to change career?

Who am I kidding? I'm useless at anything and everything else. I can't do office work, sales or marketing ... I haven't the qualifications to teach, nurse or even work in social care. I can't do anything other than cook. And taste.

My line of vision suddenly fills with my train drawing in to the platform. I slip my phone into my pocket, bundle up my belongings and drag my suitcase towards the nearest carriage.

I want to go home, and that can't happen quickly enough.

A kindly man helps me to lift my case into the carriage and on to the storage rack. Gratefully I sit in the seat opposite, babysitting my luggage, convinced that a stranger will steal my belongings and round off my holiday on a further bum note.

Funny how I trust no one now that one person has deceived me.

Ruth

Benni stares at me dolefully as I sit, phone to my ear, listening to Emma's mobile ring out.

'I'll keep trying all night if I have to,' I say across the dining-room table.

Benni sighs. This isn't how she expected to spend tonight, cooped up alongside me when she could be out dancing with Ziggy and his mates.

'What if she's done something stupid?' she asks, as I kill the connection and immediately begin to redial.

'Don't say that!' I retort, not wanting to think the worst.

'You never know. She was thrilled at the prospect of a new life, a new venture and maybe a new partner. In a matter of hours it looks like she's lost the lot.'

Her words linger in the space between us. I don't want to think about such things, so I ignore her concerns. Though deep down I know that if Emma doesn't answer soon, we might need to venture along that line of thought.

I try twice more without success, then place my phone on the table and stare at it.

We think mobile phones are life-savers. We rely on them for connection and communication, and yet in reality, if no one answers them, they're bloody useless. Overpriced bits of plastic and electronics that give us a sense of self and purpose by supposedly keeping us in touch with the world, unless someone chooses not to pick up. Or can't.

'Ruth . . . I'm frightened.'

'I know.'

'Who do we call if—'

'Stop it. She's not in that frame of mind.'

'How do you know? You said her face in the back of the taxi looked lifeless.'

I gulp. I wish I'd kept that little detail to myself.

'Well, not quite . . .'

'You said—' continues Benni.

'I know what I said. Maybe it wasn't her . . . maybe it was someone looking like her whose face was lifeless.'

'Who are you trying to kid? What're the chances of there being a near-identical woman in the same area on the same day that she does a dash for it after being stung by a greedy bastard?'

I stare at her. For one so young, Benni is very perceptive.

'I can't sit here doing nothing,' she says. 'We're wasting time.'

'Look, if all else fails, we'll call the local police and ask them to contact Rugeley police as a matter of urgency. How does that sound?'

'OK, so what time are we calling them?' asks Benni, turning to view the dining-room clock.

'Benni – don't!'

'No, we have to be realistic, Ruth. What's the time?'

I glance at the clock: 8.30.

'You last saw her at what time?'

'Three o'clock.'

'That's five and a half hours ago – plenty of time for her to get home, settle and answer her phone, even if she ran out of juice on the journey. Agreed?'

I sigh. She's got a point.

'Let's wait till ten o'clock,' she says.

I give a tiny nod.

'You keep phoning for a bit and then I'll take over. I need to find something to do,' says Benni, disappearing into the kitchen. 'I can't sit and wait for bad news.'

I know she's taking the sensible approach, but I really don't fancy calling the police and causing an unnecessary drama. Surely Emma's had enough for one day.

On the other hand, I'd hate to think . . .

Emma

'What?' I snap.

I know I should be grateful, but right now, all I want to do is sleep. My bedroom clock tells me it's 9.50.

'Emma?' comes Benni's tinny voice; even through the distorted connection of the mobile I can hear her concern.

'Yes, sorry, Benni . . . I needed . . . I just had to get away.'

'We get it, don't worry. We were worried because you weren't picking up, but now that you have . . . Can we give you a call in the morning to make sure you're OK?'

Instantly, I feel guilty. I arrived home to an empty house and was relieved that Rob wasn't here to quiz me. I knew

Ruth and Benni would be in a panic, and yet I ignored their calls for hours.

'I'm sorry. You shouldn't have to wait until tomorrow for me to explain.'

'You don't need to explain. We understand. We wanted to know that you were home safe and that you were OK, that's all.'

I'm touched by her kindness.

Her voice lifts with a giggle. 'This will make you smile, if nothing else – guess who made chocolate truffles while we were waiting for you to answer your mobile?'

'That's brilliant. I hope you enjoyed it. Benni ... can you apologise to Ruth too. I should have picked up earlier. Sorry if I've worried you both. I'm home, I'm safe and ... thank you.'

'That's fine. Get some sleep and we'll buzz you tomorrow. Is there anything you want us to do in the meantime?'

I pause. 'If you happen to see a certain man, a purveyor of ice cream, you might wish to tell him that I'll be in touch. If he thinks this is the last he's seen of me, he is quite wrong!'

'Sure will, and, Emma ... you may hear from another gent associated with said ice cream purveyor. Be kind if he calls.'

'Who? Luca?'

'The very man ... Now go and get a good night's sleep and we'll speak to you first thing tomorrow. Goodnight, Emma.'

'Goodnight, Benni, and thank you again.'

'Our pleasure.' With that Benni ends the call.

I sit clutching my phone for a few minutes until the heaviness lifts from my heart. Speaking to Benni was exactly what

270

I needed; simply knowing that other people care enough to make sure that I am home safe and well brings tears to my eyes.

Wow, how is it that some people will take advantage of you at the first opportunity while others prove themselves to be loyal friends within only a few days?

Ruth

'How does she sound?' I ask as soon as Benni hangs up.

'Not good.' Benni pulls a sad face before continuing. 'But hey, at least we know she's OK. She's home. If she needs anything I hope she'll call us, regardless of the time. I'd prefer to be up talking to her all night than for her to ... well, you know.'

'I know.'

I stand up from the dining table, where I pitched camp when we began phoning several hours ago. Benni's been active making chocolate truffles, as a means of distracting herself. I stretch my tired legs and my aching back, which seems to have creased into the shape of the hard-backed chair.

'Now what?' asks Benni, watching my every move.

I shrug.

'A double gin or even a triple over at the Queen's Arms?' she suggests. 'There's no point us waiting here – we can answer Emma's call wherever we are.'

'Sounds good to me. Come on, let's go before I change my mind.'

Benni jumps up as only a youngster can after ten o'clock at night.

'And you can tell me how your day has been,' I say. 'Because I've made a huge decision . . . well, huge for me anyway.'

Within seconds, Benni is slamming the cottage door shut as we dash over the road for our well-earned drinks.

The Queen's Arms is buzzing with customers. Marla is busy behind the bar and we manage to grab a corner table away from the blaring TV.

'Here, read this,' I say, handing Benni a brown stamped addressed envelope once we've settled with our drinks.

'Looks intriguing. Is this your big decision?'

I nod, sipping my gin and tonic.

Benni retrieves the single sheet of paper from the envelope. I know each handwritten word off by heart.

Dear Mr Saxon,

I wish to resign from my position as bank clerk at National Westminster Bank PLC. After a full-time career spanning more than two and a half decades, I have decided to explore other avenues of employment. This is a personal decision made for the benefit of myself and my family, and so I am hereby giving four weeks' notice, as required by my employment contract.

Kindest regards,

Ms Ruth Elton

Benni's face is a picture. I knew it would be.

She folds the letter and slides it back inside the envelope before passing it to me. I tuck it carefully into my handbag.

'Good for you, Ruth. I honestly thought you would dream the dream while you were down here but return to your usual routine once you were home,' she says, blushing with honesty.

'Me too. But today I walked around a beautiful apartment overlooking the harbour, and the young woman explained to me how many viewings she does a week, yet people rarely take the plunge. It struck me as being so sad. We have one chance in this world and yet we're all too frightened to chase what we truly want.'

'And?'

'And I thought, bugger it. I'm fifty-three, my mother's seventy-three – realistically, how many years have we got?'

'No one knows.'

'Exactly. I work all week and for what? To dash home to care for my mum, who's not even truly aware of what I'm doing for her. Doesn't that undermine all the effort I'm putting in? We'd be better off selling up, downsizing and moving somewhere where we can both enjoy what little time we have left together. Jack will be fine; he doesn't need us now. So I've written my resignation, and tonight, before we return to Rose Cottage, I'm going to post it.'

'Bloody hell, Ruth – are you sure?'

'Yep, it's now or never, Benni. I need to go for it.'

*   *   *

After our celebratory tipple, we scurry down the steep hill and stand before the red postbox. I'm thrilled at the prospect of pastures new but uneasy feeling the comfort blanket of routine slipping from my shoulders.

My fingers pinch the slimline envelope held aloft at the gaping mouth of the postbox.

'What if your house doesn't sell?' asks Benni, as I gently push it forward.

'It will. Houses in our postcode are snapped up in days.'

'In that case, do it!'

I push and release my grip. We hear the gentle thud as the envelope joins the other letters awaiting collection.

'Bloody hell, you did it!' squeals Benni, dancing on the spot.

'Bloody hell, I did!'

Chapter Thirteen

Thursday 30 August

Benjamina

'You're up early – did you wet the bed?' jokes Summer as I follow her along the driveway to the stables minutes after the dawn chorus breaks.

'I couldn't sleep,' I mutter, thinking back to last night's drama. After Emma's disappearing trick, two double gins and Ruth's shock announcement, I was wide awake. If I hadn't had the gin, I could have gone out with the fishermen for an all-night session hauling in their lines. At least I'd have been useful on the trawler rather than spending five hours tossing and turning whilst searching for the cold side of my pillow.

Summer begins distributing the horses' feed buckets along the rows; the yard's practice of 'first in feeds all' ensures every horse is fed simultaneously to avoid drama.

I grab equipment from the tool shed and get ready to

muck out Bruce's stable for the last time, as a final thank-you to Maddie for putting up with me. I can't begin until he's eaten his breakfast, so I lean against his stable door, watching Summer unlock and open each stable door before moving on to the next.

Bruce's head appears alongside mine and begins to nuzzle my face, his pink lips fluttering.

This is what I'll miss. The scent of the horses early in the morning, the sound of impatient hooves upon the stable floor, and the muted snorts as they communicate between stables. If I could bottle this moment, I would. But sadly, I can't.

'How's Bruce's injury?' I call to Summer, noticing the gather of stitches across his right flank.

'He's fine. Maddie's parents aren't impressed with the vet's bill, but what can they do? It looks like she'll be washing up for a month to get back into their good books.'

'And Sonya?'

'The owner of the stables collared her when she returned from her ride and demanded to speak to her parents about the situation.' Summer's voice drops to a whisper, although I'm sure we're the only ones here. 'I've been told they've been asked to consider taking Gallop elsewhere, or else rename him.'

'Can you do that with a horse?'

Summer shrugs. 'Who knows, but it isn't our problem.'

'I feel awful for letting go of Bruce's leading rein. If I'd held it tight—'

'He'd have pulled you over. Maddie's told her parents that; they also know that you ran back to get help, nearly killing yourself in the process,' says Summer, approaching Bruce's stable, the last one. 'Here, put his food bucket inside, otherwise he'll think you're teasing him.'

I do as she instructs, and Bruce starts chomping enthusiastically at his breakfast.

Ten minutes later, Maddie arrives to find that Summer has kindly manoeuvred Bruce into the empty stable opposite so that I can begin mucking out for my final time. He stands patiently, his head nosing over his temporary stable door, waiting to be led out to the paddock.

'It saves me a job, so I won't complain,' says Maddie, dragging an empty wheelbarrow nearer.

'I just wanted to say thank you for being so generous and letting me visit,' I say, but have to stop when a lump collects in my throat. I fall silent and begin work.

The simple action of turning over wood shavings, cleaning up piles of horse muck and being amongst the horses is usually therapeutic. The rhythmical action of forking the dirty straw helps my mind to drift, but with each thought, I can feel the bubble of excitement deep within me move like a carpenter's spirit level. Sadly, my bubble won't stay in the middle but constantly drifts the length of the spectrum. One minute, I'm enthralled to be here, the next moment I envisage returning to my usual routine, and my mood plummets.

Bruce neighs noisily from the opposite stable, his head twisting back and forth, his top lip fluttering.

'Can you tell how I feel, boy?' I ask, leaning my broom

against the wall and crossing to his temporary home. As I reach out to stroke his forelock, his gentle brown eyes look deep into mine, releasing a world of silent thoughts.

'He's going to miss you,' calls Maddie, resting on her broom.

'Ditto. I'm surprised how quickly I've become accustomed to seeing him . . . Strange how you get so attached to horses.'

'It's a pity you're going home. I could see you joining the team if you lived here permanently. Given time, we might have convinced you to get in the saddle,' says Maddie, fluffing up the border of Bruce's stable.

'I can't imagine myself wearing jodhpurs or sitting on a horse, given my current size. But this time next year, if I return for another fortnight in Brixham – now that's a feasible goal to aim for.'

'You could have a go tomorrow. I'm sure Marla wouldn't mind you riding Wispy around the paddock; I'd be happy to walk you round on a leading rein,' offers Maddie, her excitement growing.

'I can't. Tomorrow is officially the last day of my holiday and I've made plans.'

'What about Saturday morning before you catch your train?'

'No can do either. We need to vacate the cottage by ten o'clock, so there's no time to do anything beforehand, and I can't drag my luggage around the streets of Brixham. No, I'm afraid today's my last visit.'

Maddie pulls a face, her bottom lip protruding.

'But cheer up, I've bought you a present.' I retrieve two small boxes from my jacket pocket. 'It's just a little thank-you for you and Marla. You've both helped me out during this holiday, and it means a lot.'

'What's Marla helped with?' says Maddie indignantly, taking both boxes from me.

'One night at the cove she sat with me while the others went skinny-dipping. I was pretty miserable and she kept me company. Plus, she saved my friend's life with a favour at the Queen's Arms.'

Maddie opens one of the boxes to reveal a tiny silver horse-shoe on a delicate chain.

'They're both the same given that you're both into horses,' I say, watching the delight on her face. 'If you could pass Marla's on, I'd appreciate it.'

Amidst a series of hugs, promises to return next summer and much blinking-back of tears, I say farewell to the riding stables.

Emma

I wake with a start in my own bed. I've slept soundly all night, and now my familiar surroundings signal a new day. I fight the urge to lie back and analyse the last ten days spent in Brixham. I did enough navel-gazing on the train home yesterday.

Today I must be proactive, take a grip of my life and make some decisions.

I reach for my mobile.

'Morning, Benni, I'm ringing to say thank you again for

calling last night. Honestly, you don't know how much that meant to me.'

'You'd do the same for me,' replies Benni. 'Nice to see you're up and about bright and early.'

I glance at my bedside clock: 6.30.

'I'm so sorry. Did I wake you?'

'Nah, I've been up at the stables helping to muck out. I didn't have you down as an early bird, though.'

'I'll have you know there were days when I'd be out of bed at five o'clock to start the breakfast shift at six.'

'So how are you feeling today?'

'Brighter, thanks to you and Ruth caring enough to call me last night.'

'And have you heard anything from Martin?'

'No. I'm not expecting to until I've sent a solicitor's letter outlining my demands.'

'What about Rob; have you spoken to him?'

'I need to explain a few things about me and Rob, because I don't want you to get the wrong impression. Yes, I lied about being single. But when you've been in a toxic relationship for as long as I was, you doubt whether you can stand on your own two feet. We're not officially on a break, but we aren't in a marriage either; that died years ago because of his controlling ways.'

'So why did he drive all the way down here to deliver your wedding ring?'

'To prove a bloody point! An ego trip to show I can't outwit him, plus a way of embarrassing me to high heaven for lying. Which I shouldn't have done.'

'Do you still love him?'

'Not any more. I did once, when I was young and stupid, but I've outgrown his possessiveness and his irrational jealousy. It seemed flattering when I was younger, but really it restricts your choices, confines your life to a tiny little box and ultimately stops you achieving your potential in life. I need to be my own person and decide where my future lies.'

There's a lengthy pause before I continue. 'Benni, can you tell Ruth how truly sorry I am. I feel as if I've let you both down as much as I have myself. The holiday in Brixham felt like a good idea at the time: two weeks away, knowing that my life would change on my return to Rugeley. Pretending I was a solo made things easier all round. I just didn't bargain on Rob searching through my emails while I was away. You must think I'm such a fool.'

'Not at all. It's like I told you a few days ago: when you understand the true reasons for doing what you do, suddenly your actions make sense. I can't be angry with you. You have a valid reason for what you did.'

'You're too kind, you really are.'

'Emma, one last thing before you go.' Benni's voice has gained a giggly edge again. 'Remember I mentioned that Luca might be giving you a call?'

'Benni, please. I've got enough on my plate.'

'Please hear me out. He was gutted when I spoke to him. He genuinely likes you. It sounds like he was biding his time to ask you out, only to discover that Martin had got there first.'

'Oh Benni, there's so much I didn't share with you guys. I'm

281

mad with myself for trusting that snake. Still, at least I found out before I sold up and moved down there. What a prat!'

'He conned you. He bluffed his way into your good books and then deceived you by pretending he was single. Luca said he's renowned for having an eye for the ladies – he just took it further this time. But it's his loss, Emma. The two of you could have had a great working relationship; how is his business going to survive now?'

'On my ten thousand pounds, that's how!'

Benjamina

My mobile rings for the second time today, interrupting my breakfast with Ruth in her pink quilted dressing gown. I jump up from the table to answer, delighted that someone's calling me but saddened by the reminder that apart from Emma's earlier call, my phone hasn't rung for ten days. Maybe Mum and Dan have missed me after all. I'll apologise for not calling back after their drama to ask if everything was OK.

I reach the sideboard, disconnect my charging lead and stare at the illuminated number. I recognise it instantly. It's not home.

I don't want to answer.

'Oh no,' I groan, seeking solace in Ruth, but her expression is bewildered, as she stares from the dining table.

The phone continues to ring. A montage of flashbacks plays inside my head: Ziggy, Bruce, ice cream, the harbour, climbing steep hills, the cove, new trainers and bench pit stops for breathers.

'Are you going to answer it?' asks Ruth, watching me intently.

'If I answer this call, it will officially end my holiday.'

'So ignore it,' she says, biting into her buttered toast.

I can't ignore it.

'Benni?'

I hit accept.

The ringing ceases and I hear a familiar voice.

'Hello,' I reply, lowering my head and stepping into the kitchen, away from Ruth's watchful gaze.

'Hi, Benni, Tina here. We were wondering if you're looking for work next week . . . some shifts at Vine Yard's? Any chance that you're interested?' Her voice is crystal clear; no chance of me not hearing her request.

My heart sinks. I want to say 'no thanks, I'm sorted', but I can't . . . I daren't. I know that come Saturday I'll be home in Burntwood, slotting back into the usual routine of my life. Searching the job adverts for permanent work. Work that I actually want to do, rather than just any old low-paid position purely to avoid an empty bank account at the end of the month.

The words stick in my throat, and my head and my heart begin a tug of war over who will win. I don't need telling; I know the answer.

'Benni . . . hello, are you still there?'

'Yes.' Gone is my bubbly, excited tone as I revert to the real me: level-headed, independent and self-reliant to the core. 'How many shifts?'

'They've asked for three, but you know how it is: they always underestimate how much manpower they need on the production line. They say Monday to Wednesday but then they always bump you up to a full week with the offer of weekend work if you want it. You know how they are, Benni.'

'So, a promise of three shifts but it could be five or six?'

'Yep. I mean, there's no pressure from us; if it isn't what you're looking for then I'll call the next person. But I've always said once you get your foot in the door with these big companies, you never know what they might offer in relation to a full-time contract if you show willing.'

'No, it's fine, I'll take it.'

What other option have I got?

My heart plummets like a stone thrown down a mine shaft.

'Lovely, so that's Monday and Tuesday, seven o'clock start on both days—'

'I thought you said three shifts?'

'Did I? Sorry, no, just the two, but you know what they're like, Benni, always changing their minds.'

Bloody typical. Tina's right: everyone seems to change their mind, with little regard for others.

Ruth

It takes considerable effort to carry my painting equipment down to the tiny cove, following Benni's directions, but I manage it. And she's right: it is the perfect place to spend a morning painting once you've navigated the steep woodland pathway, the bark chippings and finally the pebbled shale.

I perch myself on the edge of a flattish rock, with a folded blanket for added comfort, and survey the scene. My pencils and watercolours are spread out beside me, and a jam jar balances precariously in a rocky crevice.

The cove is idyllic in the sunshine, with a rugged rock face towering behind me and a beautiful expanse of water stretching before me, beyond which the harbour defences cut across the horizon, with my lighthouse at the end.

Swimmers of all ages cluster in small groups beside the lichened rocks, their clothing and towels make a colourful abstract draped over the grey boulders – a stark contrast between nature and man-made.

I wonder whether to paint the lighthouse again; many artists have delivered a recurring theme or specific scene from several different perspectives. Dare I contemplate capturing it at various times of the day and from numerous angles? I can envisage the composition of each as I stare at my blank painting board. Is such a project too restrictive in terms of creativity? Or is it a canny sales plan in terms of customer appeal? Calculated or inspirational, which would I like to be?

I have no idea what Dean might advise, apart from his standard phrase: 'always complete'.

I need inspiration. As beautiful as the cove is, a composition has to have a focal point, otherwise it's simply a pretty watercolour. I don't want to produce chocolate-box images. I want to be a true artist, like the one featured in the gallery's window

– they aim high, so why shouldn't I? I need to express myself and paint with passion to capture an honest interpretation of the surrounding world.

I scan the cove, searching for something, though I'm not sure what: a glimmer of light on the water, perhaps; an interesting feature high on the rock face; any focal point other than the lighthouse.

That's when I spot it, way out from the shoreline. It's tiny at first, just a ripple breaking the surface of the sea, but as it comes closer, a seal's pointed face is clearly visible above the water line.

My breath snags in my throat; I'm spellbound.

An infectious buzz starts up amongst the swimmers, both in the water and those drying or undressing upon the water's edge. Everyone turns and watches entranced as the seal dips and dives about the cove. It appears on one side of the cove only to vanish from view again, causing heads to swivel and scan the waters to see where it will pop up next.

After a twenty-minute master class for the cove's swimming fraternity, the creature leaves as quietly as it arrived.

But not without delivering my muse.

Emma

I return home in a foul mood, having spent my entire morning in the computer section of the local library, shushing the noisy teenagers who'd rather chat than study. My heightened annoyance probably reflects my struggle to draft, scrap and redraft a feasible CV that will convey my talents as a chef, despite my limited experience, whilst minimising my deep-fat-frying expertise. I've gone overboard about my ice cream production, even creating a mini menu to entice and influence prospective bosses. I didn't realise how much places charge to print on coloured card, but needs must.

I sit and admire my slimline menus with their fancy font. I might have stretched the truth just a tad; I haven't actually attempted all the combinations listed. But if any establishment asks me for interview, I'll ensure the blends work, and even take samples with me. In my opinion, there's something for everyone in my flavour selection.

Avocado and crab
Black walnut
Roasted turmeric and candied ginger
Sweetcorn and butter
Goat's cheese and beetroot
Green tea
Lavender and honey
Cardamom and black pepper
Horseradish
Fig and balsamic vinegar
Peanut butter and jam
Rhubarb and ginger
Champagne and violet
Guinness
Pink gin

I pile the rest of my freshly printed stationery on the dining-room table to make an immediate start at folding, sealing and addressing. I settle down to the laborious but necessary task. It feels good to be doing something constructive rather than endlessly replaying events on a loop and berating myself for my foolish behaviour.

Despite the fact that I haven't seen hide nor hair of Rob since his visit to Rose Cottage, I can't ignore our situation any longer. Whether he's here to discuss the matter or not, our living arrangements are the next issue I must address, once these envelopes are in the post.

After an hour and a half, I have fifty sealed envelopes, each one neatly addressed in my best handwriting. It's going to cost a small fortune in postage, but if any one of the classy hotels in the surrounding area responds with a job offer, I won't be complaining.

I grab my car keys and head towards the post office.

Benjamina

I don a pair of yellow plastic waders, as instructed by the trawler's captain – I'm not sure he's aware just how unflattering this garb is for a girl with a fuller figure – then stand stock still on the decking amidst the all-male crew, who scurry busily back and forth. Despite the fact that I'm clutching the metal railing in an attempt to retain my balance, I sway from side to side as the trawler crashes against the waves.

'Here ... grab hold,' shouts Ziggy, throwing a bundle of netting in my direction. 'Let it feed though your hands as we lay it out to sea.'

As I follow his lead, a wave of nausea lurches about my innards. The trawler lifts and lowers in a rhythmical pattern, and my throat constricts with each move. I fear I will be sick, confirming my lack of resilience for the open waters of Brixham.

'Don't just stand there like a wet squid, girl – grab hold and start working, otherwise we might as well throw you overboard for the fishes!' barks a voice from the front of the trawler.

I daren't argue, so join the line of fishermen feeding a continuous stream of netting into the choppy sea. I can hardly see the end of it from the deck, but I imagine the net sinking deep into the ocean's inky depth to await a shoal of fish.

I thought I'd be hardy and tough on board the trawler. Sadly, I'm not. I'm a mess. A wimp, according to one of the men. I wrongly imagined that this would be a beautiful way to end my holiday, knowing that I'll soon be saying goodbye to Ziggy.

The only beautiful thing about this experience is the full moon smiling down on me. With little light pollution, the night sky is the blackest I have ever seen, with large ghostly clouds veiling the starry backdrop.

'So is it as you imagined?' asks Ziggy, gently tucking my hair into my woollen beanie and pulling it low over my ears.

From my position lying supine on a wet wooden bench, I look up at him and grimace.

'I want to go home,' I whine, as my body rocks uncontrollably from side to side while my innards rock in the opposite direction.

'Welcome to the fishing industry, but I'm afraid that won't be happening for another five hours. I'm not brave enough to ask my dad to quit a night's work because you've fed the fishes by vomiting.'

'Stop joking around, Ziggy, I'm dying here.'

I close my eyes and listen to his raucous laugh.

'You're not dying, Benni – you're just not used to it.'

'I was fine on the ferry on Monday.'

'Ah, the ferry! Benjamina, there's a huge difference between that titchy little boat used by holidaymakers and this industrial sized trawler . . . Now, I suggest you sit up and hang your head over the side when you need to, OK?'

It isn't OK, but I haven't the strength to argue that he's being unkind or unfair towards a novice fisherman. In addition, I fear the scorn of his father, who probably remembers me saying 'I'll be fine, honest – I don't get seasick.'

When I'm brave enough to open my eyes, I'm alone. I assume that Ziggy has returned to the other men to earn his money.

Emma

I sit in the armchair for the entire evening waiting for Rob to arrive home. I don't care where he was last night; I'm not interested in hearing a lame excuse involving a friend, a friend's mate or even a friend of a friend's mate.

It's none of my business any more. I officially want out.

I hear him hang up his biker jacket; I hear his boots hit the skirting board as they're removed with a flick and a kick. And when he enters the lounge, I see the look of surprise flitter across his brooding features. Despite his towering frame, he looks drawn, tired and somewhat bewildered.

'When did you get back?' is all he can say.

'That's irrelevant, Rob. I'm here now.'

I stare at the tiny gold object sitting centre stage on our coffee table. I've cleared away his dog-eared motoring magazines and the coffee-ringed coasters to ensure our discussion has focus.

'I'm not putting it back on, Rob. You've been acting like it isn't, but we've both known it for years, that this . . .' I wave my hand casually between us. 'Is over.'

He gives the tiniest of nods acknowledging my sentiment before I continue, Benni's words ringing in my ears.

'It was wrong of me to lie, I'll admit that. I should have told you about my plans for the fortnight; it would have saved you worrying and a wasted trip to Brixham, but under the circumstances, it was my choice. The life we're living . . . I'm living . . . it isn't me any more. I've got the chance to move on while I'm still young enough to start again; be the woman I want to be rather than the one I've become.'

He slowly settles into the nearest armchair, then sits back

and stares as if I'm posing a simple question about what colour to paint the lounge or where we should spend Christmas.

He says nothing.

He does nothing but stare.

I'm expecting a reaction, an argument, or even a plea to try again. But it's as if he doesn't believe me. Or believes he can talk me round, like every other time.

'I've moved my belongings into the spare room, and I've also organised a separate bank account for my earnings, though I'll make sure I transfer enough into our joint account to cover my share of the mortgage and bills.'

Still nothing.

I look down at my left hand. The white indentation on my third finger is starting to regain colour and flesh out given two weeks of being bare. I expected Ruth or Benni to spot it during the first few days at Rose Cottage, but neither of them did.

'Rob . . .' He blinks as if seeing me for the first time. 'I plan to remain in this house for a few more weeks, living as we have been, while I find a place to rent.'

I have the beginnings of a plan forming, though I feel no obligation to share the details. Anyway, it depends on whether Ruth's still contemplating her own future.

I sit and wait, allowing him time to digest and speak, but he doesn't. Instead, he simply continues to stare. I can almost see the cogs of his mind working overtime, devising a plan of action, seeking quick-fix solutions, clever words, heartfelt promises – which have always worked in the past. Tactics

I've happily accepted, which have kept me in my place in life beside him.

'Emma, we've been together for twelve years, married for just over ten . . . is there nothing I can say to make you change your mind? We could plan a holiday, if that's what you need. We can go to counselling to discuss our difficulties, or even sit down and begin talking about the family you've always wanted. What's it to be, babe?' His eyes never leave mine as he speaks; he knows I've waited years to hear him suggest the final option. Typical Rob, he didn't even pause after his original question denying me the chance to answer before he lists my options. He makes it sound as if I have choices, that I'm steering my own ship, deciding my own fate, when really, like always, they are his choices from which I must select.

I never provide the selection of choices. *Ever.*

And for twelve years his method of control has worked; his jealousies and insecurities have kept me just where he's wanted me. It's very different to the control that Ruth has encountered from her mother, dominating her life, but still Rob has called the shots in the calmest and most calculated manner throughout our relationship. There's never violence or fear, but always an imbalance of control.

'Which one is it to be, Emma?'

I answer him as calmly as I can manage. 'None. I have my own plans, thanks; my days of choosing are behind me.'

I have nothing else to say or discuss. This shouldn't be a surprise to him given how we've lived. I stand and make my way towards the lounge door, leaving my wedding band on the coffee table.

'Emma.'

I turn to see his upturned face, etched with sadness and remorse.

'I'm sorry, I truly am.'

'I know.'

I open the door and make my way to bed.

Chapter Fourteen

Friday 31 August

Benjamina

A sharp pinch to my cheek wakes me with a start. I'm bewildered by the sun streaming into my eyes. There're no curtains, no comforting duvet – just a row of stony sea-weathered faces staring at me.

'Wakey, wakey, sleeping beauty, we're nearly home,' says Ziggy, moving into my line of vision. 'I suggest you get on your feet, otherwise you'll be feeling it in your back later today.'

I raise myself on my elbows and view the wooden plinth on which I have slept the entire night.

'Sleep OK, shipmate?' asks Ziggy's father, offering me a steaming mug. A greying mop of curls pokes from beneath his woollen beanie, and his chin is a mass of silver stubble. In the morning light, I can see that Ziggy is the spitting image of his dad.

'I'm so sorry, I've never been seasick before,' I apologise while painfully easing myself to a sitting position.

'No worries, lass. Ziggy mentioned you're pretty good on the ferry, and no doubt grand when it comes to dinghies too. Let's hope you can stand long enough to help unload the catch when we arrive back in harbour.'

The sunrise over Brixham harbour looks like a painting of dusky oranges and reds. I've never seen anything so beautiful as the trawler eases closer and the distant hills rise against the backdrop with their glorious horseshoe of terraced cottages.

Ziggy stands with me at the railing, a look of concern etched upon his features.

'That was the longest night of my life,' I joke, rubbing at my back.

'Mine too,' he whispers. 'But unlike you, I didn't want it to end.'

'What's wrong?' I ask, worried that I've let him down with my lack of sea legs.

'It's ending, isn't it? You've one day remaining and then you'll head back to the Midlands and all this will be a memory to you.' I hear his voice crack, and he looks away across the water to the approaching harbour.

'It doesn't have to be,' I say. 'We can be friends, keep in touch ... Technology makes everything easier nowadays.' I reach for his hand. 'I'll be coming down as often as I can to see my dad and his family.'

'It's not the same, is it? Your dad will want to spend time with you, and how can a screen image be the same as this?'

'You could come and visit me. I'll show you the sights of Burntwood . . . I'll even show you the vinegar factory if you like.' I go to laugh, but see that his expression is stern, his jaw set, his eyes fixed. 'Ziggy?'

'Mmm.'

'Look at me.'

There's a hesitation before he turns, though his expression remains impassive, like a mask.

'You need to tell me what's up,' I urge. 'Otherwise I'll assume I've done something wrong.'

He shakes his head. 'You don't get it, do you? You're constantly putting yourself down, calling out your faults, but the truth never dawns on you.'

I wince, unsure why his hushed tone sounds so agitated.

'You, Benni, I'd simply like to visit *you*. Not the Midlands sights, not the vinegar factory, not even your family. Just you.'

I'm lost for words, so simply stare into his hazel eyes. We don't utter a word, we don't even touch – everything I need to know is visible. Despite my feet being firmly planted on the trawler's deck, I can feel myself falling. My gaze takes in his long dark lashes, the brilliant whites of his eyes, which draw me in, deeper and deeper, as though I can see a million swirling thoughts beyond the surface. I feel the same sensation as from Bruce's intense gaze; for the first time in my life, I'm standing before a person who truly understands me from the inside out.

Ruth

I feel nervous as I approach the gallery, knowing I'll be leaving with my earnings. It feels great on many levels, but wrong on others. I'm used to receiving a monthly salary for working a set number of hours spent interacting with customers over a cashier's desk, not filling a blank canvas or painting board with a series of strokes of colour.

Financial rewards feel somehow more civilised when the funds simply appear in your bank account, rather than being physically collected. This situation feels more cap-in-hand than I've experienced before.

My stomach churns at the thought of what might happen. What should I do if Dean tries to pull a fast one regarding the amount owed to me? I know we originally agreed a sixty/forty split, which seems fair given that he's providing a suitable frame for each composition, plus he does have overheads for the gallery too. And without the gallery, how would the Scottish couple have known about *Marina Mania*?

As I enter the gallery, I can't help but admire again the large lighthouse painting which still dominates the front window. One day, maybe after many hours of practice and patience, I might produce a single piece good enough to be promoted to prime position in the gallery's window.

'Wow! Loving the new you,' he says as I step inside.

'I'd forgotten you haven't seen my hair. I fancied a change. Benni says it makes me look sassy, but I'm not so sure.'

'So how are things?' he asks as he ushers me through towards the back room beyond his counter area. 'We'll chat in here. Tea?'

'Please, milk but no sugar, thanks. Fine and dandy from my perspective. I'm hoping to finish a watercolour of a seal by this afternoon, so I'll deliver that before I go home tomorrow.'

Dean drops two tea bags into a ceramic pot and adds hot water from the boiling kettle.

'Wow! Another fabulous watercolour to offer to our holidaymakers,' he says, grabbing mugs and a teaspoon. 'And the title?'

'I think *Solo Swimmer* is fitting, given that the composition depicts a seal playing amongst the cove swimmers.'

'Sounds good to me, and you can deliver that by tomorrow?'

'Absolutely. After which, I'll be back home and working on a new composition inspired by all the photographs I've taken of the area. Fingers crossed, I'll be able to produce the same quality and we can continue our arrangement.'

'That suits me, Ruth. Couriers and shipping costs will need to be taken into account, but still, that's how the majority of artists manage nowadays. If you can keep a steady flow of watercolours coming my way, I'm happy to provide gallery space. It's a lucrative market for us both.'

While the tea brews, Dean collects an envelope from a cabinet drawer and hands it to me. I blush profusely, embarrassed at accepting the money.

'This seems surreal to me,' I say. 'Literally two weeks ago, I was sitting at a cashier's till asking customers if they'd like tens

or twenty-pound notes. That was my lot in life. And now this.'
I sound overwhelmed and gushy; I can hear my inner excitement for myself, so there's no chance of hiding it from Dean.

'You've earned it, Ruth,' he says. 'I suggest you plough a little of your earnings back into your materials: widen your colour palette, purchase bigger painting boards, that kind of thing. But otherwise, enjoy!'

'I intend to. This has given me a new lease of life. Did I mention that I've resigned from the bank?'

Dean shakes his head before turning his attention back to the tea-making.

'Four weeks' notice and then I'm free to focus on being at home, caring for my mum and spending more of my time painting,' I explain, reining in my excitement for fear of spilling the beans about another idea that is slowly forming in my mind. I just need a few days back home, then I'll know whether I can make it a reality.

I stand awkwardly, the envelope grasped in my hand.

'You can count it, check it's all there,' he says, addressing the elephant in the room.

'Oh no, I'm sure it's fine.' I sound pathetic. I've been handling money all my life, and now I'm dismissing it as nothing.

'Please. I'd like to know that you're happy.'

Relieved, I open the envelope and draw out the wodge of new ten-pound notes. I can't believe that my efforts have resulted in ... I quickly finger through the notes and a few pound coins – two hundred and sixty-four pounds.

'This seems rather a lot, Dean,' I say.

He turns from the worktop.

'No, it's as we agreed. Two paintings sold for two twenty each, with a sixty/forty split. I'm no fool where calculating money is concerned.'

'Thank you, that's very kind of you,' I say, pushing the envelope deep into my handbag before taking a seat at the table. 'I can't believe the second painting sold so quickly.'

'I hardly had time to frame and display it before I was taking the payment.'

I'm stunned by this new world, everything happens so quickly. One minute you're painting, the next you're delivering and, surprise, it's sold!

'I'm amazed that customers view a painting and purchase it straight away, they don't seem to wait or buy on a second visit.'

'You can't wait, not where art is concerned.'

'Obviously, they purchase before others can.'

'And you're still enjoying the painting?'

'Of course!'

'The pressure of having to produce a finished piece isn't getting to you?'

'No, it's the best thing I've ever done ... I'm loving every minute of it. It's a pity I waited so long before I made a proper effort to use my talent. When I look back, I seem to have wasted so many years dreaming of doing something, and yet doing nothing.'

On hearing my own explanation, I understand how my sudden change of heart has occurred. I hadn't fully realised before how all the dots connected.

'Now come on . . . From what you've told me, you've raised a fine young man. More than I've done!'

He's right, but I'm not thinking about Jack, more about myself. Jack has matured into the man he is through his own efforts.

'Here . . .' Dean hands me a steaming mug of tea and settles himself opposite me.

'Would you mind if I nipped to your toilet?' I ask, standing up before he can answer.

He splutters tea on to the tabletop as I follow the sign and open the door. I glance over my shoulder to see him frantically dabbing at the spillage and waving a beckoning hand in my direction.

What on earth is the matter with him? I simply need the loo.

I take three strides along the corridor and stop, for there lies the answer. Two frames lean against the interior wall. A sheet of bubble wrap has been laid between them, but I recognise my own compositions in a flash.

I turn to call to Dean, but he's already standing in the doorway, panic etched on his face, watching my reaction.

I simply point. My mind is racing. I am lost for words.

'Ruth . . . I can explain. Please hear me out and then we'll—'
His hands lift in a calming motion.

'These are mine!' I exclaim. I don't need confirmation but my brain isn't cooperating in such confusion. 'Why isn't *Marina Mania* hanging in the young Scottish couple's dining room?'

'Please, I can explain . . .'

'You lied! You haven't sold either of them. Instead you've stashed them here, hoping I wouldn't find them.' I bend down, pulling away the bubble wrap to fully reveal my lighthouse painting, *Lonely Watch*. 'You've paid me for work you haven't even sold!'

'Please, Ruth . . . it isn't how it looks, honestly.'

'How *does* it look, Dean? Suspicious, that's what I think. Having a good laugh at my expense, were you? Poor stupid Ruth thinks she can paint; we'll boost her ego by letting her think she can. Hopefully with practice she'll improve somewhat and produce a decent composition – is that it?'

'Hear me out on this one, please.'

'No!' I sound like I mean it. It is a no-negotiation 'no' that comes out as harsh and as hurt as I feel. 'I bet you and your arty mates have had a good laugh at my expense. Is this the normal routine each summer, stringing along a gullible woman into thinking that she can achieve her dreams? Is that where your true artistry lies, in convincing others that they have a talent?'

My need for the toilet has disappeared. I hastily push past Dean, grab my handbag from beside the table and exit through the gallery.

'Ruth . . . wait!'

'No. You wait, Dean.' I stop dead and turn to face him. 'You wait until next week, when you're walking along the harbour wall and spot the next woman wanting to try her hand at something new, something that might bring a slight glimmer of hope into an otherwise bland existence.' His brow is contorted, his eyes pleading. 'Do us all a favour: save her the hassle of this bullshit and walk on by!'

I hastily depart before my tears can spill over.

My anger makes swift work of the steep hill as I speed-march towards Rose Cottage, in search of a caring friend who'll understand my anger at such deception.

Emma

It's just gone eleven o'clock when my mobile rings, interrupting my online search for catering jobs. It's a welcome interruption, given that all I can find in my area is minimum-wage employment and long, antisocial hours.

'Hello!' I say, surprisingly cheerful despite the last two hours of unproductive searching.

'Good morning, may I speak to Emma Grund, please?'

'Speaking.'

'Hello, Clarke Mellors here, head chef at the Country Club. We received your enquiry letter this morning and wondered what the delivery time is on three litres of black walnut and three litres of champagne and violet ice cream?'

My brain is still marvelling at how reliable Royal Mail is – I only posted my CV letters yesterday afternoon, and they've already started arriving – that *is* next day delivery despite people suggesting first-class postage is a waste of time – so I'm not focusing properly on what he's saying.

'I'm sorry, could you repeat that?'

'Yes, we'd like to order three litres each of black walnut and champagne and violet, but your leaflet doesn't state the expected delivery time or costings.'

This can't be happening. I stand up in shock.

'When do you require it by?'

'We've got a midweek wedding next week, and I think the champagne and violet ice cream will complement the bride's chosen dessert perfectly.'

'I see,' I mutter, playing for time as I grab a piece of paper and a pen. 'I could deliver that for Monday, at fifteen pounds per litre,' I say, cringing to my core, knowing full well I've plucked the figure from thin air.

'And the black walnut?'

'That would be twelve pounds a litre . . .'

'Sounds good to me. Could you ask for me by name when you deliver on Monday? I assume you'll invoice us?'

'Yep, yep, that's how it works,' I say, sinking down on to my haunches, not believing the giant whopper I've just told.

'Thank you. See you Monday then,' he says, before my mobile goes dead.

I remain crouching until my legs tingle with pins and needles. It feels safer than standing up to face the fear of what I've just agreed to, which feels distinctly like catering fraud, if that were an actual crime.

Ruth

I can't find Benni on my arrival at Rose Cottage. Her mobile is missing from the dining room, so I know she's been back. After last night's fishing trip, I assumed she'd still be in bed.

I grab the envelope of money from my handbag and begin to pace the dining room.

My mind is a whir as Dean's words spin about my head: 'always complete', 'invest in your materials', 'it's a lucrative market for us both' – what a bloody cheek! He's no better than Martin. Are there no decent people left in this world? Is everyone out there a cheating con man out to deceive others?

My mobile rings: Emma.

'Good timing,' I say, grateful that I can air my annoyance before my panic kicks in. 'You'll never guess what's just happened.'

'I'm all ears . . . then I'll tell you what's happened at my end,' says Emma, sounding brighter than she did last time we spoke.

It only takes me a few minutes to explain the last hour of my day, as I fire off details about Dean and his gallery quicker than an auctioneer in full flow. I tell her how cheated I feel having nearly completed the seal composition, and how I've given in my notice to the bank.

'But you've got the cash, right?' she asks as I pause for breath. 'You've still sold two watercolours and been paid for both; the fact that it's Dean who's bought them matters very little. Don't let the bastards get you down, Ruth . . . seriously, you'll find your way.'

'That's hardly the point given that Dean's thrown my plans sky high and left me in a quandary as to what I should do next,' I retort, beginning to wonder if Emma is the right person to listen to my concerns.

'You were perfectly fine knowing that the paintings were

elsewhere, so why let it bother you that for some unknown reason he stashed them? A sale is a sale, my lovely.'

I'm miffed that she isn't seeing his deception in the same light as I am, but I suppose she has a point. It's all a matter of perspective, which seems ironic.

'And you, how have things been on your return?' I ask politely, not wishing to be unfair given she had her holiday cut unfairly short.

'Rob's graciously accepted how I feel about our marriage,' she says. 'He's not happy about it, but I think that's more to do with his male ego amongst his circle of friends. I've also posted out fifty CVs ... but the most alarming news is I've accidentally become an ice cream manufacturer overnight!'

'What?' I'm bewildered with the speed with which she's found her feet. 'How long have you been home?'

'Exactly, and that's what I'm trying to say to you: forget what Dean's done and why he's done it. It's his issue, not yours. Just focus on what you want to achieve and go for it. My phone hasn't stopped ringing this morning; it seems the hotels' administration bods have opened the envelopes, removed my letter and passed the ice cream menu card to their head chefs. This morning I've taken orders that will see me busy until next Friday. How's that?'

'Amazing! But how are you going to meet the demand – surely you'll need a proper catering kitchen?'

'Ah, do you remember me mentioning that my previous boss has sold the roadside café to a developer who wants to convert it into an Indian restaurant? Well, I'm heading over there in a while to discuss renting a section of his kitchen and associated equipment, much like a hairdresser renting a chair in a salon.'

I'm blown away by her ingenuity.

'Emma, you are a force to be reckoned with, you know that, don't you?'

'Simply a case of needs must. I could just sit around moping about my lost redundancy money and Martin, crying about my failing marriage, and panicking that I can't pay the bills, but this world doesn't allow you time to wallow in self-pity. You've got to get out there and help yourself.'

'I hear what you're saying, but bloody hell, it's a scary prospect. Resigning from the job and focusing on my painting seemed legit when I had Dean's backing, but now it feels like the rug has been pulled from under me.'

'I saw the painting and I think it was great. I believe you can achieve your dream, and I'm sure Benni will say the same. What's so great about Dean – or Martin come to think about it – that you need his seal of approval before you make a decision?'

'For starters, he owns a gallery, and you don't. He's been in the art business for a long time; he has expertise, Emma.'

'So what? I've been in the ice cream business for all of four hours and I've got more work than I care to think about, and do you know what, these chefs won't have a clue that I haven't been doing it for years, because I will deliver the goods!'

'I wish I had just an ounce of your confidence, I really do.'

'You do, you simply don't realise it yet. Now go and finish

off your seal painting. You'll need to start selling online, which means you'll need a gallery of images so that potential customers can browse before purchasing.'

I tap the mobile's screen and kill the call.

I can't help but smile. I feel ten times better already. I look at the envelope of cash in my hand.

'Hello, you look pretty pleased with yourself,' says Benni, entering the dining room. 'Have you had a good morning so far?'

I'm on the brink of recounting what's happened, but decide not to.

'I have, actually, and it's about to get even better, because I'm just about to nip into town and open a new bank account.'

Benjamina

I literally don't know what I want to do. With only a few hours left before Ziggy needs to go back to work, I have no idea what to suggest.

'We could visit the cove, walk to Berry Head lighthouse, sit in the Sprat and Mackerel – though I won't be able to drink . . . It's up to you,' says Ziggy, holding my hand as we walk along the quayside. 'We could even go for an ice cream if you like.'

'I daren't in case Martin walks in; there's a good chance I'd give him a piece of my mind, and Emma doesn't need me messing up her investment for her,' I say.

'So where to? I know it'll only be a few weeks before I come up to see you, but still . . .' Ziggy frees my hand and wraps his arm about my shoulder.

'Fish and chips on our bench,' I say, unsure whether he'll laugh at my request.

'Are you sure?'

I nod. I have a million things I want to tell him, but I know I'll mess up the sentiment by attempting to say them.

It takes us ten minutes to grab our food and settle on our bench. I feel like a teenager sloping off from lessons to spend time with her first crush, rather than a twenty-five year old who should know better.

I simply can't help myself. Ziggy *is* my first crush, the only young man I've spent time with enjoying his company. I'm not worldly wise regarding relationships. I don't pretend to be knowledgeable about men. I simply recognise that I like him, and I suspect he likes me.

We pick at our chips, our chatter fading and becoming strained as time ticks by. I keep checking my watch, he his phone. We both know what needs to be said, what needs to be done, but I don't want this to end.

'Are you done?' he asks, indicating my half-eaten chips.

'Yep, you?'

'Yep. Come here.'

We slide together, our chip parcels discarded in the nearest bin, and sit in silence with our hands entwined. My fingers play with his, his thumb strokes my palm.

'Benni . . . this isn't goodbye for us,' he whispers.

'I know,' I murmur. 'Let's not talk.'

Instead we sit close and stare into each other's eyes, each of us reading the other from the inside out.

Emma

I don my clean chef's whites, adjust my hairnet to cover my ears and stand at the stainless-steel worktop to begin cracking a box of eggs into a bowl. I grab the large balloon whisk and begin beating the eggs in a vigorous circular motion.

I smile as a memory from Rose Cottage pops into my mind. Poor Benni couldn't even boil an egg, let alone whisk them properly. I recall her zigzag technique and her disgust when I complained. When she arrives home, we'll have to make arrangements for a series of cookery lessons so she'll be able to feed herself when she finally strikes out on her own.

Around me, the busy kitchen swarms with waiters and waitresses collecting cutlery and calling for table orders. Freshly prepared food sits waiting beneath glowing lights on the hot plates.

I watch the chefs yelling impatiently, hear their curt tones, and wonder if I looked that miserable cooking – correction, frying – to order every day.

I put aside the beaten eggs and reach for the measure of double cream, gently mixing the two. There's no rush, no pressure – I'll make three litres of champagne and violet ice cream in my own sweet time.

The kitchen clock already reads twenty minutes to midnight, but what do I care? I'm doing what makes me happy, and if I don't get this batch into the freezer much before one o'clock in the morning, who's to mind? The restaurant manager isn't going to complain, given that his staff will still be clearing away at that time. As long as the ice cream is frozen and delivered by Monday morning, ready for the wedding on Wednesday, everyone is happy.

Chapter Fifteen

Saturday 1 September

Ruth

I'm up with the lark. We have to pack and clean before we hand over the keys at ten o'clock, and given that we'll need breakfast before travelling back, we'd best make haste.

'Morning, Benni,' I say as I reach the bottom stair and find her entering the front door, dressed in black leggings and a baggy T-shirt. 'Have you been out?'

It's only when she looks up that I see she's not her usual self. Her eyes are red raw, her nose is running uncontrollably and her breath is laboured.

'I thought I'd . . . give jogging a go before I went home.'

'Are you serious? Over the last two weeks you've climbed hills every day, mucked out stables and raced through dense woodland to raise the alarm, but today you feel the need to try a little extra?'

'Yep . . .' she says, panting heavily. 'I'm dying here, Ruth. If you wouldn't mind . . . I need to sit down.'

I stand aside as she hobbles into the dining room and flops into a chair.

'Can I get you anything?' I ask, unsure what I'll do if she faints.

'I'll be fine. I was worse than this at the stables. I thought if I can just keep the momentum going when I arrive home, there's a chance I'll wear out my new trainers, since I haven't managed to do that in the last fortnight.'

'Such a grand fail, that, along with falling asleep on a busy fishing trawler,' I say, making my way to the kitchen to start breakfast.

'True, very true. I'm grateful Ziggy saw my true colours, so he probably won't invite me again.'

Benni's taking a shower and I'm clearing away our breakfast things – my waffles turned out nothing like Emma's – when the doorbell rings. I glance at my watch: 9.30.

I open the front door half expecting it to be the owners trying their luck and turfing us out before our time. I'm ready to say my piece, given that we've cleaned and tidied the place to within an inch of its life. I'm sure many a holidaymaker waltzes out bang on ten leaving it looking like a pigsty.

It isn't the owners. It's Dean.

'Can I have a word?' he asks, standing sheepishly on the doorstep. 'I know you're leaving today.'

'You can, but I haven't much to say.'

I stand back, allowing him to pass. His expression is doleful, his greying head lowered, possibly with embarrassment.

'I wanted to explain myself,' he says. 'Ruth, I imagine you're upset, but believe me when I say I did it for the right reasons. I've been on my own for a long time, and seeing you painting without a care in the world . . . I recognised that spirit. I know how it feels to paint with such joy and passion, and I wanted to be part of your journey. I even hoped we could strike up a rapport; that perhaps there was a chance of us getting to know each other better. You might call me a silly old goat, whatever ridiculous term best fits, but I need you to know. I like you. I like your style and I wanted to encourage you in any way I could. It sounds ridiculous, I know. I didn't do it out of spite, and I hope in time you realise that and can accept my apology. The fact that I gave you the money we agreed on proves I wasn't trying to swindle you.'

I stand motionless, listening to his words. They sound genuine. It sounds like a valid reason.

'You could have been honest, told me all this to start with,' I say.

'I could have been, should have been, but what's an old fool to say when a woman a decade his junior is holidaying on her own? I didn't want to come across as some letchy old guy, make you feel uncomfortable by asking you out.'

'Oh, I see.'

It makes sense, but still the manner in which he behaved caused me hurt and meant I didn't finish the seal painting as I'd hoped.

315

'Thank you,' I say. 'I appreciate your honesty.' I turn towards the door, knowing that time is marching on.

'I just wanted to wish you a safe journey and say how sorry I am.'

'Apology accepted.'

I am surprised as anyone that that is true.

I turn the latch and hold the front door wide. Dean pats my arm on passing but says nothing more.

Once the door closes, I lean against it and sigh.

'Did he have a valid reason?' calls Benni from the top of the stairs.

'Yep, and I'm fine with his version, but it doesn't change my plans. I'm still heading towards my new beginning.'

'Go Ruth!'

'Yeah, go me!'

Benjamina

'It's five to ten, Ruth . . . they'll be here any minute,' I call from the doorstep of Rose Cottage, keeping an eye on our suitcases stashed by the wrought-iron gate.

'I'm ready. I just wanted to check we hadn't left anything, though I'm sure they'll post it on if we have.'

I watch as two cars slowly draw up the road and stop a short distance away. One is my dad's car; the other is Ruth's taxi.

I feel sad knowing my holiday is ending. Two weeks ago, I

trundled up the hill dragging my suitcase, my ponytail sticking to my glowing skin, my elasticated waistband tight and my feet aching. Now, though my messy bun doesn't look as good as Emma's version, and my make-up is very subtle, I've managed it. My skirt is loose and I'm wearing trainers. And more importantly, I have a head full of ideas and plans for my new beginning.

'Are you sure my dad can't drop you anywhere?' I ask for the umpteenth time.

'I'm sure,' says Ruth, appearing from the dining room and closing the door firmly behind her. 'I want one last look at the cove so I can finish the seal painting properly. The driver said he's prepared to wait, as long as the meter's running. Have you returned the keys to the safe?'

'Yep,' I reply. 'I've done everything you've asked. Now come here so I can say goodbye; my dad's waiting to drop me at the station.'

I step on to the pathway and Ruth joins me, slamming the door to Rose Cottage behind us. I wrap my arms around her slender frame and hug her tight. I don't really want to let go, but I know I must.

'I'll give you a ring later in the week, OK?' I say, eager to keep in touch.

'Please do. We'll let Emma know the details and we can catch up over lunch sometime.'

'I hope your mum's on good form when you collect her tomorrow.'

'I'm sure she will be. I've phoned every morning and there haven't been any other emergencies.'

'Mind how you go,' I say, as Ben climbs from his car to greet me.

'Safe journey, Benni . . . see you soon,' Ruth replies, as the taxi driver opens the boot ready for her bags.

I take a last look at Rose Cottage, memorising the image: the wrought-iron gate, the rambling roses growing above the bay window, and the pretty lilac paintwork.

I smile.

Bye, Rose Cottage, I say silently. I've got a funny feeling it won't be long before my new beginnings truly start.

'Now remember what I said: you're welcome any time, you hear me,' says Ben, stroking my cheek before I board the waiting train. 'I don't want any excuses; we're happy for you to visit whenever you're free.'

'I promise I will. I'll phone next weekend to make arrangements.'

'And Benni, don't take any bull from your mum or Dan. Say what you want to say and let them deal with their own issues. Pave your yellow brick road and be happy.'

With that, he plants a fatherly kiss on my forehead and helps me up on to the train with my suitcase.

I step from the bus and walk the length of Redwood Drive practising my opening lines. I'm so consumed by my thoughts that I'm oblivious to the annoying rattle of my suitcase's plastic wheels.

I'm lugging my belongings home, but that isn't the weighty

issue causing me to drag my feet. My heart feels heavier with each step. If I chicken out or back down, there's a good chance I'll slot straight back into my old world. Breakfast, vinegar factory, home, bed and repeat.

I must be honest with my family, but most importantly I need to be true to myself. I have a valid reason.

I want the new me.

I want a relationship with my dad.

I want to address my diet and lifestyle habits.

I want to start enjoying my life.

I want a horse.

I pause, stop mid stride and smile.

I want a new beginning.

I want to pave my brand-new yellow brick road.

My pace quickens. I know what I want to achieve, so what the hell is there to fear?

The rows of houses fade into squat bungalows with adjoining driveways and garage frontages. The road gently descends to a dip prior to a sweeping ascent, and I stop outside our bungalow, perfectly positioned in a dip in the road's landscape. I glance towards the steep climb to my right – never before have I thought of my home as sitting within a deep rut from which I would one day need to escape.

The bungalow looks unchanged. Dan's battered Ford stands on the concrete driveway, the jokey window stickers curling, the off-side panel dented and scratched. A sense of déjà vu overwhelms me as I struggle to turn my suitcase sideways and work the plastic wheels into position to manoeuvre past the vehicle.

Is it really just two weeks since I did this on the outward journey, struggling without assistance?

I always think it strange that our family enters the bungalow via the rear entrance rather than a front hallway. Something in the bungalow's planning was arse about face, much like our existence as a dysfunctional family.

I select the back-door key and unlock the latch.

I drag my suitcase inside the tiny kitchen and close the door, looking around at the Formica surfaces, the lace net at the window and the sink full of dirty saucepans. The telly blares from the neighbouring lounge.

Nice to see nothing has changed in my absence: it's eight o'clock, food is eaten and the telly is on. Nothing ever changes.

A pair of aged rubber swirls hang from the taps; each has a droplet of water suspended from its lower edge, as if silently weeping.

Home.

How great would it be to be thrilled or even a tad excited to be back? But I'm not.

I leave my suitcase by the back door and make my way through to the lounge. Even before I get there, I know what I'll see. Mum will be sitting in her armchair, staring at the telly, the remote control resting reassuringly in her right hand. Dan will be stretched out on the sofa by the window, his socks peeled off and abandoned on the floor, either gawping at the box or asleep, snoring inanely.

I open the door, back in my familiar world, much like Lucy returning through the wardrobe.

'Hi,' I say brightly.

'Hiya,' says Mum, her eyes not leaving the illuminated screen.

'Yo,' mutters Dan, scratching his armpit and briefly glancing in my direction before returning his attention to the TV.

I stand and wait. The wall clock is the underlying beat signifying that life does exist here, regardless of the impression.

I count the seconds, slow and steady in my head, a habit from my childhood: one, two, three, four, five . . . twelve, thirteen, fourteen . . . twenty-six, twenty-seven . . .

Nothing else is said.

Is this my punishment for not cutting short my holiday to attend their drama?

Have I really been away for a fortnight? Have I travelled all the way from Brixham by train and bus merely to be greeted like this?

I stare between the two beings, both fixated on their TV.

Have my family not noticed that the third person who inhabits the bungalow hasn't been visible for the last fourteen days?

'Benni?' mutters Dan, shifting his position on the sofa. 'Put the kettle on, would ya?'

If I need a signal, the green light to give me permission to please myself, this is surely it.

Every sinew in my body wants to rejoice. I reject their lifestyle. I know Tina at the agency will be mighty peeved with me, the manager of the production line miffed at the loss of a decent worker, but I will be elsewhere, severing ties in numerous directions to pursue my new beginning, along with the new me.

I don't say a single word. I simply walk through the lounge, heading towards the hallway area and my bedroom. As I close the door after me, I hear my name again.

I poke my head back around the door jamb.

'Are you not moving your suitcase?' asks Mum, her eyes still fixed on the TV.

'No, Mum, I'm not.' I gently close the lounge door, knowing that my time here is done.

I don't know why I was nervous about their reaction. They'll cope just fine without me.

Ruth

'I didn't expect to see you quite so soon, but come in, make yourself at home,' I say, giving Benni a bear hug. She looks exactly as she did some ten hours ago: same suitcase, same attire, though decidedly more tear-stained.

'I'm so sorry . . . I couldn't think of anywhere else to go,' she says, heaving her case over the doorstep as I shuffle backwards to accommodate her. 'Are you sure it isn't a bother? What with your mother and all.'

'Of course it's not. I don't collect Mum until tomorrow. You're welcome to stay in Jack's old room.'

'Are you sure you're OK with me calling on you, like this?' I interrupt, only to repeat my welcome. It's obvious she's self-conscious about dropping in on me, but having spent the last three hours listening to the rhythmical mocking of the mantelpiece clock, I'm happy to see her.

'Top of the stairs, second door on your right . . . go up, make yourself comfy. I'll pop the kettle on. There's nothing that a decent brew can't fix,' I say, heading towards the kitchen. 'Are you hungry?'

'No, thanks, I ate on the train . . . just tea for me.' She starts to hoist her case up the stairs.

I fuss about with kettle and cups, find a packet of bourbons, then take the tray into the lounge. The clock is quieter somehow, its ticking less mocking than before, and the room doesn't feel as cold and empty as it did when I arrived home. That initial moment of putting my key in the door, breathing in the stale air of a fortnight of locked windows, instantly stole my holiday joy.

Beyond the pimpled ceiling I can hear the muted movement of life. It sounds comforting, secure and welcoming . . . as a home should feel.

'Nice place,' says Benni, bounding like an energetic pup into the lounge. I'm glad to see her mood has brightened in a matter of minutes.

'Thank you,' I say. 'I was born in this house, so I didn't choose it, but I did decorate it.' And pay for it, I want to add, but change my mind. 'Make yourself at home.'

'Anywhere?' asks Benni, pointing between the sofa and an armchair.

'Of course.' I frown, unsure of her meaning.

'It's just that in our house everyone has a specific seat, and woe betide you if you sit in someone else's chair. I wasn't sure if one belonged to your mum.'

'Nope, technically they all belong to me,' I say, though I understand what she means. When I was a small girl, my father used to sit in the armchair next to the fire, but since his death four decades ago, there've been no hard and fast rules – well, not about chairs anyway. I pour the tea to distract myself from memories, good and bad.

'What have you been doing since you got back?' she asks.

'Not much. I had a busy hour unpacking my case, loading the washing machine and opening the mail – just bills, I'm afraid. And you? How were they?'

'Still watching TV, as they were when I left two weeks ago. They didn't even ask if I'd had a nice time, can you believe that?'

I pass her a cup and saucer. She takes the cup, leaving the saucer in my grasp. I return it to the tray as the briefest of smiles dawns upon my face. How could anyone ignore this young woman and allow her to plod to her bedroom to sit alone for an hour and ponder?

'I've made a list,' she says proudly. 'An official "new beginnings" list.'

My obvious confusion prompts her to continue.

'I suppose it's like a bucket list, but maybe the list before the bucket list.'

'OK,' I laugh. I laugh more when she puts down her cup

and begins to reel off each item, counting them on her fingers as she goes.

'I want the new me, but all the time. I want to build a relationship with my dad – though my mum will probably go mad about that. I need to diet and address my lifestyle habits. I want to meet more new people and start enjoying being young before I'm actually old.' She pauses.

'What?'

'Now don't laugh but if I can achieve all those things, I would like . . . no, I *want* a horse.'

'You want a horse . . . where did that come from?'

'I've grown quite attached since I visited the stables. They're such lovely creatures.'

'So what's stopping you from doing all of that?'

'It used to be me,' she says. 'But not any more. They don't realise, but by ignoring me when I arrived home, they've given me the biggest wake-up call I could ever ask for.'

She's angry; I can see it bubbling up from her boots as she speaks.

'Do you know what, Ruth, I actually felt sorry for them when I was away. I felt awful for enjoying myself by the sea amongst strangers, seeing and doing new things, knowing that my mum and brother were back home in their usual routine. When the reality is that they don't care a jot what I do or even where I am. Well, they might be satisfied with their lives, but I'm not.'

She finishes on a high, giving herself a nod of approval.

'So?'

She retrieves her cup and takes a sip. On close scrutiny, I see a flicker of excitement in her expression.

'Tell me more,' I urge.

'I've got a plan to make my list come true,' she says, tapping her nose. 'Thing is, I didn't bargain on it starting tonight.'

'No time like the present, though, is there?'

'Nope. Do you mind if I make a quick call . . . in private?'

She's gone in an instant, her tea cooling on the abandoned tray. I'm no genius, but I'm guessing her call must be to either Emma or Ziggy.

Emma

My mobile rings at 10.50. I've been asleep for at least an hour, but I snatch it up as if my life depends upon it.

'Hello,' I say groggily.

'Emma, it's me . . . Benni.'

'Are you OK, sweet?' I'm out from under the duvet in a second, standing in the middle of the room ready for action.

'I'm sorry it's late, but I've had an idea. Correct me if I'm wrong, but legally you own part of the parlour business . . . it was a formal arrangement, wasn't it?' she asks.

'Yes, but it can't possibly remain as such given the circumstances, can it?'

'Mmm, well, I've been thinking . . .'

I climb back into bed, all ears as Benni outlines her plan of action.

'So you see,' she finishes, 'I could make it work and later expand into internet sales too.'

I'm impressed. I like her thinking. I know she'll give it her all; she's one of life's workers. I've invested my nest egg in a difficult situation, but Benni could easily take my place in a physical sense behind the counter.

A career change for her, peace of mind for me. Not a bad day's work.

Ruth

'Well?' I demand, not giving Benni a chance to settle back into the armchair.

'I phoned Emma and I've put an idea to her.'

'And?' I can hear the urgency in my tone.

'I've asked her if she'd consider putting me forward as her assistant working at the ice cream parlour.'

'That's a great idea, Benni. Obviously she'll need time to think it through properly.'

'She's fine with my suggestion, totally on board. Ruth, you know the chocolate truffles I made the other night?'

'Mmm.'

'Well, in addition to the assistant's role, I asked if she'd consider me trialling a range of truffles to complement her ice cream flavours. That way we could branch out and increase sales via the internet. She believes our difficulty will be in getting Martin to agree to our terms. Though given his recent behaviour, she's already arranged an appointment with her solicitor, so she'll include our new plan in her proposal.'

Benni's smile reflects the renewed energy charging through her body. It's been a long day, but I don't want to sleep. It seems an age since I've been this excited by anything, and it's not even happening to me.

She's on the cusp of a new life, and Emma has the power to make her dream come true.

Chapter Sixteen

Saturday 8 September

Emma

I grab for a fresh pineapple just as my mobile rings.

I bet this is Benni, telling me about a final detail she's forgotten, or checking that she has free rein on her working hours as outlined in our proposal to Martin.

But instead, I see an unknown number illuminated across my screen.

'Hello?'

'Hello, could I speak to Ms Emma Grund, please?'

'Speaking.'

'Ah, right. This is Jerry Bolstridge from the Royal House Hotel. We recently received your details and wondered if you were interested in our advertised chef's position?'

'Yes, that's right, I did contact you about a week ago.' I feel awful saying it, but I have to be honest. 'However, there have been a few developments since then and I won't be seeking a position after all.'

'No worries, Ms Grund. Thank you for your time.' He ends the call without any further discussion.

My heart is all of a flutter.

Have I just rejected what would once have been my dream job?

Instantly I address my inner doubts. I have a valid reason for saying no, and that's the fact that I have an order book filled with requests for artisan ice cream and a renewed energy for food and quirky flavours.

I pick up the pineapple and head straight for the curry powder. I suspect this combination may be a little too daring, but either way, it's worth a try.

Ruth

'What time is it?' Mum asks, her head of fine silver hair lolling against the armchair's upholstery.

I stare at the clock for the umpteenth time today.

'Half past six.'

Her wrinkled features relax and I know my words have eased her thoughts, whatever those might be.

I select a flat-pack box from the pile and fold and tuck the flaps to create another packing case to fill. I've found it's easier making them up while she's awake, then I can fill them while she's sleeping. Emptying the rooms isn't as difficult as

I imagined, as evidenced by the stash of filled boxes piled at the far end of the lounge.

Jack is still surprised by my plans to downsize and move to Brixham, but he's coming around to the idea. In a few more weeks he'll be busy making plans of his own, though not with Megan.

I didn't get the apartment I viewed, which is a pity as the harbour view was spectacular. But I've put an offer in on a similar-sized apartment in the next block: same view but a slightly different perspective, which seems to be my thing.

How did an afternoon of being nosy suddenly become a feasible plan? I suppose it all began with a tiny advert detailing a holiday let in Brixham, offering solo holidaymakers a comfy home from home with new friends guaranteed.

From that one decision to enquire about a fortnight's stay, so much has changed. I'm not sorry to contemplate life after NatWest. There are more pressing issues to focus upon. Mum's restful stay at Acorn Ridge, despite the early drama, proves how much care and attention she requires. She's returning there temporarily while I move our packing boxes to Brixham and settle in, and I've found a couple of care homes in Devon that look suitable for the long term. I'll take my time making my final decision; another visit to each before I choose.

A lump rises in my throat. I feel guilty for separating our little family, but life goes on, doesn't it? I have to make the right decision for us both. This way, Mum will have the care she needs and we can enjoy a new routine, returning to a normal mother-and-daughter relationship for this next stage of our lives.

I avert my sombre mood by reaching for another flattened cardboard box, and begin securing the bottom with brown parcel tape.

I'm looking forward to a little freedom to pursue my painting. I haven't been in touch with Dean; I wanted the dust to settle first. I meant it when I said I'd accepted his apology; deep down I think he meant well.

I glance at the far end of the room, beside the wall of packing boxes, to where my easel displays my current project. The outline sketch is complete and I've made a start on the lilac paintwork, though I'm not sure I've captured the vigour or abundance of the pale roses tumbling above the bay window. It'll take several more hours to finish, but I must do it justice. I'm surprised I allowed my first completed painting to be put up for sale; maybe I was simply too eager to prove to Dean that I'd completed a piece. This new watercolour is mine; it will hang in my new apartment overlooking the harbour, a reminder of happy days spent amongst new friends at Rose Cottage.

'What time is it?' my mother asks, her chin drooping on to her chest.

'Eight o'clock, Mum,' I say, without looking at the clock, while in my head I hear the bells of All Saints' Church chime 'Abide With Me'.

Benjamina

Tonight ends the longest week of my life. I've kept myself busy, completing three shifts at the vinegar factory and chatting to Ziggy each night until he had to go to work on the trawler.

As I walk down the shale slope at twilight, I can see a lively group of young men splashing about in the water a short distance from the shoreline. I instantly spot Ziggy's head and bare shoulders bobbing about in the centre of the group. His curly hair is pushed back from his face, and his mouth is wide as he shouts and jokes with the other guys. I stop and watch the pack dynamic, hoping that when he sees me, his playful behaviour will cease. I need to witness the before and after to confirm in my heart that I've done the right thing.

I believe I have. In fact, I know I have, but to have my feelings reinforced by his response will feel like the icing on the cake. My cake. Our cake.

The group play like young seal pups, ducking, diving, splashing and yelping.

Do men ever grow up, or do they always remain as little boys when in a group?

I continue to walk, knowing that there's a chance he'll spot me. I don't want to speak to anyone. I simply want to do as I've planned. A plan that has evolved in stages: on my long train journey, checking in at the Queen's Arms, and during what seems like the longest wait for a sultry sunset to arrive.

I'm eternally grateful to Emma for fighting my corner and

insisting that Martin honours their business agreement or she'd see him in court. I have to admit that I'm dreading meeting his wife. If she holds a grudge, then I'm in for it.

My ballet pumps crunch on the shale as I stride towards the huddle of girls silhouetted by the makeshift fire. I can just about make out Marla as she chats with the crowd. I appreciate her kind words of encouragement once she'd confirmed Ziggy would be here tonight, but I don't want anyone to notice me, make a fuss of my arrival or call out to Ziggy. I want them to continue chatting, singing and laughing until it's too late to shout a greeting.

I drop my canvas bag on the shale, flick off my ballet pumps and hastily unbutton my cotton dress. My gaze remains fixed upon Ziggy, my fingers nimbly working each button free. I slide the fabric from my shoulders, then undo my bra, allowing it to fall from my body. A gentle breeze greets my bare skin, which instantly prickles with goose bumps. My every move is electrified. I feel alive. Liberated. Free.

I begin to walk towards the water, the pebbles biting my heels. Straight-backed, my right arm lifted, cradling and covering my breasts, my gaze direct and my head held high, as proud as a peacock. Within a few steps the cold water is lapping my ankles, intensifying the goose bumps along my spine. I'm virtually naked, but I don't care who sees me. Surely they've seen flesh before, and if not, well here's a fine example.

That's when he spots me, and stops mid splash.

Gone is my shyness, my nerves and my inhibitions.

His face turns towards mine. The lack of light prevents me

from getting a clear view of his eyes, but I can imagine he's puzzled, seeking details, defining my shape against the backdrop of flickering firelight. Questioning his instinct.

He slowly wades towards me; his shoulders and waist emerge from the water and he stands stock still and staring as I move forward.

The cold water laps about my knees ... my thighs ... my hips, and with each step his silent stance is calling to me, while the others continue to splash and play behind him, providing the comparison I was hoping for.

At last, as I draw close, I see his reaction. Confidence washes the doubt away, and his shoulders square instinctively.

'Ziggy,' I whisper.

'Benjamina?'

My free hand reaches to interlink with Ziggy's. His fingers grip mine like a frightened child clutching his beloved teddy bear.

The water finally swirls around my midriff and I slowly drop my right arm as Ziggy draws me nearer, my skin pressed against his bare chest.

'You've come back ...' He doesn't finish his sentence. His lips lower towards mine and we stand wrapped in each other's arms amidst the tomfoolery of his mates.

We embrace for an age before ducking down beneath the rippling water to move aside from their noisy games.

'I thought you'd gone for good,' he explains, his face close to mine as he inhales the scent of my wet skin.

'There's so much I wanted to say, but it didn't seem right

over the phone. I knew where you'd be, and I thought, why not give you a surprise?'

'And boy, what a surprise, in all your glory.' He laughs, gently stroking my collarbone and throat. 'And you don't seem to care.'

'Honestly, I don't. The only one who watched me was you.'

'And I'm *allowed* to watch,' he murmurs, nuzzling into my neck.

I tilt my head back, lifting my gaze to the darkening night sky, a million tiny stars scattered above.

'Benni . . . let me kiss you as I want to,' he murmurs.

I lift my chin, close my eyes and let him.

Epilogue

Saturday 8 December

Benjamina

'Come in, come in, don't stand on ceremony, Emma,' I say as I wrap my arms about my friend and now employer, welcoming her to Ruth's new abode.

'Look at you,' says Emma, stepping back from our embrace to view my figure. 'You look fabulous!'

I blush. I'm still not used to the compliments. Fashionable clothing, a few hairstyle tricks and some make-up have transformed my appearance.

'I've lost nearly two stone, which is a fair amount in three months, but I'm eating healthily and I'm still mucking out the horses, which counts as strenuous exercise.'

'The results speak for themselves, lovey. You look great. I assume you're managing to resist the chocolates?'

'Only just.' I grab her hand and drag her through to the

kitchen, where Ruth is busy preparing party nibbles. 'Look who's arrived.'

Ruth throws down her oven mitts and holds out her arms.

'Is everything prepared, or do I need to roll my sleeves up?' asks Emma, returning the warm welcome.

'Not at all. You're to sit back and relax for the entire weekend,' scowls Ruth, diverting her to the nearest chair.

'How's your mum settling in at the care home?' asks Emma, making herself comfy.

'Fabulously well. She seems at peace, not as mithered as she once was.'

'And our fabulous chocolatier here can hardly keep up with the demand, can you?' says Emma, drawing me into the conversation.

'Between the ice cream parlour and the internet sales, I'm being run ragged,' I agree. 'But I'm loving it. I can't say that all your flavours are best-sellers in the chocolate range, but the dark chocolate slab with goji berries and coconut doesn't even make it to the storeroom. Straight into packing boxes and posted off to happy customers.'

'And to think that that first week you only had chocolate truffles in cellophane bags for sale,' says Emma, beaming with pride.

'Everything OK with the house?' asks Ruth. 'Nothing that you want me to arrange or fix?'

'Ruth, stop worrying, the house is fine. I'm relieved that you agreed to me renting it from you. It's saved us both a load of hassle and unnecessary bills. It's made things easier for me and Rob too. It wouldn't have been right to remain under the same roof once the divorce proceedings began.'

'Good, I'm glad to hear it ... And your artisan ice cream doing OK?'

'Couldn't be better. I've got orders coming out of my ears,' says Emma, waving her hands about wildly.

'Benni, can you grab the bubbles from the fridge?' Ruth says.

'It's only just gone midday,' I point out, conscious that we have the whole weekend ahead of us.

'If there's two hands on the clock, you can get away with having bubbles!' jokes Ruth, collecting glasses from the cupboard. 'Isn't that right, Emma ... life's too short!'

Emma blushes.

'Touched a nerve, have we?'

'You're right, Ruth. The years fly by, and if you live by all the rules and regulations that other people force on you ... well, you never have your fun, do you?'

'Don't you?' I ask cheekily, peeling the gold foil from the cork.

'Spit it out, woman ... you can't leave us hanging,' urges Ruth, lining up the glasses. 'Come on, you're blushing for England.'

Ruth is right. Emma has turned the brightest shade of red imaginable.

'Stop it, you two,' she scolds.

I quickly pour the chilled bubbles, eager to hear her news.

'Believe me when I say I wasn't interested ... right?'

'Right?' we chorus, glancing at each other.

'And I know that others will be judgemental about the situation, but—'

Suddenly her phone begins to buzz from her pocket. She fumbles, answering as quickly as humanly possible.

'Hi. Yes, I'm here ... Literally five minutes ago. Yes, I will ... Honestly, there's no problem ...' She glances from me to Ruth and back again. 'Not an issue ... we'll see you in ten. Bye.' She ends the call, puts her mobile away and picks up her glass as if we weren't present.

'And who was that?' asks Ruth, a coy smile on her lips.

'Look, you'll both be fine about it, I know. As you said, life's too short, so I've invited someone over to join us for dinner.'

'Martin?' asks Ruth, her eyebrows lifting.

Emma shakes her head slowly, her smile beaming.

'Luca?' I whisper, recognising the guilty glint in her eye.

'Mmm,' confirms Emma, blushing again.

'I told you, didn't I?' I blurt at Ruth. 'I should have guessed. He's walking around at work with a grin as wide as the harbour ... and you, Emma, well every time I speak to you, you're as happy as a sandboy!'

'That's nice,' says Ruth. 'And Martin, how's he taken the news?'

Emma shrugs. 'I don't much care. It's none of his business.' She lifts her glass and gives a wink.

'Touché!' I say, clinking my glass against hers.

Emma

I knew they wouldn't mind. True friends never do; they only ever want what's best for you. So Luca and I stay until the washing-up is dried and stashed away – though it was tricky the three of us manoeuvring round the tiny kitchen. Ziggy and Luca busied themselves at the window, spotting the wildlife outside the harbour wall. I was tempted to join them, given that Ruth's apartment does have a spectacular view across the harbour. But that would have seemed ungrateful after her efforts in cooking us a fabulous lunch.

'So where to?' asks Luca, stuffing his hands deep into his pockets as we leave the block. Instantly I sneak my gloved hand into the crook of his arm, snug and secure.

'Your choice. I'm just content to be back in Brixham under much happier circumstances than those in which I left.'

Luca smiles, his laughter lines cutting deep into his olive skin.

'First things first . . . you need to see how good the parlour's refurbishment is looking and take a peek at Benni's chocolate counter. After that, we can leave all thoughts of business behind and enjoy ourselves.'

'Sounds like a plan.'

The air is brisk and biting, the pavement grey and wet, and yet we stride happily in unison. It's effortless walking beside Luca, despite his lengthy stride and towering height. Maybe once you've found the right person, life's path becomes smoother, enabling you to pace yourself and take your time.

341

Ruth

'Well?' I ask Benni, returning to the lounge cradling a fresh coffee.

'Well what?' She lifts her head from Ziggy's shoulder to peer at me.

'Emma and Luca.'

'I had no idea. He doesn't tell me anything at work.'

'And neither does she by the looks of things,' I add, settling on the empty couch.

'Nice, though . . . they seem well suited. Better than Martin and—'

'His wife?' I quip.

'Ruth, that's naughty. Liz is OK once you get to know her.'

'But seriously, if he cheats on her each summer with who-ever he can, there's no hope left for their relationship, is there? If you can't trust the man in your life, what the hell have you got? Nothing!'

'I thought you and Dean were getting on nicely the other night,' says Benni, flashing me a knowing smile. 'You looked happy enough dining along the quayside.'

'I do believe that's called a platonic friendship. He's been a great help securing me a stall at the craft exhibition next week, so fingers crossed, I'll sell a few paintings. He's a good man, or a silly old goat as he once called himself.'

'Oh Ruth, you've got the devil inside you today!' says Benni, trying to control her giggles.

'I have, so out with it, you two!'

'Out with what?' asks Ziggy innocently.

'I've known Benni long enough to know that that smug grin is hiding something. What is it?' I ask, though I already suspect the answer.

I watch them exchange a fleeting glance, a silent agreement to answer my nosy questions.

'We're moving in together,' Benni says, her smile over-flowing. 'Martin's agreed we can rent the apartment above the ice cream parlour, as long as we decorate it tastefully.'

'Congratulations! That's fabulous news.'

'I'm glad you're pleased, Ruth. My mum wasn't too happy at the prospect, though Dan and Dad are delighted at the idea of additional weekends together now that Dan can sleep at ours.'

'Your mum will come around given time. She's accepted your relationship with your dad, hasn't she?' I add, knowing how relieved Benni was when that issue was put to bed.

'She has. Her biggest quandary was admitting the lie she'd lived for so long. I think she coped with the situation by actually believing what she'd told us.'

'Anyway, it'll save Benni having to stay at the Queen's Arms,' says Ziggy, taking her hand in his. 'Which means she can use some of her wages for other things in life.'

'There might not be enough to buy a horse and pay livery fees, but you never know,' adds Benni. 'Though having our first home together feels like another new beginning, and none of us can predict where such an adventure will lead us.'

'Maybe not, but we all know where the journey starts,' I say, glancing towards the large watercolour above my mantelpiece depicting a beautiful cottage with lilac paintwork, a wrought-iron gate and a tumble of roses above the front window.

'New beginnings at Rose Cottage,' whispers Benni, and her eyes glisten with fond memories.

Acknowledgements

Thank you to my editor, Kate Byrne, and everyone at Headline Publishing Group for believing in new beginnings and giving me the opportunity to become part of your team.

To David Headley and the crew at DHH Literary Agency – thank you for your continued support. I couldn't ask for a more experienced or dedicated team to champion my career.

Thank you to my fellow authors/friends within the Romantic Novelists' Association – you continue to support and encourage me every step of the way. I promise to repay the generosity and kindness received in recent years.

A big squeeze of a thank you to Steve, Sue, Marla and Maddie Salloway for your kind invitation to holiday in Brixham – who would have thought that amongst the boiled eggs, the guitar-playing and a visit to Totnes a brand-new book would be born! Big hugs to Maddie for showing me how to muck out a horse correctly, and to Marla for seizing the moment: 'Sometimes you just have to swim in the cove with the seal!'

Posthumous thanks to Dame Agatha Christie for delighting a shy teenager with an array of crime novels. Back then I'd spend hours consuming and second guessing each deadly deed, nowadays it feels more like a luxury as if visiting old friends!

Brixham – I'd never visited before, and you provided the most beautiful scenery, landmarks and clear blue skies under which my imagination was free to roam. I'll never hear 'Abide With Me' without recalling happy memories of the town.

Mum, thank you for always being there and for spreading the word about my books.

Heartfelt thanks to my husband, Leo: you have the patience of a saint! You never complain about the weird hours I work, the strange questions I ask or my constant daydreaming!

And finally, thank you to my wonderful readers. You continue to thrill me each day with your fabulous reviews and supportive emails. I'm truly humbled that you invest precious time from your busy lives to read my books. Without you guys, my characters, stories and happy-ever-afters would simply be daydreams.

New Beginnings at Rose Cottage

Bonus Material

If you found reading about Emma's delicious ice cream and Benni's temping chocolate truffles irresistible, why not try making them yourself with these easy recipes!

Emma's fig and balsamic ice cream

Ingredients:

300 grams ripe figs
400 grams caster sugar
A pinch of salt
5 tbsp cold water
300 ml double cream
300 ml milk
2 vanilla pods (scraped and split to remove seeds)
6 egg yolks
1 tbsp balsamic vinegar

Instructions:

Preheat the oven to 200°C.

Halve the figs and place on a baking tray, sprinkle over 150 grams castor sugar, salt and 5 tbsp of water. Allow the figs to soften in the oven for 30 mins. Once cooled, dice into small pieces and keep any syrup from the baking tray.

Add the milk and cream together in a large saucepan, add the vanilla pods (without seeds). Heat until it starts to steam and remove the pan from the heat. Remove the vanilla pods. Allow to cool for 5 minutes.

In a bowl, mix the beaten egg yolks with 250 grams caster sugar, and whisk for a few minutes.

Pour the milk/cream mixture into the bowl with the egg mix and whisk together. Place the mixture back into the pan, stirring with a wooden spoon on a low heat until thick (approx. 6 to 8 minutes). Add the cooled chopped figs, any collected syrup and balsamic vinegar – mix well. Pour the mixture into a clean bowl straight away to cool.

Leave the mixture to stand and cool, stirring occasionally, before placing in the fridge to chill thoroughly (may take several hours).

Once the mixture has cooled either place into an ice cream maker and churn or empty the mixture into a suitable shallow container and place into the freezer. If using the freezer-only method, you might wish to check on the mixture every hour or so ensuring that ice crystals are forming around the edge. Once the mixture is sufficiently frozen in the shallow tray transfer the ice cream into a suitable deep container for storage in the freezer.

Enjoy!

Benni's chocolate truffles

Ingredients
(for approx. 40 truffles):

300 grams of good quality dark chocolate (minimum
70% cocoa solids – see product packaging)
300 ml double cream
50 grams unsalted butter
Optional flavourings: peppermint, chilli or even
liqueurs (age permitting)
Toppings/coating: crushed nuts, desiccated coconut,
coloured sprinkles or cocoa powder

Instructions:

Break the chocolate into pieces and gently melt over a pan of
hot water. Place the cream and butter into a saucepan and heat
gently until the butter has melted and the cream is simmering.
Remove from the heat and pour the chocolate into the cream
mixture – mix until smooth in texture and colour.

If required, add additional flavourings to the truffle mixture.

Allow the truffle mixture to cool sufficiently to be able to handle safely.

Using a teaspoon or a melon baller, dip the instrument into hot water and then scoop a measured amount of truffle mixture. Lightly coat your hands in sunflower oil and roll the measure of truffle mix into a ball or desired shape*. Drop each shaped truffle into a coating of your choice (best poured into a shallow dish) and coat each truffle well before placing the finished truffle on to a baking tray lined with greaseproof paper. Chill the truffles in a fridge for a few hours before consumption.

Present in a small decorated box or cellophane sleeve with a decorative bow.

---

* If preferred, a piping bag can be used rather than shaping by hand.

Catching Up With Erin Green

My dream holiday destination . . .

India – where my maternal grandmother was born and raised.

If I were to be stranded on a desert island, my one luxury item would be . . .

My dog, Teddy – he's simply adorable and good company.

The first album I ever bought . . .

Paul Young's *Secret of Association* album – 1985ish!

The book I've read the most times . . .

Pride and Prejudice by Jane Austen – this is my go-to book when I need to swoon over Mr Darcy and be amongst fictional friends.

Erin Green

My guilty pleasure ...

Spending the entire day reading and drinking tea.

The last time I went to the cinema ...

Was to see *Bohemian Rhapsody*. I sobbed throughout the film, but so did everyone else.

The thing I could never give up ...

Sweetener in my tea – no sugar/sweetener is simply urgggh!

My choice of superpower ...

Invisibility – used in a good way to help others with unseen acts of kindness.

The book (by another author) that I wish I had written ...

Me Before You by JoJo Moyes – simply beautiful, powerful and thought provoking.

The best play I've seen ...

Educating Rita by Willy Russell – I was an Open University student so relate to her struggle to achieve and succeed.

The one piece of advice I would give my teenage self . . .

'It's OK being independent and liking your own company – that trait will be an asset when you're an author.'

The comedian who makes me laugh the most . . .

Billy Connolly – I simply adore his comedic storytelling with dramatic actions.

My favourite city in the world . . .

Dublin, Ireland – the people, the place and a pint of Guinness.

If I could play the starring role in any film . . .

Scarlett O'Hara in *Gone with the Wind* – she has a sassy attitude, the biggest dresses and kisses Clark Gable.

If I could go back to any time in history . . .

The Victorian era – I'd probably be a scullery maid but still . . . a fascinating time of invention and technology.

Look out for the next warm,
uplifting novel from Erin Green,

Taking a Chance on Love

coming soon!

Bookends

When one book ends, another begins...

Bookends is a vibrant new reading community to help you ensure you're never without a good book.

You'll find exclusive previews of the brilliant new books from your favourite authors as well as exciting debuts and past classics. Read our blog, check out our recommendations for your reading group, enter great competitions and much more!

Visit our website to see which great books we're recommending this month.

Join the Bookends community:
www.welcometobookends.co.uk

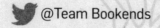 @Team Bookends   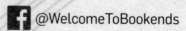 @WelcomeToBookends